PRAISE FOR CAT

Wife by Wednesday

"A fun and sizzling romance, great characters that trade verbal spars like fist punches, and the dream of your own royal wedding!"
—*Sizzling Hot Book Reviews* (5 stars)

"A good holiday, fireside or bedtime story."
—*Manic Reviews* (4½ stars)

"A great story that I hope is the start of a new series."
—*The Romance Studio* (4½ hearts)

Married by Monday

"If I hadn't already added Ms. Catherine Bybee to my list of favorite authors, after reading this book I would have been compelled to. This is a book *nobody* should miss, because the magic it contains is awesome."
—*Booked Up Reviews* (5 stars)

"Ms. Bybee writes authentic situations and expresses the good and the bad in such an equal way . . . Keep the reader on the edge of her seat."
—Reading Between the Wines (5 stars)

"*Married by Monday* was a refreshing read and one I couldn't possibly put down."
—*The Romance Studio* (4½ hearts)

Fiancé by Friday

"Bybee knows exactly how to keep readers happy . . . A thrilling pursuit and enough passion to stuff in your back pocket to last for the next few lifetimes . . . The hero and heroine come to life with each flip of the page and will linger long after readers cross the finish line."

—*RT Book Reviews* (4½ stars, top pick, hot)

"A tale full of danger and sexual tension . . . the intriguing characters add emotional depth, ensuring readers will race to the perfectly fitting finish."

—*Publishers Weekly*

"Suspense, survival, and chemistry mix in this scintillating read."

—*Booklist*

"Hot romance, a mystery assassin, British royalty, and an alpha Marine . . . this story has it all!"

—*Harlequin Junkie*

Single by Saturday

"Captures readers' hearts and keeps them glued to the pages until the fascinating finish . . . romance lovers will feel the sparks fly . . . almost instantaneously."

—*RT Book Reviews* (4½ stars, top pick)

"[A] wonderfully exciting plot, lots of desire, and some sassy attitude thrown in for good measure!"

—*Harlequin Junkie*

"Bybee concludes her popular Weekday Brides series in a gratifying way with a passionate, troubled couple who may find a happy future if they can just survive and then learn to trust each other. A compelling and entertaining mix of sexy, complicated romance and menacing suspense."

—*Kirkus Reviews*

Not Quite Dating

"It's refreshing to read about a man who isn't afraid to fall in love . . . [Jack and Jessie] fit together as a couple and as a family."

—*RT Book Reviews* (3 stars, hot)

"*Not Quite Dating* offers a sweet and satisfying Cinderella fantasy that will keep you smiling long after you've finished reading."

—Kathy Altman, *USA Today*, Happy Ever After

"The perfect rags to riches romance . . . The dialogue is inventive and witty, the characters are well drawn out. The storyline is superb and really shines . . . I highly recommend this stand out romance! Catherine Bybee is an automatic buy for me."

—*Harlequin Junkie* (4½ hearts)

Not Quite Enough

"Bybee's gift for creating unforgettable romances cannot be ignored. The third book in the Not Quite series will sweep readers away to a paradise, and they will be intrigued by the thrilling story that accompanies their literary vacation."

—*RT Book Reviews* (4½ stars, top pick)

Doing It Over

"The romance between fiercely independent Melanie and charming Wyatt heats up even as outsiders threaten to derail their newfound happiness. This novel will hook readers with its warm, inviting characters and the promise for similar future installments."

—*Publishers Weekly*

"This brand-new trilogy, Most Likely To, based on yearbook superlatives, kicks off with a novel that will encourage you to root for the incredibly likable Melanie. Her friends are hilarious and readers will swoon over Wyatt, who is charming and strong. Even Melanie's daughter, Hope, is a hoot! This romance is jam-packed with animated characters, and Bybee displays her creative writing talent wonderfully."

—*RT Book Reviews* (4 stars)

"With a dialogue full of energy and depth, and a twisting storyline that captured my attention, I would say that *Doing It Over* was a great way to start off a new series. (And look at that gorgeous book cover!) I can't wait to visit River Bend again and see who else gets to find their HEA."

—*Harlequin Junkie* (4½ stars)

Staying For Good

"Bybee's skillfully crafted second Most Likely To contemporary (after *Doing It Over*) brings together former sweethearts who have not forgotten each other in the 11 years since high school. A cast of multidimensional characters brings the story to life and promises enticing future installments."

—*Publishers Weekly*

"Romance fans will be sure to cheer on former high school sweethearts Zoe and Luke right away in *Staying For Good*. Just wait until you see what passion, laughter, reconciliations, and mischief (can you say Vegas?) awaits readers this time around. Highly recommended."

—*Harlequin Junkie* (4½ stars)

Making It Right

"Intense suspense heightens the scorching romance at the heart of Bybee's outstanding third Most Likely To contemporary (after *Staying For Good*). Sizzling sensual scenes are coupled with scary suspense in this winning novel."

—*Publishers Weekly* (starred review)

Not Quite Crazy

Also by Catherine Bybee

Contemporary Romance

Weekday Brides Series

Wife by Wednesday

Married by Monday

Fiancé by Friday

Single by Saturday

Taken by Tuesday

Seduced by Sunday

Treasured by Thursday

Not Quite Series

Not Quite Dating

Not Quite Mine

Not Quite Enough

Not Quite Forever

Not Quite Perfect

Most Likely To Series

Doing It Over

Staying For Good

Making It Right

First Wives Series

Fool Me Once

Paranormal Romance

MacCoinnich Time Travels
Binding Vows

Silent Vows

Redeeming Vows

Highland Shifter

Highland Protector

The Ritter Werewolves Series
Before the Moon Rises

Embracing the Wolf

Novellas
Soul Mate

Possessive

Erotica
Kilt Worthy

Kilt-A-Licious

CATHERINE BYBEE

Not Quite Crazy

Montlake
Romance

Published by Montlake Romance, Seattle

www.apub.com

Amazon, the Amazon logo, and Montlake Romance are trademarks of Amazon.com, Inc., or its affiliates.

ISBN-13: 9781503951730
ISBN-10: 1503951731

Cover design by Letitia Hasser

Printed in the United States of America

This one is for Kelli Martin,
my sister from a different mister.
Love you!

Chapter One

"Smells like snow."

Rachel glanced up past the skyscrapers and into the bright gray sky. "Does it?"

"It really doesn't snow in California?" Julie asked.

The two of them took a brisk pace around their building toward Romano's, where a hot lunch filled with way too many carbs awaited.

"It does in the mountains." Rachel opened the door, happy that her gloves kept the cold of the metal handle from reaching her skin. "Which I never went to during the winter."

The heat from inside the small restaurant rushed against their exposed skin and resulted in a collective sigh.

They had thirty minutes before the mad rush of lunchtime traffic in Manhattan, with lines out the doors and everyone talking at the top of their lungs.

With four patrons in front of them, Rachel took her place in line. "I'll be the first to admit I'm not ready for your winters."

"You're not ready for our summers either." Julie moved aside as a man who appeared to be wearing three jackets walked by with a tray full of soup and crusty French bread. The deli style restaurant was the way to eat when you only had an hour to do so.

Truth be told, Rachel was a little apprehensive about the weather. She'd left the ninety-degree heat on the West Coast during early September and experienced the instant cool temperatures and changing of the colors of fall in New York.

They moved forward in line as they chatted. "I should probably get some chains for my car."

Julie shook her head, straight black hair brushing against her shoulders as she did. "I don't understand why you insist on driving in."

"Public transportation scares me."

"Of all the things to be afraid of, a subway isn't one of them."

"It is when you haven't used them." They'd had this discussion before, one where Julie would roll her eyes while properly scolding her in both English and Korean.

"Tell me how it works out the first time you find yourself in a ditch on your way home."

Rachel lived a little over an hour outside of Manhattan and took the commute as any LA native would: with a smile. The commute she'd had back home was twice the time, so she looked at her current situation as a win.

"I won't end up in a ditch." As the words left her lips, she instantly saw her sporty SUV sliding into snow-covered water with her emergency lights flashing. "I'll be fine," she said to herself more than her friend. "Everyone in California has a car, and none of us use the bus."

"Like that matters in a place where it's three hundred and fifty days of sunshine and fifteen days of sprinkles."

"Hey, it rains."

Julie narrowed her already narrow eyes in Rachel's direction.

"Whatever."

They both laughed and stepped up to the counter.

Ten minutes later, the two hovered over a table as three other customers left. They slid into the recently occupied seats and made quick work of taking their first bites.

"Weekend plans?" Julie asked.

"Unpack."

"You've been here for nearly three months."

"Every room needed fresh paint and a stupid amount of cleaning before we unpacked. There are only so many hours after work and on weekends."

"Did you ever get to your room?"

Rachel had made sure Owen was completely taken care of before working on her own space. Between moving to the opposite coast, changing schools, and finding new friends, it was surprising he smiled as much as he did. He wasn't a complainer by nature, a trait he'd inherited from his mother. Rachel paused and allowed the depth of her loss to move on. "I'm finishing up my room this weekend."

"How is Owen getting along at school?"

"He likes his teachers, is passing all his class—"

"That isn't what I mean."

Rachel spoke around her food. "There are a couple of neighborhood kids who have welcomed him into their circle."

"Same age?"

"Lionel is a junior. Ford is Owen's age."

Rachel thought of the three boys the first time Owen had them over. For the first time in months, she walked into Owen's room to find him belly laughing at something one of the boys said. She'd leaned against the doorframe and watched them. And in that moment she knew they were going to be all right.

"I don't know how you do it." Julie finished her soup and nibbled on the bread that came with it. "I can hardly take care of myself."

"You'd figure it out if you had to."

"Instant mom, changing your home, your job."

"Same kind of job, different company."

Julie glanced at the man behind her who bumped into her chair while trying to climb into his. "When was the last time you went on a date?"

Rachel glared. "Are you going to ask me that question every week?"

"Yes. I am. You're too young to be hanging it up in suburbia alone."

"I'm not alone." Rachel glanced at her watch and stood.

"You have to promise me the first time Owen stays over at his buddy's, you're calling me, and we're going out. You've been in the city for a season, and my guess is you've only seen the streets on your commute and the few blocks we walk to find lunch."

Julie was right. Rachel hadn't explored the city any farther than what her work mandated. A shame, really . . . but not something she could help.

"You'll be the first to know."

The sharpness of the frozen temperature nipped at her lungs with each breath once they were back outside. She fished her gloves out of her pockets and pulled them on for the brief walk back to their building.

She was most definitely *not* in California anymore.

"Mr. Fairchild, your brother is on line two."

Jason glanced at the light blinking from his desk phone.

He signed the correspondence in front of him and lifted the receiver. "What's up, Glen?"

"Ha. Try again."

Trent. "Fifty-fifty chance of screwing that up."

"More like seventy-thirty with the amount of hours Glen puts in compared to me."

It was nice having his youngest brother back with the company. Even if it was only a couple of days a week, when he wasn't gallivanting over the globe with his wife and humanitarian efforts.

"Anytime you want to jump in—"

"Bite your tongue." Trent wasn't a nine-to-fiver, and lucky for all of them, Fairchild Charters ran like the well-oiled machine that it was.

Their planes spent more time in the air than most of their competition, the brokers found new clients every week, and their expansion across the globe had grown 15 percent in the past twenty-four months with a company growth of 5 to 7 percent annually in the past decade.

Things were good.

"So what is the uncharacteristic Friday afternoon call about?"

"I'm calling to give you a heads-up."

"Oh?"

"Yeah, Monica and Mary have been talking."

Jason leaned back in his chair and focused his gaze outside his window. "Should I be worried?"

"About you. They found out you didn't make it to Robert's for Thanksgiving."

"I was sick." Which was only half a truth. He'd found out earlier that Robert's wife had invited a woman she had been trying to set Jason up with for six months. Seems like everyone was working the find-a-girlfriend service for him for the past year.

"Monica isn't buying it."

"Monica doesn't have to buy anything."

"Like it or not, my wife cares. Neither she nor Mary will rest if they think you're alone for Christmas."

Since Trent and Monica had spent Thanksgiving in Texas with Monica's sister and her family, and Glen and Mary were enjoying fried turkey on the California shores with Mary's best friend, it was safe to assume Christmas would include someone in Connecticut. "So are they picking straws to see who is sticking around for Christmas?"

"We all are."

"So why are they worried I'll be alone?"

"They're not. But Monica is going to come over this weekend to plan, and chances are, she's going to read you the riot act for not joining Robert and Liz for Thanksgiving."

"She's coming to the ranch?"

"Yeah."

"Why?"

"Because you have the biggest place, and if you're hosting, you can't flake."

"I'm not a flake."

"Easter."

Jason thought back to the previous spring. "I was in London."

"And what, you couldn't get a flight home?"

"It didn't make sense for me to fly home for dinner when I needed to be in meetings the following week."

"Meetings you arranged at the last minute that only included a sprinkling of employees."

"Fine."

"Fine what?"

"We can have Christmas at the ranch."

Trent laughed. "Was I asking?"

No, and he didn't have to. The ranch was as much Trent's as it was his.

"I have one condition."

"Condition?" Trent didn't sound convinced.

"Yeah. No blind dates."

When Trent didn't comment, Jason knew he'd pressed a button. "Trent?"

"*I* won't set up anything."

"You won't let your *wife* set up anything either."

Trent belly laughed. "Have you met my wife? I don't tell her what she can or can't do. It's what keeps me aboveground."

"I mean it, Trent. No setups in my own house."

There was a pause. "I'll see what I can do."

Jason moaned.

"If you just brought your own date . . ."

"Yeah, yeah." Outside his office window, he noticed the sky growing lighter. He stood at the glass and looked up. "Are you home?"

"Yeah, why?"

"Is it snowing?"

"Started about a half an hour ago."

Jason frowned. "Was it in the forecast?" He usually paid attention to those things.

"Couldn't tell you."

He returned to his desk and clicked around his computer until he found his weather station. From the looks of the sky, he'd already lost his opportunity to helicopter home.

"If there isn't anything else, some of us have to work."

The sound of Trent's dogs barking brought a smile to Jason's face. "See ya."

He hung up and found his eyes drawn to the window again. The season's first snow was most often welcomed, but the last one was cursed . . . especially if it extended into spring.

Resigned to the long drive home, he returned to his desk and turned to the never-ending stack of papers he needed to sign.

———

Everything was fine, peaceful even, until Rachel reached the city limits. How so much snow could pile up in only five hours, she didn't know. She hugged the right lane and let the natives in the area buzz past her on the left. She'd already sent a text to Owen, letting him know she would likely be home late. He responded with half a dozen emoticons ranging from snowflakes to snowmen. For him, the snow would be nothing but a reason to put the video game aside and get outside.

On the highway, the snow fell at a slow, even clip . . . almost like a sprinkle of rain. When she reached her exit, those tiny flakes turned into quarter-size monsters that settled on her windshield wipers like drifts of sand that didn't want to wash away with the tide.

It didn't take long for the asphalt to disappear, only to be replaced by the tracks of previous cars that had driven ahead of her.

"Slow and steady," she repeated to herself.

Each stoplight was met with apprehension and white knuckles.

"Stay green."

Her foot hovered over her brakes until she passed through. When she drove through the last town before the long stretch of nothing leading her home, it was after seven. Thankfully, the roads were all but empty.

She reached a stop sign at a crawl. For one brief moment her tires locked up, and she slid.

Her heart squeezed in her chest, even though there wasn't any opposing traffic to hit. Rachel pumped her brakes until she managed a stop.

Closing her eyes, she sucked in a deep breath and continued on even slower than before.

"First thing tomorrow, chains." Not that she knew how to put them on. How hard could it be?

Less than five miles from her neighborhood, Rachel loosened her grip on the wheel. Confidence that she wouldn't be the California girl taken out by her first snow washed over her.

The two-lane road with its tiny hill gave her pause. She felt her tires spin at the base, and instead of staying in the slick tracks of the drivers before her, she inched to the side of the road and let her chainless treads grip the fresh snow.

Lights from a car behind her came up fast. Well, fast for the crawl she was doing.

One eye on her rearview mirror, one eye on the empty road in front of her, Rachel mentally told the other driver to go around.

She reached the top of the small hill as the driver behind her moved in close.

Lights blinded her briefly before the other car shifted to the side to pass.

At the crest of the hill, with no other illumination in sight, the other driver pulled around.

One second she was releasing a long-suffering sigh, the next her heart kicked hard in her chest.

The other driver lost traction, and the back end of their car started to slide.

Rachel hit her brakes, realized her mistake as it happened.

Everything spun a full circle before she managed to regain control. When she did, she was headed straight into the other car, which had settled in the ditch on the side of the road. She swerved, missed the car by inches, and came to rest beside the same ditch without dipping into it.

Her heart sped, her hands held the wheel in a death grip.

Lights from her rearview mirror told her the driver behind her hadn't fared as well as she had.

She shoved her car into park and jumped out. The boots on her feet were meant for the office. She slipped as she walked back to the other vehicle.

"You okay?" she asked long before she reached the passenger door. For a brief second she didn't see the man inside moving. She grasped the door handle and pulled.

Locked.

Then he looked up and shook his head before disengaging the lock.

"Are you okay?"

"Great, just great for a guy with his car in a ditch." He looked up, and Rachel forgot to breathe.

Chapter Two

Jason wasn't sure which had zapped him more, the fact that he'd managed to ditch his car or the bright blue eyes of the woman staring him down. No jacket, her light brown hair hung close to her face while snow settled on top of her uncovered head. Her cheeks were flushed with the cold, her lips . . . good lord, he needed to look past her lips or he'd start talking like a teenage kid with an instant crush. He blinked, breaking the contact, and moved to unbuckle his seat belt.

With the car at an angle, he needed to crawl over the center console.

The woman extended her gloved hand. "Here."

With the grace of an elephant, he managed to get one leg over and into the passenger seat, and then the other, before taking her small hand.

Outside the car, he stepped into half a foot of snow, and his Hugo Bosses slid.

She glanced down. "Looks like you're about as prepared to deal with this as I am."

He took in her footwear. "At least you have boots."

"I don't think this is what Steve Madden thought of when he designed them." She shivered, closed her arms around her waist. "You sure you're okay?"

Jason looked back at her car, the flashers blinking over the snow with every blip. "My pride is bruised, my bones are fine." He reached into the car, removed his overcoat, and retrieved his cell phone.

She started moving from foot to foot, the cold obviously settling in.

He handed her his coat.

"Let's call from inside my car."

"Do you let strange men into your car often?"

Those lips smiled and his stomach flipped.

"Only during blizzards."

"This isn't a blizzard."

"It is to me. C'mon, I won't bite." She didn't take his coat before walking back.

Jason followed, his eyes moving to her license plate before he opened the passenger door and climbed inside.

She already had the heater on high. Rubbing her hands together, she shook her head, sprinkling melting snow over the both of them. "Thanks for stopping," he said.

"I almost bit it myself. Still kinda surprised I didn't, to tell the truth."

"I noticed your plates. California?"

She nodded, her cheeks turning redder as her body warmed. "My first snowstorm. I had no idea this was in the forecast, or I would have bought chains."

"Took me by surprise, too."

She found his eyes, and he realized he was staring.

He remembered his phone and dialed for help.

Nathan answered on the fourth ring. "Hell of a night, Jason." His mechanic and keeper of the family's personal aircraft had a thick Scottish brogue.

"Tell me something I don't know."

"What can I do for you, lad?"

"I managed to park my car in a ditch."

When Nathan stopped laughing, he asked, "What are ya drivin'?"

"The Audi."

"Well, that would be your first problem. This is a Jeep kind of day."

"Your words of wisdom astound me, Nate." He proceeded to tell him where he was and noticed his female companion looking at her watch. "How soon can you come?"

"I need to finish up here and I'll be on my way."

"Finish up where?"

"I'm at Betty's. Her power is out and she needed a proper fire set."

The widow Betty was on a property adjacent to his, but far enough away in a snowstorm to delay Nathan's trip.

"So how long?"

"Her road isn't plowed. I need to get back to the house and collect the truck. Might take a little time to find a tow. At least an hour."

"An hour?" On a good day he wasn't twenty minutes from home. He considered asking the woman with eyes as blue as the sky to drive him there. But she looked about as anxious to drive in the snow longer as he was to sit in his car for an hour waiting for a ride.

"Longer if you keep yammering at me."

"Fine."

Jason hung up, knowing he wasn't going to rush a man twice his age.

"An hour?" his companion asked.

"Yeah. Tow trucks will be at a premium tonight. I can wait in my car."

She looked at him like he was crazy. "And watch as another car comes over that hill and plows into you?"

He glanced over his shoulder. She had a point.

"I live close by." She looked at her watch again. "And I need to get home. Why don't you wait there for your friend?"

He wanted to ask if her husband would mind but realized how that might sound to a woman alone on the side of the road, much as he wanted to know her marital status.

"You sure?"

She lifted her pink lips in a half smile. "You're not an ax murderer, are you?"

"Gave that up last week. Messy."

She grinned and looked through her rearview mirror. "Need anything from your car?"

"My briefcase." He opened the door.

"You might want to put your flashers on," she told him. "A dead battery is better than a smashed in hood."

Jason's eighty-thousand-dollar car sat sadly in the ditch, and all he could think of was the next hour of his life in the company of a woman who looked like an angel.

I hope you're not married.

———

"Thank you for this," Jason said as they inched away from his abandoned car.

"It's all good."

He watched her hands gripping the steering wheel and noticed the tightness of her jaw as she concentrated on the road in front of them. "Does this have four-wheel drive?"

"I wish. When I bought it back in LA, I never thought I'd be driving in the snow. First time for everything, I suppose."

She crawled through a right-hand turn, her eyes wide.

Jason stopped staring at her hand when her words registered in his brain. "This is your first time driving in the snow?"

"Yep."

His heart skipped a beat and his hand moved to his seat belt. He'd driven in the snow since he was old enough to reach the pedals. Easy to do when you grew up on fifty acres of private property that housed an airstrip. There was no lack of motorized toys growing up, and he and his brothers raced them all against each other.

There was no risk of this woman racing.

He tried to see the speedometer reading on the car but couldn't without making his intention clear. If he had to guess, she wasn't going over fifteen miles per hour, which would normally make his skin itch to press the gas.

"You're doing well," he said.

She turned her head, briefly, and flashed a smile. "I think a turtle could move faster."

He almost agreed before she turned down a residential street and pulled into what he assumed was her driveway. Her sigh was short of comical when she cut the power to the engine.

"You don't park in your garage?"

"I'm not completely unpacked." She glanced at the closed garage door. "It's still full of boxes."

"Oh."

She grabbed her purse from behind his seat and pushed out of the car. Jason followed her a few short steps along a snow-covered path to a small patio. He found himself holding his breath as he awaited what was on the other side of the door.

One step inside and his hope that this California bred, reluctant snow driving woman was single plunged.

"Owen?"

She's married. Of course she's married. Why wouldn't a woman with a snow-melting smile be married?

"In here."

A young voice.

Married with children.

She shook the snow from her jacket by the front door and started to take it off when a teenage boy walked around the corner. "I was starting to worry."

Jason stared.

The boy stopped short and sized Jason up from head to toe.

"I made it. I told you I could handle it."

The boy spoke without looking at her. "You driving in the snow is like me taking a semi to school tomorrow . . . who is this?"

The kid was young, probably not old enough to drive himself, but he had spunk.

She turned to him. "This is . . ." Her smile fell. "Oh my God, I don't know your name."

"Jason Fa—"

"You don't know his name?" Owen turned an accusing stare her way.

"He was stranded on the side of the road!" She placed her hands on her hips. "Don't look at me like that."

"Like what? Like you're crazy for bringing a stranger home? Like that?"

"I'm a good judge of character."

Owen didn't appear convinced.

"I'm not an ax murderer," Jason told him.

Owen rolled his eyes.

"Go get your dad. I'm sure I can convince him."

Owen pursed his lips together and narrowed his eyes.

"His dad isn't here," she told him.

Jason was fairly certain there were several colorful words that exploded out of Owen's mouth under the cloak of a grunt before he articulated, "Don't tell him that, Rachel. He could chop us into tiny pieces by morning. No one knows us here enough to look for the parts he leaves behind." On that, Owen turned on his heel and stormed away.

"Owen!" Rachel turned to him. "I'm sorry. He's protective. Just give me a minute." And then she was gone.

Jason slowly set his briefcase on the floor and undid the buttons on his jacket.

Rachel, her name was Rachel.

Dad wasn't there.

And her son was black.

———

"He drives an Audi." Even as the words left her mouth, she realized how lame they sounded.

Owen stared her down like a man and not a fifteen-year-old boy.

"Jack the Ripper was a surgeon."

He had a point.

She tried to make light of it. "But Ripper didn't drive an Audi."

"Was it an R8?"

Rachel didn't even pretend to know what that was. Her eyes must have given her away.

"You're hopeless."

"He's just waiting for his ride. It's freezing out there." She paused and shook her head. "Why am I arguing with you?" *I'm the adult.*

"Because even your parents told you not to bring strangers home."

No, technically her parents told her not to talk to strangers. Not bringing them home was a given.

"You're right."

Owen opened his mouth and then promptly shut it.

She looked over her shoulder. "I'll drive him back to his stranded car."

"No."

She stopped. "He needs to leave."

"You can't get into a car with a stranger."

"I just drove him here."

She saw the moment his brain short-circuited with her problem. "How long before his ride gets here?"

"I don't know, an hour . . . I think."

Owen muttered something under his breath and rubbed the top of his head like a man twice his age. And in that second, he reminded her of Emily. God, Em would often pull her hair out while solving a problem.

"Why are you smiling?"

Rachel attempted to stop, knew she failed.

Being stared down by a kid half your age made you laugh.

She bit her lip.

With a roll of the eyes, Owen turned and walked back into the living room.

Rachel followed and watched him track the stranger with a turn of the head when he walked past and straight to the kitchen. The rattling of a utensil drawer followed his disappearance into the other room.

"Is everything okay?"

"It's fine."

Something crashed to the floor, Owen muttered something she was certain wasn't appropriate. Then he emerged from the swinging door, holding a butcher knife and the cordless phone.

"Owen!"

He set the knife and the phone down next to what looked like the homework he was doing on the small dining table between the living room and the kitchen. He resumed his seat and glared.

"Maybe I should wait outside for my ride."

"Don't be ridiculous." Rachel took a step toward the table. "Owen, that's enough."

"As long as Mr. Suit doesn't do anything, I won't do anything."

Rachel placed both hands on her hips. Her amusement over Owen's actions started to turn sour. "You'll just end up cutting yourself."

"I'll go."

"No!" Rachel pointed toward the couch. "Sit. I'll make us some coffee. You!" She moved that finger to Owen. "Finish your homework and stop acting like you were raised in Compton." With that, she stormed through the swinging door into the kitchen. Forcing a deep breath, she looked at the mess Owen had left from the frozen pizza he'd managed to make for his dinner.

"Wow, she's bossy," Rachel heard the man say . . . what was his name? Jason. He looked like a Jason.

Owen said something she couldn't quite hear. The swinging kitchen door had felt a little retro when she'd bought the house, now it felt cumbersome. She hurried to put the coffee on.

By the time she stepped back into the living room, Jason had removed his coat and sat on the couch. She caught his eyes and looked at the top of Owen's head, which was ducked into his homework. When she looked back, she mouthed the word *sorry*.

Jason offered a smile and shook his head.

"Coffee will just take a minute."

"That's great. What's your address? I'll let Nathan know where I am."

Rachel gave it to him and moved to Owen's side.

"What are you working on?" She tried to ease the tension in Owen's face.

He glared at her.

She accepted his anger so long as he maintained a level of respect.

They sat in silence while Jason finished his short call. "He's about a half an hour out."

Rachel wanted to tell him not to hurry, but the tension in the room wouldn't go away until he was gone. "That's fine. How do you take your coffee?"

"Black is fine."

She poured the coffee faster than a coffee shop waitress and brought it back.

Owen hadn't moved a muscle, and she was fairly certain he hadn't progressed on his homework either.

"This is good, thanks."

She took the seat opposite of Jason and tried not to stare. Short brown hair, blue eyes, strong jaw, the kind you knew Clark Kent would have, if he were real. Wide shoulders that looked at home in his suit. He didn't wear a tie. She wondered if it was a casual thing, or if he'd lost it before getting in his car for the long drive home. Without thought, she looked at his hands for the first time. No ring.

A strand of wet hair fell across her face. She closed her eyes to stop staring. The need for that hallway mirror was now pushed to the front. Not that she needed her reflection to know she looked a mess. Still, it would be nice to casually glance at herself and know she wasn't a complete disaster.

"You weren't kidding when you said you're not moved in."

She followed his eyes to a box that doubled as a coffee table. "Not yet. I've been doing the home improvement thing on my weekends before I clutter the space."

"Looks like it's coming along."

"Thanks. Owen and I have mastered the art of the paint roller. Isn't that right, Owen?"

He grunted.

Outside the living room window, the snow falling with the streetlight behind it looked like a scene from a movie. "This isn't going to be gone by morning, is it?"

"Probably not."

"At least tomorrow is Friday. I'll only have one round-trip into the city."

"You mean to drive to work tomorrow?"

"It's a new job. It's not like I can call in for a snow day."

"I wasn't suggesting that. You can take the train."

She cringed. "No, no." Yet even as she said those words, she knew it was only a matter of time before she had to overcome the anxiety around public transportation. "I'll leave early."

Jason looked as if he wanted to say something, glanced at Owen, and changed his mind.

"The trains are safe. Trust me, I've lived here all my life."

"I've been told." She sipped her coffee. "I'm just . . . not . . ."

"She's paranoid of being mugged," Owen announced.

Rachel sighed.

"Really?" Jason asked.

"There aren't a lot of trains in California."

"Do you take the bus?"

"God, no."

"Germs and mugging," Owen chimed in.

Jason glanced around the space. "Germ phobic?"

"No!" she said, as if that was ridiculous.

Owen opened his mouth again, and she cut him off. "Drinking out of a water bottle instead of a drinking fountain is just smart. It doesn't count as a phobia."

"Do you fly?"

She blinked, happy to finally say yes to something. "Sometimes."

"Twice." Owen kept announcing her secrets.

Jason stared at her as if she'd grown a horn on her head.

"It's a control thing." Owen kept talking.

"It is not," she denied.

"I told her she needed to get over it before I get my driver's permit."

She glared. "Don't you have homework?"

"I know someone who used to be afraid of flying," Jason said. "Maybe you should talk to her."

"I'm not afraid of flying." She glared at Owen. "I just like to drive myself," she said with a straight face.

Lights flashed through the window as someone pulled into the driveway.

Jason stood. "That would be my ride."

Rachel walked him the short distance to the door.

He took a moment to put on his long coat. "Nice meeting you, Owen."

She opened the door and walked him onto her porch, slid the door almost closed behind her. "Thanks for understanding him."

"He's being protective. Gotta give the kid points for that."

"The man of the house collides with a teenage attitude daily."

Jason smiled.

Rachel shivered.

He reached out his hand. "Thank you for braving a stranger in the storm."

His hands were warm, despite the cold. "You're welcome. Good luck with your car."

Jason hesitated, then turned and walked away.

Chapter Three

Rachel allowed herself an extra hour to get to work, and she was still late.

She skirted past the smaller cubbies and around the corner to her less tiny workspace. Julie popped her head up, looked around as if to see if anyone else noticed Rachel's lateness, and then started laughing.

"What?" Rachel tucked her purse inside her desk and pulled her coat from her shoulders.

"The look on your face is priceless."

"You mean the *I'm late and don't want my supervisor to notice* look?"

"Yep, that one."

"Too late." The male voice behind her made her cringe.

Rachel squared her shoulders and turned to face her boss. "I'm sorry, Gerald. I thought I gave myself enough time—"

Gerald looked past her and toward Julie. "You owe me ten bucks."

Julie pulled out her purse as she laughed.

Both of them were smiling.

Julie reached past Rachel and handed Gerald a ten.

"What's that about?"

Gerald waved the bill in the air. "Julie didn't think you'd make it here until nine, I had faith you'd make it before eight thirty."

"You were betting on me?"

"I'm kinda shocked you made it in at all," Julie confessed.

The tension in Rachel's shoulders started to ease. "The streets by my house were a mess." Luckily, the snow in the city streets had been pushed to the side.

Gerald waved a hand toward the high-rise window. "Most of this will melt before tomorrow."

"That's good."

"Do we have the Google proposal ready for Monday's meeting?"

Rachel and Julie both said yes at the same time. "Just fine-tuning the PowerPoint."

Gerald turned and started walking into his office. "Rachel, I need a minute."

Just when she thought she was off the hook for showing up late.

She glanced at Julie, who offered a shrug of her shoulders.

In his midsixties, Gerald was one of the longest lasting company employees and a close personal friend of the owners.

"I'm really sorry I'm late," Rachel started.

"I know you are. Please sit."

She clenched her hands together and sat on the edge of the chair opposite his desk.

"Winters in New York can be brutal."

"I've been told."

"And driving into the city is a colossal waste of time."

"I've heard that, too."

Gerald lifted his eyes to hers. "When we offered this position, we knew you were coming in from California and sweetened the deal with six months of city parking. More than enough time for you to come to the conclusion that driving in is something you may want to reconsider."

She felt an intervention coming on. "If I need to leave home at four in the morning to get here, I will."

"And what happens if Owen needs you at home and it takes you three hours to get there?"

She blinked a few times.

"I like you, Rachel. You bring a freshness to marketing we haven't seen in a while. You have the ability to pinpoint issues before they become problems. You're a leader, and quite honestly, I think you'll fit right in with the management team before your first year with us is up."

That had been the goal since she moved. "I'd like that."

"If you opt out of the city parking, we will give the allowance in a cash sum that will pay for a monthly train pass and parking at the train station you'll need to drive to for over a year."

Rachel opened her mouth to respond, only to have Gerald cut her off.

"Not to mention toll fees and gas."

The denial of need sat on her lips.

She swallowed it.

"I'll consider the offer."

"Good. Your first nor'easter is just around the corner, and that snow takes weeks to melt, trash piles up . . . it's not pretty. You haven't lived until it takes you two hours to drive four miles in this city."

She didn't think that was possible.

One look at Gerald and she knew he wasn't bluffing.

"Now go fine-tune your PowerPoint."

"Owen?" Rachel walked into the house, tossing her car keys in a bowl by the front door and shedding her coat to keep the drops of water that fell off of it from trailing all over the house.

"We're up here," he yelled from upstairs.

The familiar sound of cars skidding on pavement and the occasional outburst from a teenage boy told her he had a friend over who was racing him on a virtual track in a video game. Owen's laughter met her ears halfway up the stairs. Rachel paused and smiled. Hearing the sounds of normal lifted her spirits.

She poked her head through the crack in the door to find Owen and Ford perched on the edge of his bed, controllers in hand, eyes glued to the flat-screen on Owen's wall.

"Hey, Ford."

"Hi," he said, his eyes never leaving the screen.

She looked around the room; an empty bag of corn chips lay on the floor, a half empty bottle of water sat beside Owen. "Did you eat?"

"I'm starving," Owen announced.

"Dude, knock it off." Ford turned his controller with his whole body, as if that would make the online car move in the direction of his arms.

Owen obviously didn't knock the *whatever* off that Ford was talking about. Not that it mattered, both boys continued to ram their virtual cars into each other while they laughed.

"I'll get something started for dinner."

Rachel was sure neither kid heard her.

"Are you staying for dinner, Ford?"

"That would be great."

As she turned to leave the boys to their task of crashing and racing, Owen announced, "There was a package at the door when I came home from school. I left it on the table."

"Okay."

She stopped by her unfinished bedroom, pulled off her boots, and replaced them with a thick pair of socks. The hardwood floors kept the old house the temperature of its basement, something she had yet to get used to. California homes didn't have subterranean space for storage, laundry, and spiders. Luckily there were a few high windows down there that helped brighten up the place. But she'd vowed to drywall as much of the open room as she could and paint the whole thing in a shade of white before summer. Basements like hers belonged in scary movies with screaming women. Neither of which she wanted anything to do with.

Back downstairs, she clicked on her speaker and linked her Internet radio station in. A new pop song had her humming as she walked into the kitchen. Before Owen moved in with her, dinner on a Friday night at home would be half a bottle of wine and a salad. Now that Sister Responsibility was her middle name, the wine was replaced with iced tea, and something had to go along with the salad. With two teenagers eating, tonight would be something filled with carbs. She scanned her pantry, hoping the meal would jump out at her.

Pasta.

Easy, quick . . . and she could heat up sauce and boil noodles without a recipe.

She added half an onion and a handful of mushrooms to the sauce, nothing fancy, but something to make her feel like she was actually cooking. A morphed cucumber and a moldy tomato ended up in the trash, reducing their salad to lettuce and carrots.

A Saturday trip to the grocery store was in order.

While the water boiled and the sauce simmered, Rachel found the stack of mail on the dining room table. She fingered through a few bills and tossed the junk to the side to add to the recycle bin. The box Owen had spoken of didn't have a mailing label. In fact, all that was written on the plain brown box was her name, her first name.

She peeled away the tape, not knowing what to expect. Once she folded the lid back, she saw a handwritten envelope on top of a white canvas bag. It took a little effort to lift the noisy bag from the box—the sound of metal hitting metal struck her as odd. She set the envelope aside, unread, and opened the bag.

Chains.

Chains for the tires on her car.

"Who . . . ?"

She thought maybe Julie, perhaps Gerald . . . then she opened the note and a second paper fell out.

Rachel

Thank you for braving this stranger in a storm and keeping me from frostbite. I thought maybe Owen would like to replace the kitchen knife with skills. I know the owner, first month is on me if he is interested.

Welcome to Connecticut.

Jason

Below his name was a phone number.

Rachel glanced at the paper that had fallen out. A flyer for a tae kwon do studio and a name, address, and number were attached to a simple note that said, "Tell Bruce I sent you."

Something inside her stomach flipped, the buzz a teenage girl feels when she notices a popular boy watching her from the other side of the classroom. Or maybe she was reading into it. Maybe this was just a thank-you, a friendly gesture from a grateful, stranded traveler.

Before she could consider her options further, the sound of water boiling over on the stove directed her attention to dinner. Back through the door in the kitchen, she relit the flame on the stovetop and turned down the temperature of the sauce.

Ten minutes later, Owen and Ford were sitting at her small table, passing the salt. The boys were animated in their conversation about the video game they'd been playing and about the football team at their school. Neither one of them was on it, but each of them had an opinion on whether or not the team would make the finals.

Rachel listened and would occasionally try and say something worthy of hearing. The boys entertained her comments but redirected the conversation back to what only the two of them knew anything about.

"We should probably get there early," Ford said during the quarterback debate.

"Yeah, it's gonna be packed."

Rachel pushed her plate aside, catching on to their discussion. "Are you guys going to the game tonight?"

"We talked about this earlier," Owen told her.

"We did?" She remembered something about a game last weekend but hadn't remembered to put anything on her calendar.

"It's your turn to drive," Owen said, his voice more than a little annoyed that she'd forgotten. "Unless you let me use the car."

She narrowed her eyes. "Nice try."

Owen scowled.

"You boys clean the dishes, I'll change."

Owen stared. "You don't have to stay at the game."

She shrugged her shoulders and pushed back from the table. "I don't have anything else I'd like to do tonight more than go to a high school football game."

Owen looked between her and Ford. "Fine, but we're not sitting with you."

She almost laughed. "I wouldn't think of it."

An hour later, half frozen among several hundred teenagers and excited parents and alumni, Rachel tried to remember any redeeming value of sitting in the stands in arctic temperatures when she could be at home painting a bedroom. Her gaze traveled to Owen, who sat with Ford, Lionel, and two girls she didn't recognize. "I'm only here because you would have dragged me along with you, Em."

The lady on Rachel's right glanced out of the corner of her eye. Speaking to herself probably wasn't the best way to make friends.

Rachel smiled and pretended to pay attention to what was happening on the field.

The quarterback of East Ranch High looked like he was either on his sixth year at the school or belonged in college. And one of the linebackers had enough facial hair to be the spokesman for the crew of *Duck Dynasty*. Rachel didn't remember boys looking like men when she was in high school. And much like most of the adults in the stands, she wasn't that many years away from that time in her life.

While she watched the spectators, something happened on the field, and half of the people in the stands stood and started to cheer. She stood, just to put some circulation in her legs.

Their team had the ball and had stopped at the five-yard line. The cheerleaders did their job of inciting the crowd, and on the next play, East Ranch scored the first points in the game. Rachel let the fans' excitement pump her up as she cheered. Her eyes landed on Owen once again. This time he was looking back at her with a smile. She offered a thumbs-up before he turned back to his new friends.

Yeah, that was why she was there. When you stepped into the mom role, you went in with both feet. Out of the blue, she wondered if he would be interested in something like tae kwon do. Her thoughts immediately turned to the chains sitting on her table at home.

She pulled the note Jason had left with his gift out of her pocket and reread it.

Her cheeks warmed.

Assuming he gave her a mobile number, Rachel opted to send a text. Besides, trying to talk to him in this crowd was pointless.

Hello Jason. Owen and I received your gifts. They were incredibly thoughtful. Thank you.

She read her note over, twice, then pressed "Send."

Off it went, wherever notes went as they traveled faster than Superman in cyberspace. It was a good thing she understood marketing, because technical anything ping-ponged around her head until she was dizzy. If it weren't for Owen, they would never have managed to hook up the speaker system and DVR at the house.

The phone in her hand buzzed, reminding her she was holding it.

Is this Rachel?

She grinned.

Do you leave gifts on everyone's doorstep in town?

Dot. Dot. Dot. It is nearly Christmas.

Was he flirting? It had been some time since she'd sent a text to anyone outside of the friend zone, so she couldn't tell. So you double as Connecticut's Santa Claus?

Shhh. Don't tell anyone. It's a secret.

Well, he wasn't *not* flirting. I'll keep my mouth closed on one condition.

Oh? What's that?

Rachel's eyes no longer lingered on the field. I want to meet Vixen. She's always been my favorite.

I thought Vixen was a he.

She giggled. A boy named Vixen. That's just cruel.

Good point. I'll see what I can do. The team is on a strict curfew until after the holiday.

Rachel found a rolling eye emoji.

What are you doing on this balmy Friday night?

She glanced at the field, then found the back of Owen's head in the stands. Freezing my butt off at a high school football game.

Does Owen play?

No.

She found Owen again, noticed him talking with one of the girls. The girls are here.

Ah, yes. I remember. Smart kid.

She stared at her screen for a full minute, wondering how she could keep their conversation going. Thank you again, for the gifts.

You're welcome.

She hesitated. Maybe Jason was just being nice and what she thought was flirting was just nice to another level.

The visitor fans cheered from the other side of the field. After glancing at her messages and not seeing a dot, dot, dot, she went ahead and put the phone in her pocket.

He was just being nice.

A minute later it buzzed.

Rachel?

Yes

Dot. Dot. Dot. Would you mind if I text you again sometime? For personal reasons.

She squeezed her fist, grinned like a fool. Owen cheered from below. Did she really have time for this right now? My life is a little complicated.

I like complicated.

She rubbed her ear through the beanie holding the warmth on her head. You've been warned.

Is that a yes?

Rachel giggled. Yes.

Enjoy the rest of the game. I hope your team wins.

It felt as if her team already had.

Chapter Four

"When was the last time this place saw Christmas decorations?" Mary wiped dust off a plastic box Jason hadn't seen in years.

Glen stood beside him. The sadness in his eyes matched the feeling in Jason's heart. "It's been a while," he told his wife.

Truth was, none of them wanted to warm the estate for Christmas after their parents died. It wasn't that they made a conscious effort *not* to decorate, but they hadn't taken the steps to deck the halls either.

Mary pulled out a stream of garland. "Do you have pictures of where this goes?"

"I'm sure we do," Glen said.

"All the albums are in the library," Jason told her.

Mary stood, brushed her hands together. Her gaze found her husband's, then she turned to Jason. "Oh." She paused. "Are you guys okay with this?" The therapist in her emerged. "We can always buy new decorations if this is too painful."

Jason shook away the memory of his mother decorating the house and directing them to trim the tree, and the years he'd seen the same garland draped from the stairway banister.

"Don't be ridiculous," Glen said.

"We're good," Jason assured her. "That goes on the stairs."

"Right, with the gold ball things I always managed to break," Glen added.

Mary approached Glen, patted his arm, and headed toward the library.

"C'mon. Only fifty thousand more boxes to bring in."

Glen moaned and followed him to the storage shed. Although *shed* wasn't a fair description of the thousand-foot building, complete with electricity and an alarm system. Nothing at the estate was done small. His father had spared no expense when it came to building his castle for his wife and children. He would talk about the day all of them were married and grandchildren would fill the empty rooms.

"Good God. I forgot how much Mom loved Christmas."

"Dad was just as bad." Jason placed his hand on the shelf containing the massive train that didn't just circle the tree like a Norman Rockwell painting but encompassed the entire expanse of the family room, disappeared through a tiny tunnel and hidden door behind one of the curtains, and zigzagged up a grade and onto an elevated track in the formal dining room. Yeah, the train system was an engineering marvel that took twenty-two minutes to make a full rotation.

Glen came up behind him and paused. "Should we?"

"Would it be the same if we didn't?"

Glen shook his head and pulled down the first of a zillion boxes.

It took a village of effort to make a dent in the decorations.

Back at the house, Trent, Glen, and Jason tackled the train while Mary and Monica trimmed every surface with green, gold, red, and silver.

Lyn, the housekeeper, who had been with the Fairchild house for fifteen years, lived in a small guesthouse on the estate. Now in her midsixties, she'd raised her own children before coming to work for Jason's parents, and lost her husband to cancer only five years ago. Lyn helped direct Mary and Monica and made the effort to prepare an after-decorating meal, which filled the house with the warm smell of roasting beef and onions.

Outside, Nathan worked with Randy, an on-site groundskeeper who bunked with him in the accommodations by the hangars. Randy was new on the property and not someone Jason thought would last for long. He liked the job, and did it well, but he was more of a designer than a gardener. Time would tell.

"It's a good thing Dad was anal about his train," Trent said as he peered over the schematics, written down as if the scaffolding for the toy were the plans to build the Empire State Building.

Glen unfolded the aluminum risers that would eventually hold the rail system. "He loved this thing."

"We all loved this thing," Jason said. "Especially when Grandpa was around. Remember how he used to disappear in another room and fill the empty cars with candy and tell us it was Santa's elves?"

"I miss that man."

"I miss them all," Trent said.

Glen patted Trent's back. He'd always blamed himself for their parents' accident. He'd found out that the woman he thought he loved, the woman he had considered marrying, was already married. He asked his father to fly her home, and their mother had gone with him since it was a night flight. The plane went down, killing all three of them on board.

Jason looked over the mess they were making, which would eventually be magical. "Not to sound all mystical and stuff, but it feels like they're here."

Trent's eyes welled, and Jason looked away, pretending he didn't notice. His own throat clogged with emotion.

Glen cut the melancholy. "Yeah, and Dad is laughing at how long it's taking us to get this up."

"Right!"

Half an hour later, Jason took a break to check on the progress outside. A lighting service was there with two cherry pickers, and a team of five guys was tacking Christmas lights along the eaves lines.

Nathan played foreman and made his way to Jason's side. "This makes me smile, lad."

"It's a lot of work."

"Celebrating our good Lord's birth is worth it, don't you think?"

"This would be easier if this place wasn't so big."

"But it wouldn't be your home."

True. He'd never lived in a modest home. Ever.

His thoughts turned to Rachel. Was she a tree and lights kinda woman, or did she have Santa throw up everywhere? Or maybe she didn't do anything at all.

He dialed her number to find out.

"Hello." She sounded surprised.

"Good morning."

"It's one o'clock."

"Good afternoon, then."

She laughed. The kind of nervous laugh that said his call may have flustered her. He liked that thought.

"I was wondering about something," he started.

"Oh?"

"Yeah. I was calling to see if you were a decorate the house for Christmas like it's a department store kind of person, or a simple tree and string of lights and call it done."

He heard her take a deep breath. "You're calling me to find out how I decorate for Christmas?"

He considered how that sounded. "I called to hear your voice. Christmas lights were my excuse."

She muttered something he didn't quite get. "You're making me blush."

"Good."

"I haven't given it much thought," she told him. "I probably should."

He thought of her son. "Kids like Christmas."

"Right . . . oh, geez. I should probably get a tree." Her playful tone was replaced by distress.

"Did you bring your decorations with you on the move, or are you buying new?"

"I need to go shopping."

That answered that. "You sound stressed."

"I have a lot to do. This Christmas will be hard enough on Owen, I need to make it as normal as possible. That means a tree." It sounded as if she were talking to herself. "And presents. Like from Santa. I'm sure he doesn't believe in Santa, but I should probably still make the effort, right?"

Was she asking for his opinion?

"I'm sure your son knows the big man in the red suit is really just you."

"My what . . . oh. No, no. Owen isn't my son."

It was Jason's turn to be surprised. "He's not?"

Rachel paused. "His mom, Emily, was my best friend. She . . ."

Jason closed his eyes, knew what was coming.

"Cancer. Rare and aggressive. She asked me to take care of Owen when she died. Not that she needed to."

"I'm sorry."

"I told you my life was complicated."

"And I like complicated." He wasn't sure that was completely true, but he was sticking to his words.

"She passed in May. Between the move, my new job, and taking on Owen, Christmas decorations haven't entered my mind."

He thought about how long it had taken for the Fairchild men to redecorate after the loss of their parents. "It's not a priority."

"Yeah, it is. Owen is still a kid. He had to grow up a lot after Em. I need to make this work."

"I'm sure you'll do fine."

"I'm guaranteed to screw it up. But I have to try. Do tree lots deliver? I don't even know what a tree costs." She was doing that talking to herself thing again.

He thought of the tree arriving later that day for the family room. The cost of the thing almost matched the delivery fee because of its size.

"I have a truck."

"I couldn't ask you . . ."

"You didn't ask."

Silence.

"I was going to ask you out for dinner, but tree shopping was my second choice."

Crickets.

"I haven't dated since Owen," she told him. "I don't know how this fits."

"It's tree shopping. Bring Owen along."

"I don't know."

"Wednesday night," he said. "Just a friendly thank-you from the stranger you met on the side of the road. Practical, since I have a truck." It was actually Nathan's truck, but he wasn't about to split hairs over it.

"Wednesday?"

She was considering it.

"I'll bring a thermos of hot cocoa."

She laughed. "Okay."

Jason hadn't worked that hard for a first date in years. Most women jumped. "Seven?"

"Seven should work."

"I'll see you then."

After he hung up, he gave a celebratory fist to the air. He turned to go back into the house and found Monica watching him from inside. She questioned him with her eyes.

He waved and walked back around the house to avoid any questions.

It was almost as if Jason's mention of Christmas illuminated the holiday in Technicolor. Everywhere Rachel went after his call screamed Santa. Thanksgiving had been rather low-key, a meal at a restaurant, a few tense moments when Owen went to bed early and Rachel heard him crying in his room. There hadn't been many of those times since they'd moved to the East Coast. But they happened enough to remind them both of their loss. Every month proved easier. The grief counselors told her that the first set of holidays would be the hardest. Which meant Rachel needed to do everything in her power to allow Christmas to live.

She'd spent a lot of time in Emily's condo during the holidays. She always had a tree and really loved red and white lights. Rachel hadn't really bothered. A tabletop tree, if she remembered, and the presents she'd buy were store wrapped to perfection. The single woman in the group didn't do the entertaining, so decorating wasn't a priority.

She pulled into her driveway and stared at her house.

She'd never strung Christmas lights in her life.

"How hard can it be?" she asked herself.

With her arms loaded with groceries, she looked up the street to see one of her neighbors standing on a ladder, hammer in hand. Across from him, another man was blanketing his shrubs in a netting of lights.

Yep, Christmas was everywhere.

"Owen?"

"Yeah?"

"Help with the groceries."

Footsteps down the stairs followed her request. He brought in the rest of the bags and helped her unpack. He opened a package of cookies from the in-store bakery before putting one thing away.

"Hungry?" she asked.

"Always."

He was past the age to tell him not to make a meal out of sugar. Most of the time he policed himself, anyway.

"Where do you think we should put the Christmas tree?" she asked as they moved around the kitchen, putting things away.

"Christmas tree?"

"Yeah." She watched him from the corners of her eyes. "In front of the window? In the corner of the living room?"

"We're getting a tree?"

She looked straight at him. "It's Christmastime, isn't it?"

He pushed open the door leading to the living room, cocked his head to the side. "In front of the window."

Smiling, she said, "Jason volunteered his truck to help us out on Wednesday."

"Stranded Car Guy?"

"Yeah."

He met her eyes, didn't look away. "He likes you."

"Maybe."

"He sent you chains."

Nothing screamed romance like snow chains. "Which was very thoughtful. Have you given more thought to tae kwon do?" She mentioned the free lessons after the football game. He said he'd think about it.

"We'll see after Wednesday. If the guy ends up being a jerk, I don't want to take anything from him."

"That's a good rule to follow." Not that she'd give back the chains. She needed them.

Later that night, after she and Owen had made a trip to a big box store in search of lights and glass balls for the tree they planned on putting up, Rachel tackled the door leading to the kitchen. What she first thought was charming now became a nuisance. It took a hammer and a flathead screwdriver she used as a battering ram to knock the bottom hinge free. The top hinge proved more difficult. As she pounded away, she estimated the weight of the solid wooden door. She cautioned herself to wait until Owen was home from his friend's house but decided against it. Like every home repair she'd managed since moving in, she did it herself. Even if it took three times as long. There was a sense of accomplishment about it. Having lived in a turnkey condo most of her adult life, there wasn't anything to fix. And if something did break, she'd always called someone. Now that she was playing caretaker for Owen, she needed to watch what she spent. And that meant checking out a crap-ton of YouTube how-to videos.

Em had left Owen what money she had. Social security kicked in a monthly check. All of which was funneled into a college account. The money Rachel didn't spend on repairs was for Owen's future car, insurance, which she knew would be steep, and all the other crap that came along with taking care of a teenager. At this point she wasn't struggling, but that was due in part to frugality.

She knocked at the stubborn top hinge as years of rust sprinkled to the ground. Fifteen minutes of pounding later, the pin pulled free. To her surprise, the door didn't fall to the ground. It stayed in the same location, as if suggesting she was a fool for trying to remove it.

Rachel stepped down from the tiny stepladder she had and grasped the door with both hands. She shoved. Nothing moved. Apparently the rusty pins weren't keeping the door in place. The weight of the door kept the hinges fused. She used the hammer to knock away at the hinges, wiggling the door after every swing. Giving up wasn't an option. With her luck the damn thing would fall in the middle of the night and give her a heart attack.

Finally, an hour into what should have been a ten-minute job, the door broke free.

Unfortunately, she caught it with the side of her head. She managed to keep from crumbling under it and not so gently set it aside. Her forehead above her right eye screamed. When she removed her hand, she expected to see blood but didn't.

In the downstairs bathroom, she checked the damage. Already a goose egg formed, which meant she was going to have a black eye by Monday. Her first impression on the owners of the company she worked for, and she was going to look like she took a punch in a bar fight.

She left the door where it lay, and filled a plastic bag with ice. Maybe the cold would mitigate the damage. The ice hurt, and her forehead already felt as if a skipping stone sat under the surface of her skin.

"Know your limits, woman," she told herself. Her intention was to take the heavy door to the basement, but she decided the trip down the old stairs would be pushing her luck.

Ice in hand, she picked up her mess, except for the door, and admired the difference with it gone. Then she noticed the casing and layers of paint that needed to be scraped free. The kitchen cabinets on the other side of the wall . . . could they go? It would work so much better with the space completely opened up. Removing the cabinets would probably result in stitches.

Good thing Jason was helping with the tree.

Jason. If he had a truck, chances were he had a ladder.

She checked the time, decided it wasn't too late for a text.

Do you have a ladder I can borrow? It wasn't until after she pressed "Send" that it dawned on her that she was asking a favor of a man she'd known for three days.

When Jason didn't respond right away, she wondered if he was out on a date. It was Saturday night.

I do and you can. Why do you need it?

Perfect. One less thing she needed to buy. **Christmas lights.**

You're putting them up?

Her hand traveled to her head. **Between Owen and I, we can manage.**

Do you want me to bring it by tomorrow?

Wednesday is fine. Maybe by then she'd be able to cover any left-over bruises up with cosmetics.

I'm looking forward to it.

I am, too.

Chapter Five

Owen laughed every time he looked at her. The swelling had reached its height by Sunday morning, and by the afternoon the red and purple weren't colors she was going to cover with foundation. Wearing dark sunglasses when it was raining stood out just as much as a bruised face.

"It's not funny."

"One look at you and Stranded Car Guy is gonna run the other direction."

"Men aren't that shallow."

"Yes, they are. Lida had a massive zit right on the tip of her nose, and Lionel didn't ask her to the winter formal."

"Zits don't last forever."

"It was huge. Not as big as that thing you're growing on your head, but close." He started laughing again.

"It will be better by Wednesday."

"You keep telling yourself that."

Rachel laughed. "Your mom used to say that all the time."

They both stopped talking, locked in a memory.

"I miss her," Owen said quietly.

"I do, too."

Sure enough, Monday morning was met with a massive headache and her right eye swollen and bluish purple. Her rainy commute added to her stress, especially when she barely made it to her office chair before she was officially late. She and Julie had planned to arrive half an hour early to go over their PowerPoint one more time before they presented it to the owners of the company.

"What happened to you?" Julie exclaimed.

"I had a fight with my kitchen door. The door won."

"You're not kidding. Should you even be here?"

"Today is a big day." Otherwise she would have called in. Her headache alone was hitting migraine level. "I might try and cut out early."

"I'm sure no one would complain."

From the looks she'd received walking in, Rachel knew no one would.

Julie pushed away from her desk. "Let's get everything set up in the conference room."

Their meeting was set for eight thirty sharp. Gerald arrived a few minutes early, took one look at Rachel, and scowled. "What the . . . ?"

"Don't ask," Rachel said.

Julie laughed. "Her kitchen door beat her up."

"What?"

"It's a long story." It wasn't, but she didn't want to go into it.

"We can postpone this," Gerald offered.

"As bad as this looks"—she pointed to her face—"postponing is worse. Besides, maybe the owners will see that I'm willing to take one for the team."

"Whatever you say."

Gerald took his seat when three members of the advertising team walked in. Julie ran interference by telling everyone about her door punch.

Rachel ignored the giggling and willed her stomach to settle. She'd really wanted to go into this meeting poised and confident. As much as she knew her presentation was exactly what the company needed, delivering the message and selling it to the CEO and CFO didn't need the distraction of a bruised face getting in the way.

There were only two chairs left that needed filling, and it was eight thirty-five.

When she heard voices behind the closed conference door, she turned around to gather her strength. Public speaking was easy for her, she knew her material . . . but damn, her head hurt, messing with her psyche.

A chorus of good mornings spread around the room.

Rachel sucked in a breath, blew it out slowly.

"You remember Julie Kim," Gerald said.

Rachel painted on a smile and turned.

"And this is our newest member of the team. Rach—"

"Rachel?"

Maybe the hit to her head was harder than she thought. "Jason?"

"What the hell happened to your face?"

"What the hell are you doing here?"

Jason stood beside another man, close in stature, their power suits perfectly pressed, not a hair out of place. He was just as easy to look at as she'd remembered.

"You two have already met?"

Two giant steps and Jason was at her side, his hand reaching up to brush her hair back. The gesture and the concern on his face would have wooed her if he wasn't standing in the middle of her office doing it.

"She had a fight with a door," Julie said from the side.

"Have you had this looked at?" Jason asked.

Rachel shook him off. "No. What . . . what are you doing here?"

The room was perfectly silent, and the seed of doubt spread in her gut. She glanced around. The man Jason had walked in with had his hands tucked in his pockets as he rocked back on his heels, a mischievous grin on his face. The advertising team was exchanging glances.

Julie looked at her and shook her head; the hidden message she was attempting to send was lost on Rachel.

She felt sick.

Gerald was the only one who found his voice. "Rachel, this is Jason Fairchild."

"Fairchild." She blinked several times, trying to register everything coming in at one time. *Stranded Car Guy.* Her Wednesday night tree trimming date . . . was her boss. She closed her eyes, shook her head. "No, no . . . this isn't . . ." She was thinking out loud.

"Are you okay?" Gerald asked.

She opened her eyes, pushed her chin in the air.

"I think you should sit down," Jason suggested.

How could he be her boss? "I'm fine." Her tone was harsher than she meant.

"This is highly entertaining." The man with Jason approached. "I'm Glen . . . *Fairchild.* Jason's brother."

Rachel attempted to compose herself, reached out to shake Glen's hand. "Rachel Price. It's a pleasure."

"It sure is."

The staff in the room started to mutter among themselves.

She took advantage of the noise and leaned closer to Jason. "Why didn't you tell me you were my boss?"

He leaned in. "You didn't tell me where you worked."

Glen started laughing.

"Now that the introductions are formally done, should we get started?" Gerald moved them along.

Rachel couldn't help but glare at the man she was supposed to be impressing.

"Fine."

A long drink of water later, she asked that Julie dim the lights, which didn't help much to hide the man staring at her. The fact that he sat at the head of the conference table, directly opposite her, his smirking brother to his right, Gerald to his left, made her acutely aware of the fact she'd flirted with her boss.

Her boss!

She stopped looking at him and started to speak.

———

What the hell happened to her? It looked like she'd been punched. Her eye was swollen damn near shut. She kept rubbing her temple, a sure sign it hurt. He had a strong desire to pull her out of the meeting to quiz her and make sure a doctor had given her a clear view of her health.

Glen kicked him under the table.

Jason glared.

His brother nodded toward Rachel, making him aware that he wasn't listening to her new approach to online marketing.

". . . so if we're going to capture the millennials and push Fairchild Charters to the top of the private jet food chain, we need to spend a serious effort online." The image on the screen showed early twenty-somethings holding cell phones while sitting in a bar.

For the next hour, Rachel offered an impressive array of facts, including the sheer number of kids under twenty-five who were self-made millionaires. Many of them living in Silicon Valley, working for companies such as Google and Yahoo, both companies that had their own fleet of jets but didn't offer them to everyone. Rachel suggested frequent trips and networking with these companies and other tech enterprises to encourage private charters as an alternative for their travel needs. It helped that she had worked with these businesses when she lived on the West Coast.

All in all, the presentation was well thought out and left room for very few questions when she was finished.

Jason was impressed.

"If we start rolling out my plan now, we should see a bump in charters by early summer. By fall I'd like to see Fairchild Charters land a corporate account with Yahoo, Google, or Amazon."

"Or all three," Julie added.

"I won't oversell that idea, but it's worth a try."

"You already have contacts in Palo Alto?" Jason asked.

"I do." She didn't offer more.

"I like it," Glen said. "We'll need our team to create a budget."

"The big accounts are obviously where it's at, but the long-term plan with young CEOs will be our bread and butter in ten years," Gerald added. "I think Miss Price has given us a lot to consider."

"I want to see more numbers," Jason told them. "Projections on how much staff will be needed, cross-training cost."

"We can do that," Rachel assured him.

She rubbed the side of her neck and quickly looked away.

"I'd like a report in two weeks."

"I can do it in one."

His gaze traveled to her bruise. "Two weeks is fine. It is the holidays."

She winced.

Glen stood and someone turned up the lights.

"Thank you, Rachel, Julie," Glen told them.

"Our pleasure." Julie spoke for both of them.

Julie patted Rachel on the back while Jason's advertising team funneled out of the room.

"Progressive thinking." Gerald stood in front of him, cutting off the view of the two women whispering.

"You said the new blood we'd hired was coming to us with innovative ideas," Jason said.

"Rachel knows her stuff."

"How do you know her?" Glen asked Jason.

Jason looked around Gerald, wanting to catch Rachel before she left the room. "Long story."

Glen chuckled. "Great, you can tell me over lunch."

Gerald and Glen left the conference room together.

Julie and Rachel started toward the door. "If I can have a minute," Jason said.

Julie looked between them, muttered something, and left them alone.

Rachel set her laptop down. "Why didn't you tell me you were Jason *Fairchild*?"

"It wasn't intentional."

"You're my boss."

"Technically, Gerald is your boss."

"You own the company."

"It doesn't change anything."

She looked at him as if he had an IQ of five. "It changes everything. I can't have my *boss* texting me for *personal reasons*."

"Gerald's married."

Did she just growl at him?

"Dating the man who signs my checks is the fastest way to lose my job."

"Glen is married, too. Technically he signs your checks."

"This isn't a joke, Jason."

He knew it put a ripple in his plans, but that wasn't going to stop him. "I like complicated, remember."

She waved a finger between the two of them. "This can't happen. I need this job. I need to make things work here for Owen. Sleeping with the boss is never a good idea."

So she was already picturing him in bed.

He liked that.

"Stop smiling." She raised her voice.

"Did you see a doctor for that?" He purposely changed the subject.

"No. It's just a bump."

"It's a knot, and it should be checked."

"I'm pretty sure if it were serious, I would know by now."

"Do you have a headache?"

She rolled her eyes. "Of course. There is a golf ball under my skin."

"Are you eating?"

"Are you my mother?"

Her evasion of his question gave him the answer. "I'm your boss, as you keep trying to point out. And if you're not well enough to be at work, you should be at home, resting . . . after you've seen a doctor."

"Would you be telling me this if my cell number wasn't in your phone?"

He didn't answer.

"Exactly. Which is why we can't date."

"We can date."

She tried to smile, huffed out a breath. "I'm sorry. I'm flattered, really, I am. I'm attracted, obviously, or I wouldn't have . . . but I'm *not* stupid—"

Yeah, well . . . that made one of them.

Jason took a step toward her and stopped her rant with his lips.

He could almost taste her simmering anger as it softened. Rachel gasped but didn't pull away. He touched her cheek and held her close. Oh yeah, this was going to happen. When was the last time he'd had butterflies when he'd kissed a woman? When was the last time one had reluctantly melted in his arms?

She opened her lips, and her tongue dipped inside his.

All the blood in his system dumped south before Rachel pulled away.

Her face was flushed, her breathing too quick.

Accomplishment settled in his system.

She stared at him without words.

"Rachel . . ."

She pressed a finger to his lips before gathering her computer and walking out the door.

The inquisition began the moment Rachel returned to her desk.

Julie rolled her chair over, ducked her head. "How do you know Jason Fairchild?"

"He's Stranded Car Guy."

"The guy you ran off the road?"

"I didn't run him off the road, he tried to go around. In an Audi." A really nice Audi, if she remembered.

"He acted a little familiar for a guy you helped stay out of the cold," Julie said.

Rachel glanced over Julie's head, didn't see anyone watching them.

"We've been texting all weekend. He left chains for my car at the house on Friday. He was going to help Owen and me get our Christmas tree on Wednesday, since he has a truck," she whispered.

Julie squealed.

Rachel shushed her. "Stop it. That can't happen now."

"Why not?"

"He's my boss. I can't date my boss."

"Every great soap opera has a chick doing her boss."

Rachel glared, whispered harshly, "I'm not *doing* anyone!"

"Rachel?"

She swung her head up too quickly, winced at the pain behind her eye. Gerald stood a few feet away, his expression unreadable.

"Yes?" How much of their conversation had he heard? This wasn't good.

"Good job today."

"Thank you."

He looked at her forehead. "That looks like it hurts."

"It does, which is why I got off to a shaky start. I promise my delivery is smoother than what you saw."

"It appeared there was more than one reason for that wobbly start." She wasn't sure how to respond.

Gerald was. "Cussing at the owner of the company probably didn't help."

"I cussed?" Seeing Jason there blocked her common sense.

"You did," Julie said.

Rachel closed her eyes, tried to replay what happened. "It won't happen again." Not in public, anyway.

"That's probably for the best," Gerald told her. "Now why don't you celebrate by going home early and nursing that black eye?"

"It's okay, I'm—"

"That wasn't a request, Rachel."

She stopped talking, and Gerald returned to his office.

"I cussed?" she asked herself again.

Julie just laughed.

Chapter Six

"You ended up in a ditch?"

Jason knew he would never hear the end of this. He managed to get out of lunch with his brother, but that didn't stop the man from showing up in his office after two.

"I'm not proud."

Glen leaned back in the chair he offered himself when he walked in.

"Are you dating this woman?"

Jason flipped through the work on his desk, wondering how to answer that question. Was he dating her? No. Did he want to . . . yes. Did he want his brother to know?

"Maybe."

Glen was obviously amused. "Well then, this should put Monica and Mary off the matchmaking campaign."

Jason looked up. "There's a campaign?"

"Not anymore." Glen unfolded from the chair.

He knew his brothers' wives were up to something.

"No blind dates, Glen. As if I need to say that aloud."

"I told Mary that."

Somehow Jason didn't think she listened. Both of his brothers were hopelessly in love with their wives.

"Rachel does have some great ideas for pushing the company forward."

"I thought so, too."

"She's obviously dedicated . . . coming to work with that shiner."

Jason went back to the paperwork on his desk. "I already saw to it that Gerald sent her home."

Glen hesitated at the door. "Risk management would advise you not to date someone on staff. So would our lawyers."

He'd had a few hours to think about that fact.

"Rachel said the same thing."

"She's a smart woman."

And beautiful, and witty . . . and someone he wanted to know better.

"Their advice isn't going to stop you," Glen said.

"Not this time."

———

God, she loved Google. *Cosmo*, eHarmony, *Insider* . . . there wasn't a magazine or website that didn't weigh in on why you shouldn't date your boss.

He holds power over you, he overlooks your faults . . . your colleagues will hate you.

Oh, yeah . . . one more tiny, itty-bitty thing.

You'll lose your job.

Fired.

Or be forced to quit.

No matter how you spun that bottle, dating your boss was a recipe for a last place in line at the unemployment office.

Rachel tucked her feet under her on the couch and watched the rain outside her front window.

Owen was at school, not due home until three. She should probably be painting, or removing the casing around the door that attacked
her. Something. Instead she stared at the drops of water falling from
the sky, contemplating her life, which was stupid. She'd only known
Jason for a few days.

It didn't matter that he was the only man who had turned her head
in close to a year. Wait . . . more like a year and a half.

What did she know about him, anyway? Aside from the driving
himself into a ditch, or his thoughtful thank-you gifts?

He was gorgeous. She knew that.

Rachel shook her head as if her brain was an Etch A Sketch that
would remove the image of him.

She tapped her finger against her knee.

What did she know about him?

Jason Fairchild.

She jumped up from the couch, caught herself when her head
swam, then moved with a little more caution to grab her laptop from
the dining room table.

Once settled, she googled again.

She'd googled potential dates in the past, but never . . . and she did
mean never . . . had there been so much information about one person
who was interested in her.

He had a *Wikipedia* page.

Rachel closed her eyes. How could anyone who had their own
Internet encyclopedia page be interested in dating her?

She started there.

CEO of Fairchild Charters, which he owned jointly with his two
brothers. Yeah, yeah . . . she knew all that.

Net worth . . .

Rachel rubbed her eyes. How could anyone who needed a ride from
her be worth that many zeros?

He'd taken over the role of CEO after the unexpected death of his parents. Rachel found herself following the bouncing ball of Beverly and Marcus Fairchild.

They weren't even sixty, and both of them fell out of the sky while on a short flight in bad weather. Some reports suggested a lightning strike, others said pilot error. The brothers argued against anything their father could have done to cause the plane to crash.

She found a picture of the Fairchild brothers standing over their parents' graves at a funeral.

A tear dropped off her cheek. Jason stared forward, while Glen, the man she'd met today, had his arm around the youngest son, Trent. Her gaze found Jason again. Chin high, his eyes glazed with loss. The picture had been taken eight years before.

Sadly, Rachel understood death all too well.

She moved on.

The information on Jason's personal life was limited to appearances at charity and corporate events. Most of the time he arrived solo, or on occasion he would have a date that consisted of a "family friend" or "colleague." He wasn't one to have the paparazzi following him, so Rachel found herself back on his *Wikipedia* page.

He lived in Connecticut. She knew that.

His philanthropic efforts were for orphaned children, and the company was actively working with Borderless Doctors and Organ Transfers. She had questions about the latter part of that equation. Why was this something she had to look up to hear about? Wouldn't Fairchild Charters want to advertise that information? A company with a heart . . . literally? She wondered just how much money the company she worked for gave up for these efforts.

She bounced around again, this time on social media. She hashtagged Fairchild Charters. The usual shout-outs came from passengers who weren't used to flying in private jets, friends of those who were paying the bill. Most of this she'd seen while doing her research on the company's marketing. She added Borderless Doctors to her search and found a few old splashes of information, mainly about Trent Fairchild and his wife, Monica. For the next hour she read the media's take on their story, starting with a tragedy in Jamaica and ending in Trent being the first of the Fairchild brothers to get married. She wanted to know more about that.

The front door opened, pulling her out of her research.

"What are you doing home?" she asked Owen.

"Ahh." He looked around as if she'd asked something crazy. "School's out. What are you doing home?"

"It's early . . ." Only the time on her computer said it was after three. Apparently the Fairchild family did a good job of keeping her busy all afternoon. "Oh."

"Why are you home? Get fired?"

She jerked. "No. Of course not! Why would you ask such a thing?"

"I was joking." Owen blew past her, straight to the kitchen.

Her heart raced at the mere mention of getting canned. "I wasn't feeling well."

"And you look like crap."

She scowled. "I should probably be telling you not to talk that way."

He laughed. "Yeah, probably."

She heard the pantry door open, the rustling of paper, suggesting junk food. "How about an apple?"

Owen laughed as he left the kitchen and ran up the stairs to his bedroom with a bag of chips and a can of soda.

"I suck at this mom thing."

In an effort to make up for her lacking parenting skills, Rachel cooked something that required more than boiling water. While she wouldn't be winning any culinary awards anytime soon, her chicken casserole had a fair amount of vegetables that should counter some of the junk that sustained Owen's metabolism.

The pain in her head had eased as the day went on, even though the bruise was at its peak. Or so she hoped. Either way, she was going to work in the morning and went to bed early to ensure she had enough rest. Once in bed, she took a minute to check her own personal social media pages. The usual kitten and kid pictures littered her timeline. There weren't many personal messages, even after she posted the picture of the snow she'd managed to get through over the weekend. No, it was as if her life in California never existed. She reminded herself that her closest friend was gone, and the time before Emily's death was buried in her illness. Fostering friendships to withstand a cross-country life hadn't been a priority. So people forgot about her. To be fair, she wasn't going out of her way to keep in close contact with those back home either. She'd hoped that while she was clicking around on her media pages, someone would pop up who would spark a conversation, and she could vent about her current crazy life.

That didn't happen, and instead of finding a friend to talk to, her mood plunged further down.

Loneliness had a cousin named self-pity. And she was a bitch. Picking up the phone to talk to Julie about her dilemma was out of the question. Talking about it online was job suicide. Her mom would tell her to date the man so she'd get fired and somehow be forced to move back to California, which couldn't happen even if Rachel wanted it to. She didn't have a sister, and her brother, as much as she loved him, lacked the common sense gene. He was three years younger than she was and already had one divorce behind him. Relationship advice wasn't something she was going to go to Steve for.

This was a job for Em.

"I shouldn't get anywhere close to him, right?" Rachel glanced at the ceiling in her bedroom as if Emily was right there.

Only there wasn't an answer.

"You're not helping."

Still no answer. Not that she expected one.

She plugged her cell phone in by her bedside, turned off the light, and crawled under the covers. Even though her mind hadn't turned off all day, she managed to fall asleep quickly, and when she woke up, the image of Jason kissing her lingered over her morning cup of coffee.

———

Jason knew Rachel was at her desk, and it took every ounce of willpower to not go over to see her himself. He knew if he started frequenting the marketing and PR departments, he'd churn the office gossip. He'd kissed her in a closed conference room without a witness, and he'd lay money that Rachel hadn't told anyone about his advance, since she was hell-bent on not dating him. He hated that his head was torn with these thoughts. For the first time in forever, a woman sparked his interest beyond the physical, and she worked for him.

Yeah, he wanted to pretend she was managed by Gerald, or even Glen, but no . . . her living was made by Fairchild Charters, of which he was the CEO. A technicality of being the firstborn was complicating his love life. Truth was, being the firstborn had always complicated his life. The expectations, the pressure of keeping everything together after his parents had died. With both of his brothers married and settled, he'd stopped offering all big brother advice, which was often mistaken as parenting words of wisdom. Truth was, Jason had felt the need to step into everything his father had left behind. It was surprising he hadn't had any major health problems.

So why did he wake up at two in the morning, trying to figure out how to make Rachel forget who she worked for? The fact that he thought about convincing her that he was dateworthy while at the same time concerning himself with who might have seen them kissing was enough to send an older man to the hospital with chest pain.

When he closed his eyes, he saw the flush that rose on her cheeks. The smile she tried to hide when she pulled away from his lips . . . the doubt in her eyes. He saw it all. While his head swam with the negativity of an office romance, his heart—and maybe another organ—suggested he continue the path he'd started down.

A knock on his office door interrupted his thoughts. His six-months-pregnant secretary walked in with his acknowledgment.

"I have today's schedule."

He grasped a pen to make notes while she took the seat opposite him.

"How is Junior today?" he asked.

"Kicking way too much for my taste."

Jason couldn't help but smile. Audrey had been his secretary for four years, and in those years she was always either planning a wedding or picking out colors for a nursery. Like many New York executive women, her pregnancy hardly showed through the stylish office clothing and coats. She'd finally settled into shorter heels at the pleading of her husband. But that had taken five months to make happen.

"Don't push yourself," he found himself saying.

"You're sweet. I'm fine."

She looked fine. He'd heard pregnant women had a glow about them, and he'd seen it for himself once Audrey revealed her status.

"You have a meeting with Chuck and Gerald to go over the new marketing plan at ten. You have lunch with Mr. Lewton at Fleming's."

Jason jotted that down with a moan. Lunch with Matt Lewton meant martinis, and the last thing Jason wanted on a Tuesday was a desire for a nap by two. Some clients needed his attention, and martini lunches were part of the job.

Audrey slid a paper across his desk with the heading *Holiday Office Party*. "I know you hate this, but it has to be done today. I tried to make it as easy as possible."

The paper looked like a high school multiple-choice quiz.

The first bullet point had the words *gold, silver, white, silver and gold, silver and green*, and *gold and green* with check boxes next to them.

"What is this?"

"I made it easy. Just check off the box with your preferences."

"It's Christmas," he said as if she didn't know. "Red and green."

"Nope, can't do that. Remember the Starbucks cup debacle? Nineteen percent of the staff is Jewish. We don't want to offend."

He doubted anyone cared as long as they got free booze and a bonus.

"There has to be someone more qualified than me to do this." Jason was pretty sure he'd said the same thing every year since he took over for his father.

"I suggested you hire a coordinator last October, but you put me off," she reminded him.

"So hire one now."

Audrey blinked a few times. "Every event planner in the city worth hiring is booked. Have been since the first week in November. Which was why I bugged you in October."

He pushed the paper to the side, determined to put off the details again. His mother had always taken care of the office parties, and in the last year, he'd managed to enlist Monica and a couple of her family members to take care of some of the details for outside events. The annual holiday party wasn't one of them, but maybe he could wiggle out of it now that Mary had been added to the family.

"I'll take care of it."

Audrey didn't look convinced. "Today. I need to give the caterers the menu and the decorators a direction."

"I got it. The first week in February, we hire an event planner."

"I'll be out on leave at the end of January."

"So the second week in January."

She took a note.

"Do we have your temporary replacement yet?" He'd put Audrey in charge of finding three in-office candidates who could fill her shoes for the four months she was planning on taking off.

"I will have a list for you before Christmas."

"Perfect."

She stood and clasped her notepad to her chest. "Remember, I'm leaving today at three thirty to see my doctor."

Which explained his lack of afternoon appointments.

He grinned and tapped a finger on his holiday to-do list. "So this really doesn't need to be back to you until the morning."

She frowned. "Jason!"

He laughed. "Fine, but if I leave something blank, you make the decision."

She turned and walked away. "I don't take laundry to the cleaners, or buy flowers for girlfriends . . . or pick colors for Christmas."

The first two he'd never asked of her, the last one, however . . . her argument in years past was that food allergies made her the last person to ask about culinary choices, and she blamed being slightly color-blind for her inability to oversee the other part of event planning.

"How about some coffee?"

"That I can do."

He chuckled as she walked out the door.

The grocery store screamed Christmas, from the bags of candy on the end of every aisle to the music piped through the PA. Rachel reached for one too many sugary sweets and added eggnog to her cart.

She didn't even care for eggnog. Still, like the obligatory fruitcake, one needed to buy it even if it just ended up in the trash on December twenty-sixth.

Her phone pinged, letting her know she had a text message.

She looked at Owen's name and opened her messages.

Get frozen pizza

Rachel turned back toward the frozen aisle.

And soda

How about juice?

A frown emoji preceded his response. I'm 15 not 5.
Rachel bought both.
Her phone pinged again. She looked at the message, not the sender.

Silver and gold, or gold and green?

She paused. *Is this a trick question?*

I'm planning the Christmas party.

Rachel scratched her head. What party? She hit "Send" before she realized it wasn't Owen who was texting her.

No, it was Jason. The man who she'd thought about all day long at work and yet hadn't seen or heard from once. To tell the truth, she was surprised and slightly disappointed he hadn't made an excuse to talk to her. Even though it would have been a mistake to do so.

The company Christmas . . . excuse me, holiday party.

Rachel moved out of the way of a woman trying to get to a box of Dr Pepper and huddled over her phone. Wait, you run a billion dollar company and you don't have someone else planning the Christmas party?

Long story, starting with my mother. I'll tell you when we pick up your Christmas tree tomorrow night. So, silver and gold or gold and green?

"Oh, you're smooth," she muttered to herself.

Gold and green. Tomorrow is a bad idea.

He didn't take long to reply.

My phone is about to die. Pick you up at seven. Dress warm, it's supposed to snow.

Her fingers moved fast. I told you we can't date.
He didn't reply.

Jason!

Nothing.

I don't believe for a minute your phone is dead.

Still nothing.

Jason!!!

Zillion-dollar-company CEO and he doesn't have a charger? She tossed her phone into her purse and made her way to the checkout.

Chapter Seven

Rachel must have checked her messages a dozen times an hour, every hour, right up until she left the office the next day. Jason had her in the palm of his hand. If she made a personal appearance in his office on the premise of cancelling their tree-buying date, she'd create the very gossip she was trying to avoid. If she didn't, he'd show up on her doorstep.

She practiced how she was going to blow him off in person and give him a little piece of her mind about ignoring the dozen *answer your messages* she'd left on his cell phone. That was until she closed the door leading in from the garage and was greeted by Owen.

"Hey."

"Hey, back," she said.

"We're getting a tree today, right?"

Oh, shit.

"I moved the couch away from the window to make room."

She followed Owen from the back door through the kitchen and into the living room. Sure enough, Owen had made room for a tree and had even pulled the vacuum out and cleaned in places that hadn't seen attention since before they'd moved in.

"Looks like someone is excited."

He smiled. "Mom would want us to get a tree and make the most of what is gonna suck without her."

Rachel stared straight ahead as his words sank in. "Yeah, she would."

"What time is Stranded Car Guy getting here with the truck?"

"Seven," she said, absently.

"I'll pop a pizza in the oven so we're ready to go. He's not coming for dinner, right?"

"No." No, he wasn't coming for dinner, and now she wasn't going to be able to deliver her premeditated speech.

"Cool." Owen disappeared into the kitchen, leaving her staring at the empty space in the living room.

She closed her eyes, huffed out a long-winded breath, and went upstairs to change.

Jason turned onto Rachel's street, his hands gripping the wheel. Sixteen . . . she had texted him sixteen times telling him they couldn't date. She scolded him for not returning her texts, accused him of ignoring her to get his way. He deserved her wrath and was in fact ignoring her texts. Now, if she'd started saying things he wanted to hear, perhaps his phone would have miraculously returned from cell phone hell. The fact that she didn't outright tell him to stay away gave him comfort that she wouldn't close the door in his face. It didn't hurt that he was her boss, as she had pointed out many times. Not that he would hold that against her if she really wasn't interested. But she was. If she wasn't, she wouldn't have flirted with him over the phone. That was his theory, and he was sticking with it until she proved otherwise.

He was thirty minutes early. An extension ladder rattled in the back of the truck, a hammer sat in the front seat, and hooks used to hang Christmas lights filled a bag from a local hardware store. Along with a timer and outdoor extension cord. He wasn't about to see what damage she could do to her face with a ladder if a simple kitchen door gave her the shiner she'd come to work with on Monday. He'd wiggled the details out of Gerald and earned the man's unwanted advice about interoffice relationships.

Gerald had worked with Jason's father long before Jason finished college. He was filling in as the head of marketing and at the same time keeping the company broker management in line. Gerald had worked in just about every end of Fairchild Charters with the exception of the mailroom. Anytime they lost a senior manager, Gerald was the one they called on to help fill the seat. He said he enjoyed the diversity, and the truth was, once under his guidance, the levels he managed took care of themselves. The man was invaluable. He was also fast approaching retirement, something Jason didn't want to think about.

Rachel's driveway was empty, but lights inside the house gave him hope that she hadn't stepped out for the night to avoid him.

He removed the ladder from the truck first and set it up on the west side of the house. He considered starting the job of getting the hooks up before telling her he was there but decided against it. It was better to gauge the barometer of her mood before testing his parameters.

In a warm down jacket, prepared for rain or possible snow, and blue jeans and boots instead of his office attire, Jason knocked on her door twice and stood back.

Owen opened the door, a piece of pizza in his hand. "You're early."

Heat from inside rushed out.

"I am. Thought I'd get those lights up for you guys before we get the tree."

Owen looked beyond the threshold and toward the ladder. "Good idea. I'll get the lights from the garage."

He turned and left Jason standing in the doorway. Once Owen disappeared from view, Rachel stepped around the corner. She wore a beige sweater and blue jeans that hugged her hips, it was hard not to stare.

"So your phone is dead, huh?"

He blinked a few times and met her eyes. "Yeah. I thought it was the battery, but then . . ." He opened his palm and made a noise indicating the thing had blown up.

"Uh-huh . . . right."

She didn't believe him.

She was smart like that.

"So, single strand or . . . ?" He turned back to the outside, closing the cell phone conversation.

"Are you always this stubborn?" She'd crossed to the doorway and stepped out on her welcome mat.

"I don't know, you'll have to ask my brothers." Jason smiled at her, noticed her holding back.

She glanced over her shoulder and lowered her voice. "The only reason I'm agreeing to this is because Owen is excited about the stupid tree."

Jason wasn't opposed to using Owen to have his foot in Rachel's door.

"Trees are important."

She narrowed her eyes and shivered.

"I got 'em," Owen said as he walked back into the room. He set the boxes down by the door and reached for his coat. "I can help."

"Okay, then. Let's get this done." Jason glanced at Rachel, flashed what he hoped was a charming grin, and turned back outside.

Owen was a great assistant. He stood at the foot of the ladder and handed Jason what he needed as they inched along the eaves, tacking in the hooks.

"This is the first time I've hung lights outside," Owen told him.

"How is that?"

"My mom and I always lived in a condo."

Jason took note of the fact that the kid didn't mention a dad. He tacked in a hook. "Rachel said it was cancer."

"Yeah."

Jason looked down at Owen. "That sucks. I'm sorry."

He shrugged. "I try not to think about it."

"How is that working out?"

Owen gave a partial smile. "Not very well."

Jason turned back to the eaves, pounded another nail. "I lost my mom, too."

"Really?"

"Plane crash. Both her and my dad on the same day."

"That bites. Were you young like me?"

Jason stepped down from the ladder, moved over a few feet as they spoke. "No. I was an adult. Still, they were young."

"Yeah, it's never good. I mean, unless they're really old and stuff. Even then I bet it sucks." Owen handed him another hook and nail.

"It's good you have Rachel."

The mention of her name had Owen clamming up.

"Did she really hit her head with a door?"

Owen laughed.

Jason took that as a yes.

"It's probably a good thing I'm up here on the ladder, then."

"She'd probably break a leg," Owen said.

Jason opened his mouth to comment, and closed it when the front door opened and the woman in question emerged.

He and Owen both kept silent.

"How's it going?"

"Almost done with these."

Owen shined a flashlight up on the last four feet.

"You know, you really didn't have to do this," Rachel told him. "I could have managed."

Jason looked at the fading bruise she tried to hide with makeup. "How's your eye?"

"*That* was an accident."

He turned to place the last hook in before descending off the ladder. "Time for the lights, Owen."

The strands were plugged in at the power source on the side of the garage. It appeared that the previous owners had purposely placed the plug up at the eaves for the sole purpose of holiday lighting. Jason imagined how many years of struggling they'd managed to skip when it came to stringing extension cords and making lights look right in places you didn't want them. He wondered if his house had the same thing. A crew of half a dozen men put the lights up at the estate, so he didn't know.

The brand-new, multicolored lights were perfectly balanced from the west side of the house to the east. The second story had dormers over the windows that Owen said they hadn't accounted for when buying lights. Still, once they were up and the timer was set to go on and off, Jason stepped away from the ladder one last time to see his work.

Rachel and Owen were standing at the edge of the lawn, taking it all in with soft smiles.

"I like," Rachel said.

"Looks good."

"Not bad," Jason said. "I bet we could squeeze a couple more strands up by those windows."

Rachel shook her head. "No, that's okay—"

"I think that's a great idea," Owen interrupted.

"I'll be back on Friday, then." Jason ignored the glare from Rachel as he smiled at Owen.

"I wouldn't want to take you away from your *busy* schedule," Rachel told him. "If you leave the ladder, I can take care of it."

Jason lifted an eyebrow. "She who dances with doors should probably stay away from heights."

Owen laughed out loud.

"Says the man who drove himself into a ditch," Rachel said with a tiny grin.

"I would feel responsible if you got hurt."

"I would feel guilty for monopolizing all your *valuable* time."

Jason glanced at Owen. "Don't you have a new job?" he asked Rachel, assuming she hadn't told Owen about Jason owning the company.

"I do." Her eyes shifted to Owen, then back.

"If you got hurt and had to miss work, wouldn't that impact your new position?"

She narrowed her eyes. "Probably."

Jason smiled, rolled his shoulders back. "Then you're in luck. Because I've had my job for some time, and if I get hurt, I still get a paycheck. So I'll be back Friday, or better yet, Saturday morning, while it's still light out."

They stared at each other, neither backing down.

"Great, now can we go get the tree?" Owen asked. "I'm freezing out here."

Rachel looked away first. "Fine. Let me get my purse."

———

Dances with doors! Who said things like that? In search of hot chocolate, Owen broke away from them once they hit the tree lot. "What about *we shouldn't date* did you misunderstand?"

Jason kept his eyes forward. "If we were dating, I'd be holding your hand."

Rachel glanced at her hand swinging beside his. When was the last time she'd held a man's hand?

"I'm sure you have better things to do on a Saturday morning than hanging more Christmas lights."

"You're right."

"Ha!" Maybe he was seeing his way to her point of view.

"I could be taking the beautiful new woman in my life out for brunch, or maybe dinner. But since she's playing hard to get, I have to settle for hanging her Christmas lights instead."

Maybe not.

"Jason!"

He stopped at a twelve-foot noble fir. "This one's nice."

"I have ten-foot ceilings."

"That might prove tight." He moved across the aisle to the shorter trees.

"I'm not going to date you."

His eyes told her he wasn't convinced. "Fine."

"I need this job."

"You've told me that."

"I mean it, for better or for worse, Owen and I need to stay here until he turns eighteen."

"Why is that, exactly? Was it something his mother wanted?"

"No, Em wouldn't want us anywhere near here."

Jason stopped looking at trees. "I don't understand."

Rachel looked over her shoulder, then back. "It's complicated. If Owen walks up, I'm dropping the subject."

Jason glanced around, didn't see Owen. "Fair enough."

"Owen's paternal grandparents live close by. They haven't had a relationship with Owen at all." She glanced up, then moved closer and lowered her voice. "When Emily died, she had made it clear I was to be Owen's guardian. But the Colemans thought differently."

"Owen's grandparents."

"Right. They immediately hired lawyers. I knew ultimately they could win, especially when they said they were going to get Owen's father involved."

"Does Owen know his dad?"

"Barely." She looked up, stiffened. "There is more to the story that has to wait. Bottom line, we're here to avoid a battle I would lose. And I can't afford to live here without my job."

"There you two are." Owen's words stopped the conversation in half a second.

Rachel painted on a smile. "I see you found cocoa *and* candy."

Owen stirred his hot beverage with a candy cane.

Two kids ran past them and darted into the thick of the trees.

"Never enough sugar." Owen licked the candy and turned around.

Rachel found Jason watching her, his smile a little less cocky, his eyes a little more serious. "What kind of tree do you like, Owen?" he asked.

"One that smells like pine."

Rachel giggled. "I think we're good, then."

Thirty minutes of pulling trees aside and making sure they didn't have massive empty spots where the wind had taken out the branches during their growth, and they finally had their tree.

Jason attempted to pull out his wallet, something Rachel bet was a common thing for him, but she refused. "My home, my tree, my bill."

He scowled.

"You've helped enough already."

He stood back and let her pay.

Chapter Eight

The tree overtook the living room. Owen's smile outshined it all.

It was past nine when Jason secured the tree in the stand and made adjustments to Rachel's satisfaction. Owen opened a box of unused lights and went to work.

"We really can take it from here," Rachel told him.

Jason said nothing and stared.

She rolled her eyes. "Okay, fine. Coffee?"

"That's more like it. I'd love a cup of coffee."

She disappeared into the kitchen; the sound of cupboards opening and closing emerged.

"She doesn't like asking for help," Owen whispered.

"I can tell," Jason whispered back.

"I've been trying to paint her room for over a month, but she's never gone longer than a few hours when I'm not at school."

"Her room needs to be painted?" Jason glanced at the stairs, had a sudden desire to see the inside of her personal space.

"Everything in this house needed repairs and paint. I helped a little before school started, but she's done most of it herself. You should take her out to dinner so I can surprise her."

The kid was smooth, Jason gave him props. "I'll see what I can do." He lifted his hand, palm up. "I'll give you my cell phone, and we can coordinate."

Owen grinned, looked beyond Jason's shoulder, and handed him his phone.

Rachel walked back into the room, coffee cups in hand, before Jason finished typing it in. "So that's how you do that?" he said to Owen, handing over the phone.

Owen laughed. "Yeah. It came with the new update."

"I'll have to try it out." Jason kept the ruse going.

"With your broken phone?" Rachel asked, handing him his cup.

Faking innocence, Jason said, "Right."

She shook her head. "Did you want cream or sugar?"

He took a drink. "Black is fine."

"Ha. That's what she said," Owen chimed.

"Very funny." Rachel sat on the sofa, facing the tree.

Jason didn't catch the joke. It must have shown on his face.

Owen pointed a finger at his face. "Black."

Jason's laugh started slow and built. "That was funny."

"How are those lights coming?" Rachel pushed. "You do have school in the morning."

Half an hour later, the lights were perfectly set, and the boxes of brand-new ornaments were empty. Jason didn't remember the last time he trimmed a tree, and this year he'd done it twice. There had to be a message in there somewhere.

"My work here is done!" Owen dropped a plastic bag as if he were exiting the stage and dropping a microphone.

"Not bad for our first attempt." Rachel rested with her back against the sofa, her legs crossed at her ankles and propped on the coffee table.

Owen stretched, looked at his feet. "Much as I'd love to help clean this up, I have school in the morning."

"Don't worry, I'll leave it for you to take care of when you get home."

Owen shook his head and walked toward the stairs. "Thanks for your help, Jason."

"Anytime."

Owen looked between the two of them. "She has to work in the morning," he said.

Jason noted the suggestion. "My boss hates it when I'm late, too."

"Okay, then. Good night."

"Good night," they echoed back.

"He's a great kid," Jason said once they were alone.

Rachel didn't take credit. "Emily did a fantastic job."

"You're picking up the pieces like you know what you're doing."

She shrugged. "Trial by fire, I'm here to tell you."

"You make it look easy."

She finally looked in his eyes. "Thank you."

"So, Owen's grandparents . . ." The questions had burned in his brain all evening as he'd waited for a little time alone with her to understand the details of her situation.

Her smile fell. "They agreed not to file a custody suit if we moved here. I had to buy, not rent, as proof that we weren't going to just leave."

"So you found a job in Manhattan and made the move."

"This year has been hard enough on Owen. I didn't want the threat of him being forced to move away hanging around us for six months to a year, then see him here without living with me once the Colemans won."

"You're sure they would have?" Not that he wanted her to fight and move away. She was a valuable employee, and there was that whole hand-holding thing he wanted to eventually get to.

"They have money. They have a blood relation. And if TJ demanded custody, it would have happened sooner than later."

"TJ is the dad?"

"Yep, Tereck Junior. He and Em had a thing for about a year. He went off on some photojournalist job when she found out she was expecting Owen. She never kept it from TJ, but according to her, he would have sucked at the dad thing, and they both agreed that Owen should stay with her."

Jason had a hard time with any man who didn't take on the weight of his own child. "Did he help her out, at least?"

"Sometimes. She didn't demand it. I asked her about it a few times, especially when money was tight . . . she told me she'd always wanted to be a mother but didn't see herself being a wife. That if Owen hadn't have happened when he did, she might have taken matters into her own hands and never let the dad know."

"That's harsh."

"It probably happens more than we think. In vitro is great and all, but expensive when you consider the alternative."

"Does Owen know TJ is his dad?"

"Yep."

"He seems well-adjusted, considering the man isn't around."

"Emily always said that having no dad, or not one you expected to be around, was better than thinking you were important to someone only to be disappointed." Rachel sighed, looked at him briefly, then back to the tree. "She didn't have a great relationship with her father."

"Obviously."

"But she didn't stop TJ from having the chance with Owen. She simply never sugarcoated the man to Owen, never said he should be or shouldn't be anything. It helped that TJ wasn't around in the early years, and by the time Owen met him, he was old enough to take the man with a shrug."

Jason couldn't wrap his brain around the whole thing. "But the Colemans want custody?"

"Yeah. Early on they wanted nothing to do with Em. Thought she was after their money or some stupid thing. My guess is, since TJ never settled down and hasn't given them legitimate grandchildren, they want a shot now that Em isn't in the way."

"Forcing it isn't the way to go," he said.

"That's what I told them. I can't argue with a grandparent wanting to know their grandson. Even TJ made it to Emily's funeral. After everything settled, I realized that if something happened to me, Owen wouldn't have anyone. I mean, my parents would step up, but they'd be just as hard for Owen to live with as the Colemans. So as long as everyone plays nice, Owen and I will stay here and make a new life."

Jason paused. "And if everyone doesn't play nice?"

She made eye contact and smiled. "I hear Panama is nice this time of year."

It sounded like a joke, but he wouldn't put it past her. "It is, actually."

"You've been?"

"I own a company that flies private jets. I've been everywhere."

She squeezed her eyes shut, as if she'd forgotten who he was. "What are you doing in my living room?"

He lifted his coffee cup. "Drinking cold coffee and giving you a chance to know me."

"Hardly. I've done all the talking."

Jason pushed forward on the chair. "That means we'll have to do it again so you can dig into my secrets."

She unfolded her legs from the coffee table. "About that."

He held up his hand. Looked at it. "We're not hand-holding. I have dinner with lots of my employees."

"You put up my Christmas lights."

He pointed two fingers in her direction. "You have me there. Still . . . nothing here is job-ending-worthy."

She glanced at the clock on the wall. "Well, showing up late is, so . . ."

"I get the hint." He stood along with her, and she walked him to the door.

He slid on his coat.

"Thank you again. For everything." Rachel opened the door.

He turned to her.

She held on to the door, her hands fidgeting with what looked like nerves.

"You're welcome," he said, not making any attempt to hug her, hold her hand and kiss the back of it . . . push her against the door and taste the back of her throat. No, he was quite reserved, given the fact he wanted to do all three of those things.

"I'll see you later," she said.

"Good night, Rachel."

"G'night, Jason." There was a tiny sigh in her voice. Whimsy or want . . . either way, he liked the way it sounded.

Less than thirty minutes later, he was climbing the stairs to the master suite of the estate . . . the walls of the house quiet, the lights outside illuminating the halls through the windows. He pulled his cell phone from his back pocket and shot off a quick text. Your lights will go off at eleven. If that's too long I'll change it on Saturday.

A quick dot, dot, dot flashed. It's a miracle, your phone is alive!

He laughed as he walked into his room. Don't you have to work in the morning?

Don't you?

I'm already in bed. Well, he was sitting on his bed, taking off his shoes, and texting. I bet money you're cleaning up empty decoration boxes.

When she didn't reply right away, he knew he was right.

Rachel?

Nothing.

You're cleaning up, aren't you?

Crickets.
Did your phone die? Like his had.

Ha! It fell in the fish tank.

Jason pictured her living room. You don't have a fish tank.

I'll work on that.

He managed to kick off one boot. Goodnight.

Goodnight.

Jason tossed his phone to the side of his bed and forced the second boot from his foot. For the first time since he'd moved into the master bedroom, he took notice of the color of paint on his walls. A decorator had removed his parents' life before he'd moved into it. His mother was a buttery yellow kind of woman, and his father had let her decorate the house as she saw fit. Everything except the master suite had stayed the same, but the soothing yellow had gone away in order for Jason to make it his. Shades of olive and brown matched the style of the rest of the house without making the room overly masculine. He'd approved a picture and returned after a European business trip to have it completed. Much like hanging Christmas lights, he hadn't painted a wall since he was a teenager. And that had to have been one of the walls in the guesthouse Nathan occupied on the property. The man had made it his business to give Jason and his brothers a space they could make mistakes in. Not that his own parents cared that they would screw things up, it was just that the main house was too large to ever consider tackling a project such as painting a room. He liked the feeling of accomplishment something as simple as hanging a strand of lights gave him. There was a lightness inside his chest that he hadn't felt in a while.

He liked it.

———

Halfway through Thursday, Trent made an unexpected appearance at Jason's door. The youngest brother came to the office twice a week at most. He headed the vacation helicopter tour section of their business, and then spent the rest of his time working from home or flying all over the globe with his wife, Monica, helping relief efforts. Flying in medicine or flying out a heart, the two of them had made it their quest in life to help others. They'd been married for four years and still looked at each other with lovestruck eyes.

"To what do I owe the honor?" Jason pushed a pile of papers aside and stood to shake his brother's hand.

"It's my day in purgatory."

Jason smiled at Trent's reference to the Manhattan office. "You don't hate it as much as you carry on."

"That's debatable."

They sat down.

"What's on your mind?"

"Cut right through the bull, eh?"

"I do have a schedule to keep here in purgatory."

Trent leaned forward, rested his hands on his knees. "I'll keep it short. Monica and I want to use the ranch for a charity fundraising event in early spring."

Jason paused. "You don't have to ask."

"Yes I do."

"It's just as much your home as it is mine."

Trent lifted a hand in the air. "Fine, but you live there."

No matter how many times he told his brothers his permission wasn't needed, they always asked. "All right. Yes, you can use the estate. Just tell the staff."

"We'd like to make sure you can attend."

Jason sat up. "Well, now we're talking a different thing." He opened his calendar on his desktop. "When are you thinking?"

"Last weekend of April or the first weekend of May."

"Has to be May. I'll be in the London offices the last week in April."

"Perfect. I'll tell Monica." Trent stood to leave. "By the way, it's going to be an auction event. Monica wanted to let you know that if you didn't bring a date, she's threatening to auction you off for a night out with the CEO."

Jason stared in silence for several seconds. "I'll have a date."

"Really?"

Jason paused on purpose. The kind of waiting that made the other person listen to what was going to be said next. "Yes, really."

Trent grinned. "I'll tell her. Anyone in particular?"

Now it was time to move things along. "Good-bye, Trent."

His brother lifted both hands in the air as he walked out. "Okay, okay. Just asking." He turned before walking out of the office. "I heard you left work early on Wednesday."

Jason narrowed his eyes. "Yeah, so?"

"You never leave work early."

Jason saw right through his little brother's questioning. "Good-bye, Trent."

While Rachel worked diligently to have her report on her marketing plan ready for Jason and the senior executives on Monday, she spent an awful lot of time looking toward the hall, wondering when Jason would show up.

He didn't.

She thought about texting him.

She didn't.

Julie glanced around the divider separating them and caught her staring out the window. "Pssstt."

Rachel jumped. "What?"

"Any chance I can talk you into drinks after work?"

"Happy hour?"

For a minute, Julie looked hopeful.

"I remember happy hour . . . it's that time before you need to get on the freeway and make sure the kid living with you is home and has dinner."

Julie pushed her chair back behind the divider separating them. "If you took the damn train, you'd be home in time for all that and still have an hour for some happy in your life."

Rachel squeezed her eyes closed and pinched the bridge of her nose. "I'm sorry, Julie."

"Whatever."

She felt as if she was screwing up the only friend she'd really managed since moving to this city.

Rachel pushed her chair around the cubby to see her colleague. "Julie."

She kept typing.

"I don't know how to balance this. It isn't like Owen has been my responsibility for fifteen years and I know the boundaries."

Julie stopped and met her gaze. "Is he a latchkey kid now?"

Rachel blinked.

"Does he come home from high school, turn the lock on the door, and you're not home?"

"Yes."

"Can he microwave a meal, shove a pizza in the oven?"

Rachel felt the walls closing in. "Yes."

Julie took a few breaths. "Then he won't miss you for an hour while you try and be a single adult."

She hated that Julie was right. Much as Rachel didn't like stepping out of her newfound comfort zone with Owen, her friend was right.

"Next week."

Julie rolled her eyes and looked away.

"No, really . . . I'll tell Owen I'm staying in the city for a night out and will be home late. One Friday night won't hurt . . . right?"

Julie slowly let her lips pull into a grin. "You're sure?"

No. "Yes. Even Em and I would go out on occasion." In the early years, Em would get a babysitter. Still, Owen's mother managed to play adult once in a while.

"I'm holding you to it."

Rachel tried to smile.

"And if we have the night, bring a little black dress. You can change at my place."

The walls started to close in. Why did she have to suggest a night, when an hour would have made Julie happy?

"Black dress. Got it." She pushed back to her space. "Wait, it's winter. I'll be cold."

"Little. Black. Dress." Julie's staccato couldn't be missed.

"Okay."

"And a coat. No reason to be pissing cold."

Rachel placed her head on her desk and mumbled, "Oh my God."

"Don't even think about backing out on me!"

Her head popped up. "I'm not."

"Good!" Julie peeked around the corner. "You're gonna love New York."

Rachel skipped the high school football game that night and used the time to shop for a few more boxes of Christmas lights and presents. The shopping center closest to home was shoulder to shoulder people herding through the department stores. Parents dragged small children around after their bedtimes, resulting in tears and tantrums. The line to sit on St. Nick's lap wrapped around like a summer day in Disneyland. Holiday music blared as if it was yelling at the shoppers to enjoy the damn season.

Rachel didn't recall a Christmas when there was this much stress mixing in with mistletoe. Then again, her role in any gathering consisted of bringing a hot dish or a bottle of wine. She normally opted for the liquor. Now that she was responsible for a kid, a very grown-up teenager, but a kid nonetheless, everything was different. Instantly Christmas became something it had never been before.

A chore.

She scolded herself after walking into a video game store to pick out the latest must-have on Owen's list. The line to the register was out the door. She should have just shopped on Amazon like everyone else. She glanced around. "Almost everyone," she muttered.

A massive display advertised the game she sought, along with a zillion copies of the disk. She snagged her copy and found the last person in the long line. "How long have you been waiting?" she asked the lady in front of her.

"Five minutes."

The man in front of her chimed in. "I've been here ten. The people at the register haven't moved."

The teenagers manning the store appeared to be dealing with an exchange for one customer, and only two registers were open. To be fair, there were only two places the employees could check people out.

Five minutes later and the line finally moved up by one. Behind her it had grown by three.

Rachel fished her cell phone out of her back pocket, searching for a distraction.

She opened it up to find a missed text from Jason. Who is winning the game tonight?

She snapped a picture of the long line and sent it off. Couldn't tell you.

That looks brutal.

Shoot me now, she joked.

I do my shopping in June.

They moved forward by a family of four.

I take it there are no kids in the family. Because if there were, early shopping just meant more shopping. Kids had a tendency to change their minds, and since technology was the big turn-on for teens, stuff was dated in six months.

Rachel ignored the woman who backed into her, the lady's bags nearly taking out the display standing in the aisle.

Nope, not yet.

That was interesting.
Yet?

I assume it's only a matter of time. Glen has been married a year and a half, Trent just over four years.

She was down to two customers in front of her.

I'll try harder to get this all done online next year.

You still have time this year.

She glanced up, moved forward, then ducked back into her phone.

Other than a couple of video games, Owen didn't ask for anything. I think he feels guilty.

Maybe I can get some ideas out of him tomorrow.

Much as she wanted to wipe the smile off her face at the thought of Jason coming back over, she didn't. That would be great. Any idea is better than me buying the kid socks.

Now that she thought about it, socks weren't a *bad* idea.

Poor Owen. I'll see what I can find out.

Thanks.

Is 9 too early?

That's perfect.

See you then.

Rachel tucked her phone away and noticed the lady behind her glaring.

A register had opened and no less than five people were snarling at her. "Oh, sorry." She skittered up and tried to ignore the not so nice words from those in line behind her.

Chapter Nine

It was the first time Jason had been to the house during daylight hours. The Cape Cod style boasted lots of molding around the windows and more wood than stone accents. The small porch was large enough for one chair, or maybe a two-person swing, if it angled toward the door, but it didn't have either. Someone had given the entry a fresh coat of paint in the not too distant past. Jason wondered if that was something Rachel did after she moved in, or if the sellers had put in some effort. He could see where there was more work to be done once winter lost its grip on the East Coast.

He rapped on the door twice. Like last time, Owen answered with food in his hand. This time it was a bagel. "Hey."

Owen stepped aside.

"Hey," Jason mimicked back.

"Rachel?" How the kid could get that loud with a mouth full of food was quite a talent. "Jason is here."

She replied from upstairs. "Coming."

Owen nodded. "Come on in."

Jason entered the warm space and smiled at the Christmas tree, which hadn't changed since he left on Wednesday.

Owen waved his bagel in the air. "Have you eaten?"

"I'm good."

The sound of Rachel as she double-timed down the stairs had him turning around.

Her hair was wet from the shower, her face void of makeup. Her cheeks were flushed and her skin was damp. Jason had a strong urge to lean in and sniff. "Good morning," he greeted her.

"You're very prompt."

"All my flights arrive on time."

Those dusty pink lips pulled into a grin.

"You're a pilot?" Owen asked.

"I know how to fly a plane."

Owen's eyes grew wide. "That's epic. Did you know Rachel works for some highfalutin private jet company?"

"She did mention it." Jason caught Rachel's tense posture and lack of adding anything to the conversation. "So are you ready to string some more lights?"

"Would you like some coffee first?" Rachel asked.

"After, when I'm wet and cold."

Rachel looked over his shoulder and out the window. "It's raining?"

"Drizzling."

"You don't have to do this today."

Jason opened the door. "This isn't California. If we waited for good weather, we wouldn't get anything done here."

"Okay. Let me know if you need anything."

Owen grabbed his coat and walked out. Jason followed.

———

Her boss. No, the *owner of the highfalutin private jet company* was on her roof, in the rain, for the second time in a week. She'd bet money there weren't any other employees of Fairchild Charters who could say that. She and Jason might not be dating, but there certainly was something going on here she didn't know how to navigate.

She'd sat down to put on makeup before he arrived and stopped herself. It shouldn't matter how smooth her skin looked or how expressive her eyes were if he was just being neighborly. He didn't seem to notice, and he hadn't run away. Not that she applied her cosmetics with a heavy hand . . . well, she had that week due to the black eye, but as a norm, she didn't.

From the window, she watched Owen and Jason set up the ladder as they had earlier in the week. Jason went up, and this time she heard footsteps on her roof. She cringed and really hoped her boss knew what he was doing and wasn't going to be part of her landscape with a wrong turn.

Instead of standing by the window and stressing herself out, she went through the kitchen to her mudroom and out into the garage to gather the tools she needed for her indoor activity.

Removing the kitchen door left a frame that needed to come out. She'd become well acquainted with chisels and hand sanders. Wood putty did a great job of hiding her mistakes before she added a new layer of paint to cover it all up. After setting up her workspace, she took her hammer and chisel and went to work.

There was a harmony in the pounding going on outside as she went at it inside. Much as this was work, it also calmed her soul. She liked the diversity of the tasks she'd managed to accomplish since moving to Connecticut. There was a first time for everything, and Rachel had experienced many do-it-yourself ones.

It quickly became apparent that the simple doorway, which should have taken an hour of careful destruction, was going to take much longer. Like other places in the house, the kitchen threshold had no less than a dozen layers of paint. And to make it worse, the semigloss stuff used in the high-moisture room seemed to stick better. Or maybe that was the years of grease built up. She gave up kneeling on the ground and took a chair from the kitchen table to make things easier on her back. She hummed a popular country song while she worked and lost track of time.

A gust of cold air followed Jason and Owen as they came back inside.

"That was quick," she said, looking up from her perch.

"We've been out there an hour and a half." Owen shook off his coat and hung it by the door.

Jason followed his lead.

Rachel glanced at the clock, then back at what little she'd accomplished. "I'm never gonna get this done before tonight," she said to herself.

It only took a few steps for Jason to reach her. "What are you doing?"

"Taking away the rest of the door that bit me."

He assessed her work. "You could just rip the whole thing out and put in new wood."

"I could. If I owned the right kind of saw to cut it, or had a truck to carry the supplies I'd need from the hardware store." She glanced up. "And no, that wasn't a request to use your truck again. What I'm doing works fine. It takes longer, but it's something I can do without all the aforementioned tools."

"I told you she likes to do it all herself," Owen said.

"Hey," she scolded him. "I didn't hang the lights."

"You would have," Jason said under his breath.

She couldn't argue that.

Brushing the flaky paint from her palms, she stood. "Ready for that coffee?"

Before Jason opened his mouth, Owen said, "No, but hot chocolate sounds dope."

"Dope?"

"Yeah, like awesome, only better."

Rachel rolled her eyes. "Fine." She glanced at Jason. "Coffee?"

He hesitated. "Actually, hot chocolate does sound dope."

"Right?" Owen asked.

"You're both incorrigible. Fine, two hot chocolates and one adult coffee coming right up."

Owen took that as his exit line and turned back to the living room. He plopped on the couch and sank into his cell phone.

Jason followed her into the kitchen.

"Thanks again," she said over her shoulder as she took milk from her refrigerator and moved to the pantry to find the chocolate stash.

"You're welcome."

"I seem to be saying that a lot to you this week."

"I'm glad I can help."

Jason was a big presence in the tiny kitchen space. She had to move around him to reach the cupboard with her mugs. She lowered her voice. "So did he give you any gift ideas?"

"As a matter of fact," he whispered, "there's this—"

"Hey, why is it so quiet in there?"

"We're not being quiet," Rachel said, louder than she intended.

"You're not making out or anything, are you?"

Rachel knew her face shot bright red. "Of course not."

"No such luck," Jason said.

Rachel was close enough to push at Jason's shoulder. "Stop it. Don't encourage him."

"Why? It's a nice switch from him grabbing a butcher knife the night I ditched my car."

Rachel moved around him again to reach the stove and warm the milk. "You can tell me later," she managed to say softly enough to avoid Owen overhearing her.

Jason seemed to like the fact that she had to spin around him, since he didn't volunteer to move out of her way. Finally, when she'd veered to the left and then to the right one final time, she placed both hands on his shoulders and pushed him to stand against the threshold. "There. This is a one-butt kitchen, and yours is one too many."

He laughed. "One-butt? I've never heard that before."

She turned on the flame, poured in the milk. "Only one butt can cook in this kitchen at the same time or you'll fall over each other. Which is why I took out the door. If Owen is walking in and out, it makes it even harder to get around."

Jason looked around the space as if sizing it up. "I wonder if you can take some of this wall down? Open it up a little."

"That's what I thought. It would certainly feel less cramped in here. But I won't have as much cupboard space if I did."

He walked to the back of the room and around the wall to the mudroom and the doorway to the garage and the basement.

"What's this lead to?"

"Basement."

"Finished?"

"No. I wish. I hate it down there. Saw one too many B horror flicks growing up."

Jason smiled. "Mind if I take a look?"

"Knock yourself out."

He disappeared down the basement stairs, the smell of the musty space wafting from the open door.

She was pouring the milk into the mugs when he reappeared. "You have a lot of space under this house."

"Really? I wouldn't know. I run down, put a load of laundry in, and run up before the boogeyman gets me."

Jason started laughing.

"Laugh all you want. The chick always dies in the basement, usually tied to a pole in her swimming suit."

He laughed harder.

"Do you want to drink this or wear it?"

"With threats like that, the boogeyman wouldn't come anywhere near here."

She topped the drink off with marshmallows for Owen, then looked at Jason. He eyed the white, fluffy sugar drops like a puppy stares down a treat.

She topped Jason's drink off, too.

After pouring herself a cup of coffee, she put a dash of cream in and then took Owen his cup.

"Thanks."

"No problem. Thank you both for putting up the rest of the lights."

Owen sipped his drink, leaving marshmallows on his lips. "Have to make a good impression on the weather killers."

Rachel cringed.

"Weather killers?" Jason asked.

"My grandparents," Owen said before Rachel found her voice.

"Why do you call them weather killers?"

Owen pushed on. "Because if it wasn't for them, we'd be enjoying a seventy-degree Christmas in California. But no, we had to move here, killing our perfect weather."

Rachel glanced at Jason before focusing on Owen. "They just want to get to know you."

"Whatever! When are they coming tonight, anyway?"

"Six."

Owen closed his eyes and tilted his head back. Rachel took no joy in his pain. Neither of them could avoid the couple. She just hoped it would get easier the longer they were close by.

Jason questioned her with a look.

"Dinner with Owen's grandparents. It will be the first time they've come here since we moved in. We've met them once a month since the move."

Jason digested the information with a single nod. "Is it so bad, Owen?"

"They're rich snobs. I can't believe I'm related to them."

"They're not that bad." Well . . . they were. But downplaying their faults was something she had to try. The longer things were peaceful, the better.

"They walk around with their noses in the air."

Again, Jason's eyes questioned her.

She answered with a single nod and a half smile. The Colemans did sniff the room before walking in.

"I bet they find something to bitch about tonight."

"They can't find fault with our lights," Jason said.

Owen looked at Jason. "Or the tree, but they'll find something."

Rachel didn't argue.

"That bad?" Jason asked her.

"I'm sure it will be fine," she answered.

"Ten bucks says they complain about something within ten minutes of getting here."

"Stop."

"See, Jason, Rachel won't even bet against me. She knows I'm right."

"Have you tried pouring the sugar on when they get that way?" Jason asked.

"Like what?"

Jason set his cup aside, leaned forward with his hands resting on his knees. "My mom used to tell me to compliment the hell out of complainers. Every time they complain, tell them you like the color shirt they're wearing or how it matches their eyes. Anything to distract and force them off the negativity path."

"That works?" he asked.

"Most of the time. When it doesn't, everyone else in the room starts to catch on, and before you know it, you've made a game out of calling out the person putting a downer on the party. Compliments get you everywhere, Owen."

"Only if the person you're complimenting is slow on catching on," Rachel said.

Jason picked up his cup again, took a sip. "This is really good, by the way. Did you get a lot of practice in LA with all that sunny weather?"

"It was cold on occasion."

"Well, this is perfect."

She cared that he liked it.

Then she noticed both Owen and Jason staring at her.

"Oh . . . you just . . . I'm not slow."

Jason sipped his drink again. "Hard to stay negative when someone's pouring sugar. But this is really good."

"Touché."

Owen finished his hot chocolate and set his cup aside. "I'll try it tonight and let you know if it works."

"I will expect a full report on my desk by Monday."

Rachel almost made a comment about the report she did owe him on Monday but decided now was not a good time to tell Owen that Jason was her boss. Not that there would be a good time.

"That sounds like homework."

"Speaking of, don't you have finals this week?"

"Next week." He stood. "But I probably should pick up my room. Wouldn't want Grandma Frown Face to pop a blood vessel behind an eyeball, looking at a dirty room."

Jason commented once Owen was halfway up the stairs, "He really doesn't like them."

"He doesn't."

"Are they that bad?"

"I haven't been looking for the positive, to be honest. I'll pour my own sugar tonight and come up with something."

"At least the black eye is nearly gone and they won't speculate on the cause."

"You wouldn't believe the looks I got this week. A lady at the mall handed me a business card with a domestic abuse hotline on it."

"That's funny."

"Big sunglasses when it's raining aren't exactly inconspicuous either."

"At least your boss didn't think you took up bar fighting and question your character."

He had the sexiest smile when he tried to tease her.

"He was too busy putting up my lights to notice my stocked liquor cabinet."

Jason stared at her lips, and without trying, made her moisten them with her tongue. Her heart jumped just looking at him watching her.

Her boss.

She shook her head. "Well, I should probably get back to my doorway."

"Want some help?"

"No," she said too quickly. "No, I have it. Then I need to run to the grocery store and figure out dinner."

He pushed off the couch. "That's my cue to leave."

She walked him to the door. "I can't thank you enough."

He tilted his head. "You could go out to dinner with me."

"I could . . ."

Jason did a double take.

"But then we'd end up with a drink or two. I'd let my guard down and find you holding my hand, maybe you'd even let your arm linger on my waistline after opening the door for me." The image caught in her head, and her stomach warmed.

"The food would be spectacular, especially since I didn't have to cook it," she continued. She closed her eyes and imagined buttery scallops and vegetables that melted in your mouth. Fresh bread. "Candlelight . . ."

"I can make all that happen," Jason quietly said.

"We'd probably do more than hold hands."

The touch of Jason's fingertips on her arm made her open her eyes. The warmth in his face hadn't been there a moment before.

Rachel swallowed and let reality in. "Then we'd start seeing each other more at work. People would start to talk. Next thing you know, I'm getting called out for you playing favorites. I mean, if I missed my deadlines because of you, you'd probably understand."

"I'm an understanding guy."

"Next thing you know, we're fighting over work, or schedules . . . or toothpaste."

Jason smirked.

"Or maybe you find someone that suits you better, or an old flame returns."

"I doubt—"

"Feelings change. Most romantic relationships float in and out of our lives. No harm, no foul. But feelings always get hurt in the end, and then I'll be in need of a new job. And I like my job."

"I wouldn't—"

She lifted two fingers in the air and cut him off. "Unemployment is exactly what the Colemans would use to gain custody of Owen. If I'm unable to provide for him, the courts wouldn't favor me."

Jason dropped his arm.

"I'm sorry, Jason. You're thoughtful, charming . . . superhot, even when licking marshmallows off your lips." Why had she said that?

"But . . . ," he said.

"Owen comes first. I promised Emily."

They stood there staring at each other for a full minute. "I understand," he finally said.

Disappointment sat in her chest. The first decent guy to ask her out in forever just had to come with serious strings.

"No dating."

"No dating," she agreed.

"No hand-holding."

She glanced at his long fingers and sighed. "No."

"Coming over for hot chocolate and decorating for Christmas is okay?"

"Of course. I'm happy to advise you on the company Christmas party and drive you away from ditched cars in return."

He turned and placed his hand on the door. "Got it. Friends and favors." He opened the door and looked back.

"Thank you."

He smiled. "Let me know how dinner with Frown Face works out."

"I will."

With a single nod, he bundled into his coat and walked to his truck.

She watched as he pulled out of her driveway and down the street.

"Damn."

Chapter Ten

Deyadria Coleman was a tall, willowy woman who apparently didn't stand in line when they were handing out curves. Deyadria's slight height advantage over Rachel had her picking an outfit with a pair of boots with a couple of extra inches. That way she was eye to eye with the weather-killing woman when she walked through the door.

"Welcome," Rachel greeted the couple. "I hope you didn't have any trouble finding the place."

Tereck helped his wife with her coat. "No problem at all," he said. The kinder of the two, Tereck had more salt than pepper in his hair, probably a result of being married to his wife for a few decades. The man was not a slave to a gym and carried a few extra pounds around his stomach.

"Where is my grandson?" Deyadria asked before Rachel could take her coat.

"Owen?" Rachel called up the stairs, knowing damn well he was waiting until the last possible second to join them.

Somewhat satisfied that Owen was in the house, Deyadria moved deeper into the room. "Very quaint." Compliment or insult, Rachel wasn't sure how to take her comment.

"We like it."

Deyadria lifted her nose and turned.

Insult, Rachel decided.

"It's very nice," Tereck said.

"Isn't it a bit small?"

"Owen and I fit perfectly," Rachel told the woman.

Deyadria dismissed the Christmas tree with a sniff and glanced at the stairway.

"Can I get you something to drink?" *Arsenic, eye of newt?*

"Perrier with lime," Deyadria requested, as if she were in a restaurant.

Rachel tried hard not to cringe. "Fresh out of sparkling water, I'm afraid. I have wine, coffee, tea, soda . . . bottled water with lemon?"

"Herbal?"

"Mint or chamomile?"

Deyadria huffed. "Chamomile, I suppose."

"Just coffee for me," Tereck said, glaring at his wife.

"I'll see what's taking Owen so long." With that, Rachel double-timed it upstairs and found Owen in his room with his earbuds in. "Dude!"

He pulled the cord and looked up from his phone. "What?"

"The weather killers are downstairs. Help me," she said in a curt whisper.

"That bad already?" Owen swung his legs off his bed.

"She asked for Perrier."

"What's that?"

"Never mind. Just help. I have to make tea."

She left his room, Owen on her heels.

"I hate this," he said.

"Shhh, they'll hear you." With a painted on smile, she forced her shoulders back and made nice.

What is Perrier?

Jason stared at the text for a full minute before figuring out who was asking the question.

Owen?

It took two minutes for a response.

Yeah.

Carbonated water.

Owen responded with two letters, TX.

Jason waited to see if Owen would elaborate on why he asked the question. Apparently the kid wasn't long-winded.

Why do you ask?

Frown Face asked for it, and now Rachel is mumbling Perrier under her breath in the kitchen.

———

Her lips were going to crack before they sat down to eat.

Rachel placed Deyadria's herbal tea on the coffee table and handed Tereck his coffee.

Owen sat in a chair, his cell phone in his hand. No one was talking when she entered the room.

"Thank you," Tereck offered.

"Do you have honey?"

Rachel's ass had touched the sofa before she popped back up. "Of course."

Once behind the kitchen wall, her smile fell. "Perrier, honey."

Owen walked in behind her. "Don't leave me with them," he whispered.

"Don't leave them alone."

He grabbed a soda from the fridge and walked out. Rachel found the honey, lifted her chin, and entered the torture chamber.

"Here you go."

Rachel was proud of herself for not tossing the honey at the woman.

"How are you doing in school, Owen?" Tereck asked.

Owen shrugged.

Rachel glared.

"It's okay."

"He's getting *A's* and *B's*," Rachel added.

Deyadria placed a tiny drop of honey in her tea and proceeded to stir. "What is that *B* in?"

"Math and science."

She stopped stirring long enough to stare. "Both?"

"I hate math and science."

"*Hate* is such a strong word."

Owen glared. "I *don't care* for math or science."

Deyadria smiled, as if she had changed Owen's language for good with one suggestion.

"Much like I *don't care* for a festering, pus-filled pimple on my butt."

Tereck spit a tiny bit of coffee, and Deyadria choked on her tea.

Rachel tried hard not to laugh.

Owen sipped his soda and burped quietly.

"Owen earns *A's* in English," Rachel pointed out.

She's bitching about my B in math.

Jason looked down from his monitor to see the text message lighting up his screen.

Did you try complimenting her?

She's a hag.

Jason leaned back in his chair with a grin. Calling her a lovely hag won't work.

––––

Rachel sat at the head of her table, the roast she'd been cooking all day was perfect, the gravy was free of lumps . . . all the sides that she normally didn't bother with played nice and didn't undercook.

"How is that new little job of yours?"

The woman could cut her with a simple word. Nothing about her position at Fairchild Charters was *little*.

"It's working out really well."

"Are you still driving in instead of taking the train?" Tereck asked.

"For now." Rachel took a bite, found it hard to keep eating when her appetite was zip.

"For the price you pay to park in the city, you could have had a bigger home," Deyadria said.

Rachel held her fork a little tighter. "The company pays for my parking."

Deyadria didn't look convinced. "What was the name of it again?"

"Fairchild Charters."

"Oh, yes, that's right. *Plànes.*" Deyadria pushed the food on her plate around before taking a tiny bite.

"They're already talking to Rachel about a promotion," Owen said.

She smiled across the table, liking the praise in his voice.

"I would think that would be hard in a company that big," Tereck said.

"Oh, please, Tereck. Rachel is young and beautiful. I'm sure if she smiles at the right person, she'll manage free parking *and* a pay raise."

Rachel placed her fork aside. "Actually, Deyadria, I'm really good at my job."

"Is that so?"

It was hard to talk when your back teeth were grinding together. "Did you ever work outside the home?"

The woman held her head high. "I graduated from Columbia."

"Yes, but did you work?"

"Tereck and I met when we were young."

"So, no."

Silence filled the table. Rachel wanted to gloat.

"That's a pretty sweater, Deyadria. It matches your eyes."

All three adults turned to stare at Owen.

"What a lovely thing to say, Owen. Please call me Grandma."

Rachel saw the internal struggle on his face.

"Let's give that more time," he suggested.

Rachel reminded herself to hug the kid when this was all done. Hard.

It totally worked!

Jason had turned his phone ringer on high so he wouldn't miss any of Owen's messages.

What did you say?

I told her the gray sweater she wore matched her eyes.

Jason started to reply but Owen beat him with his next text. Gray like dark clouds in a storm from hell . . . but I left that part out.

He was really starting to like this kid.

Good choice. How is Rachel holding up?

Dot, dot, dot filled the screen long enough for Jason to think Owen was distracted from giving the answer.

The hag started to make digs about Rachel's job. Rachel started questioning if the hag ever held a job. It was getting ugly.

The skin on Jason's neck prickled. What does the hag know about Rachel's work?

Probably nothing. That doesn't stop the hag from putting it down. Told you she was a total b*tch.

At least the kid used a character instead of spelling out the whole word.

———

Rachel cleared the table, tossing most of her food in the trash. Tereck ate his, much to the complaining of his wife, who reminded him of his cholesterol. Of course she said something more to the tune of "Careful, Tereck, your cholesterol is a bit high, wouldn't want to waste the extra points on too much of this."

Because Tereck had taken her up on more coffee, she was stuck with them for another thirty minutes, minimum. She wasn't sure she'd survive it.

". . . Rachel is doing a lot of the work herself on the weekends."

"What did I miss?" she asked when she walked back into the living room.

"They were asking about the doorframe." Owen pointed to the half ripped out project leading into the kitchen.

"Oh, that."

"Owen was telling us you've done a lot of projects since you both moved in." Tereck was working hard to speak before his wife ever since the woman's snarky crap about her job.

"I've gotten very used to sanding and painting."

"We counted eight layers of paint in my room," Owen told him.

"Sanding?" Deyadria asked.

"Sadly, yes. I suppose it's better than a gym membership."

"How old is this house?" she asked.

"It was built in 1965."

"Is that so?"

"Yes, why?" Rachel was certain there was a nasty comment hovering in the woman's head.

When Deyadria smiled, it unnerved her.

"We have some good news for you, Owen."

Owen and Rachel exchanged glances, then turned to Tereck.

"Oh?"

"Your father is coming to town just in time for Christmas."

Owen paused. "You mean your son."

"He means your father, Owen."

"Right . . ."

"You don't seem happy," Deyadria said.

"I've seen the man six times in my whole life, the last time at my mother's funeral. Why should I be happy to see him?"

"That wasn't his fault."

Rachel watched the emotion on Owen's face. This wasn't going to end well.

"And whose fault was it?" Owen asked.

"If your mother hadn't kept you away . . ."

Owen snapped. "Don't talk about my mom."

"Deyadria. Leave Emily out of it," Rachel warned her.

"Owen has the right to know his father."

"He knows your son."

"Not as a boy knows his dad. He needs a man in his life."

Rachel wanted to call the woman out. Wanted to deck her for the pain she put in Owen's face.

"Just because your son isn't in my life doesn't mean there aren't men in my life."

"Is that so?" Deyadria asked.

"Rachel has a boyfriend. He was here just this morning helping put up the Christmas lights. Something my *father* has never done."

"A boyfriend?"

The word repeated in Rachel's head, too. "He isn't really a boyfriend."

"What is he, if not a boyfriend?"

"A friend."

"Just a friend? Isn't that convenient. What kind of influence are you setting, bringing men around my grandson?"

Tereck stood. "Deyadria, *honey*. I think we should leave."

"One minute, *darling*." She glared at him, then back to Rachel. "This friend that isn't a boyfriend . . . that has such a hold on my grandson that he defends the man . . . is he African American?"

Rachel didn't see the question coming. "What? No, why?"

"Then he can't possibly be the right man in Owen's life. He needs a man with our culture and our values. Something Emily obviously didn't nurture when she chose you as Owen's guardian."

Her jaw dropped. Words escaped Rachel's reply.

Owen, on the other hand, used many.

"You mean sanctimonious and prejudicial values?"

"Owen!" Deyadria scolded.

"Not to mention rude." Owen stood and walked to the door, grabbed Deyadria's coat. "This is a nice coat. You should put it on before we kick you out of the house." He tossed it on the floor and ran up the stairs.

"He is out of control."

Rachel picked up the coat. "Actually, I think he used a lot of restraint."

"Oh—"

She didn't let the woman speak. "You're out of line. Pick on me, my cooking, my home, my job . . . fine. But pick on that child's mother, and you deserve whatever he throws at you."

Deyadria had the good sense to shut up.

"When TJ is in town, have him call me." Rachel thrust out the coat, making it clear she wanted them gone.

Tereck accepted it, held it open for his wife.

"TJ is planning on staying." Deyadria pulled her collar high and buttoned the front.

"Good for him." Rachel couldn't care less.

"He wants to settle down."

Her back tingled.

"Our boy wants to know his son," Tereck said.

"Great." *Not great, not great at all.* "Have him call me."

"What, to ask your permission?" Deyadria didn't know when to quit.

"No." Rachel opened the door. "To ask Owen's."

She locked the door the second they were on the other side, and climbed the stairs. "Owen?" She rapped on the closed door twice.

"Yeah."

He was on his bed.

"You okay?"

"I hate them."

She sat on the edge of the bed, by his feet. "I don't care for them either."

He blinked at her a few times.

"I don't care for pus-filled pimples on my ass either." Rachel mimicked Owen's voice.

Owen smiled through the pain.

She smiled back and started laughing.

His bright face was a relief to see.

"I about died when you said that."

"I was proud of myself, too."

He released a long sigh when they stopped giggling. "If they ever get custody, I'll run away."

She placed a hand on his leg. "You won't have to run. I'll be there with you."

"Are you okay? They were pretty shitty to you tonight."

"I'm not that bad. Although I might open a bottle of wine and be unfit to drive in about an hour."

He smiled. "I'll stay away from sharp objects and a need for the ER."

Rachel patted his leg and left his room.

Once downstairs, she made good on her threat and opened a bottle of merlot.

———

Don't leave me hanging. How did the rest of the night go?

It had been an hour since Owen's last text, and Jason felt as if he was watching the last episode of the season and needed to know the outcome of the show.

They started a fight about my mom.

Jason was ready for a snarky remark and didn't see Owen's words coming.

No!

Yeah, the hag has no right.

No, she doesn't. I'm sorry, Owen.

My mom and Rachel warned me about them. I didn't expect adults to act like kids.

Jason started to give advice. You're more grown up than a lot of people twice your age.

Don't talk too soon. I might have told the hag and the hag's husband that you were Rachel's boyfriend just to get them to shut up about me needing a male influence in my life.

Jason smiled at that thought. I'd call that thinking on your toes and using the resources surrounding you. Very smart.

It kinda backfired. The hag tossed it back at Rachel, saying she was bringing men around the house.

He squeezed his eyes closed. Poor Rachel.
How is Rachel?

She said she was going to suck down a bottle of wine. I haven't seen her do that since before my mom got really sick.

Should he call her?

What is the hag's real name? Looking up *hag* on the Internet probably wouldn't do any good. Owen gave him both their names, which Jason wrote down.

Let me know if you need me. I'm not far.

I will. Thanks.

Jason took his laptop from his office and settled into the den. He stretched out and typed in the old hag's name.

Chapter Eleven

Two glasses of wine and Rachel's head spun. Since when was she such a lightweight?

It didn't help that she'd barely eaten, but still, the wine did the job of relaxing her shoulders. For an hour after the Colemans left, she researched custody cases in Connecticut. Just like in California, the favor would be for the Colemans, and most definitely TJ, if he in fact wanted to fight. If they were going to be complete assholes, she wouldn't have a choice.

She knew they wouldn't have kind things to say about Em, but she hadn't expected them to put the woman down. Didn't they realize they were ruining any relationship with Owen by doing that? Or were they that stupid? People used to getting their way all the time did tend to lack the common sense gene.

"I see why you didn't nurture a relationship with these asshats," Rachel said to the ceiling.

Emily had told her early on that Owen's grandparents were opinionated snobs. Information she'd managed to get through TJ. They'd never attempted to know Emily or Owen until after her passing. Rachel often wondered why that was but couldn't question Em now and certainly wasn't going to quiz the Colemans.

Rachel yawned as her cell phone rang.

Jason's name lit up and she smiled.

"Hello?"

"Hey, how was it?" he asked.

She closed her laptop and flopped back on her couch. "Awful. A zillion shades of horrid."

"You want to talk about it?"

She did, for a good half an hour. And Jason listened. "It's as if she didn't get any reaction from any of her complaints until she hit the right button. Telling Owen his mother was anything but a saint, and wham. Game over. He beat me to it. I wanted to hit the woman."

"Violent tendencies won't grant you custody."

"Wanna know the worst part?"

"I don't know, do I?"

"The Colemans said that Owen's dad is coming around."

"For a visit?"

"Permanently."

Jason sighed through the line. "That doesn't sound good."

Rachel rubbed the bridge of her nose. "I have guardianship over Owen only because Em requested it in her will and TJ didn't stand up. If he stands up, the court would grant him complete custody unless I can prove he's unfit."

"It doesn't matter that Owen doesn't know his father and doesn't want to live with him?"

"No. I could have fought the ugly grandparents and been heard. The court might listen to me suggest TJ not be given custody, but he will win."

"This isn't good."

"I tried to avoid any of this by moving here. Owen and I both decided it was in everyone's best interest to give the grandparents a chance to get to know him. TJ wasn't a factor."

"How did Owen feel about the whole move?"

"Better than most teenagers, I think. He was so wrapped up in Em's passing that he hadn't kept any close friends during the last year. And staying in California, passing the same grocery stores he used to go into with his mom . . . it was hard. Moving erased some of that."

Jason's voice softened. "What are you going to do?"

"Nothing. I could lawyer up, but I don't have the money for that. And right now there isn't anyone petitioning for a different custodial situation. I'll try and make nice with the Colemans. Invite TJ to get to know his kid. But at the end of the day, there isn't a thing I can do until they move to make the situation different." And that's what sucked the most. The not knowing what the other parties were up to.

"Is there anything I can do to help?"

She smiled, knowing already that he'd jump in if she needed it. "No. You've already helped a lot. Owen really likes you." Which proved there was a point to the Colemans' argument that Owen needed a man in his life. Rachel had never seen Owen attach to anyone like he had with Jason. And in less than two weeks.

"He's a great kid."

"He is. I wish I could erase all this stress in his life."

Jason paused. "You're a decent person, Rachel. Not everyone would take on the responsibility like you're doing."

She shook off his compliment. "Who would walk away? Emily was my best friend. I've known Owen since he was five."

"Lots of people would walk away. You know that. I'm glad you're the kind of person who has more integrity than that."

She glanced at the time. "Thanks. And thanks for checking in."

"Anytime."

"I need to get to bed. I have a report to finish up for my boss on Monday," she teased.

He laughed. "Yes, you do. Don't think your boss is going to play favorites just because he knows you."

"Good night, Jason."

"Night, Rachel."

———

Rachel knew she'd be presenting a more detailed plan to Jason and his management team, but she didn't take in the scope of how many people were going to be in the conference room. The space she'd used the previous week sat twelve, and there had been a few seats unoccupied. Now she stood in a room that comfortably sat twice as many chairs, and several extras were brought in and placed along the walls.

The teams filed in, marketing, advertising, public relations . . . all part of the same general team. Risk management, the heads of the broker department, and the staffing manager rounded out the attendees. Rachel lost track of everyone's names. Several executive secretaries were there as well. Toward the tail end of the parade of people, Jason walked through the door.

Her heart shouldn't leap when she saw the man, she told herself. But her chemical reaction wasn't something she could control. He was such a contrast in a suit and tie to when he was climbing on her roof, hanging Christmas lights.

"Try not to cuss at him this time," Julie whispered in her ear.

Rachel lowered her head and softly laughed.

"Good morning, Rachel," he greeted her with his hand extended.

"Good morning, Mr. Fairchild." She nearly choked on his name, not sure if she should address him as Jason or not.

He grasped her hand, an amused grin on his lips. "Really? I think you can call me Jason."

"Fine."

He squeezed her hand before letting go. "You remember my brother, Glen."

She shook his hand. "Nice to see you again."

He winked. "You look much better without the black eye."

Rachel's hand lifted to what was left of said bruise, and she shook her head. "You should have seen the other guy."

The employees around them laughed.

"I don't believe you met Trent." Jason turned her attention to a man she'd seen in pictures on the Internet when researching Jason. "Trent is in charge of our helicopter vacation tours division."

He looked as if he'd just returned from a sunny vacation, complete with a tan and hair that needed a trim.

"I'm also allergic to the office, so if you need to get in touch, call."

"That's the truth," Glen agreed.

"I'll do that," Rachel said.

Trent turned to the blonde on his left. "And this is my wife, Monica. The ambassador for our volunteer relief flight program."

Rachel smiled. "I'm so glad you're here," Rachel said, clasping the woman's hand. "I've read about what you're doing and have some ideas on how to reach farther for your efforts."

"We have all the flights we can handle," Trent said.

"I mean more financial backing outside of Fairchild Charters footing the bill."

Monica had expressive blue eyes that lit up when she smiled.

"I like that idea," Glen said. The man in charge of the money portion always liked spreading the spending outside of the company.

"Are you free for lunch?" Monica asked.

"Lunch sounds perfect."

Out of the corners of her eyes, Rachel noticed all three Fairchild brothers exchanging glances as if they were having a wordless conversation. "What?" she asked.

Jason glanced between Monica and her. "Nothing. We should get started."

For the next two hours, Rachel ran through a more detailed, global plan to expand Fairchild Charters' reach. She had a laundry list of things to do for each department and suggestions on who would be best to handle each task. She mapped out goals and how to monitor and reach them. She suggested the use of interns, fresh out of college, or those who needed the experience for their grades, to help keep their hiring costs low. "Everyone bags on the millennials as entitled young kids who would rather sit on the beach with their laptop than go into an office."

"Sounds like me," Trent said.

The majority of the people in the office laughed along with him.

"My point is, we can tap into that lifestyle and benefit from it. Use the empty legs we have sitting around as incentive for each team reaching their goals. Travel incentives for the new grad are more attractive than a dental plan."

Melissa, the head of staffing, leaned forward in her chair. "It sounds like you're gunning for my job, Rachel."

Rachel put a hand in the air. "No thanks. I have enough to do with mine. My approach to marketing, and this plan, will reach out to the millionaire millennials and the working-class millennials. They speak the same language."

"You act as if it's a foreign language," one of the brokers said. His name escaped her.

"In a way it is. In one breath they'll talk about pros of personal jet travel to meetings for work, and the next connect because they both zip-lined in the Swiss Alps. There is an entirely new generation of professionals out there that understand there is a time for work and a time for play. If you give them a task, they will complete it on time, but if you force them into an office to do it, you might be nudging them two days after the task is due for the results."

"I'd be firing them," Gerald said.

"That's my point. You won't have to, because this generation understands the power of the online world better than anyone. That getting things done, and getting it done quickly and efficiently, means they have more time to skydive. How many of you have teenage kids?"

Half a dozen hands went up.

"Their phones are attached to their fingers day and night, right?"

"My phone is attached to my fingers," Glen said.

"I would guess it isn't for the same reasons. Teens today grew up with technology in ways even I didn't. And I think I'm a bit younger than some of you in this room."

Several people smiled. One of the secretaries muttered something about asking her kid how to use her phone.

"Generation Z, that's kids born after 1995, are the fastest growing consumers. They have an attention span of about eight seconds. Which means you win or lose them quickly. Seventy-six percent of them are on Instagram, which is why you see me speaking of social media in all aspects of marketing."

"This generation doesn't have money."

"You're right, but their parents do. Seventy percent of the parents say their children influence their spending."

Hayden from accounting piped in. "Yes, but how many parents will charter a flight for their kid's birthday?"

There were several of the staff who obviously thought Rachel was blowing smoke up their asses. "When I was in LA, I was known to join my friend for her son's holiday programs at the local elementary school. Do you know what it costs to make a playground a winter wonderland when it's seventy degrees outside? Snow . . . man-made snow?"

The laughter stopped.

"Children influence their parents. From snow to a sixteen-year-old in a brand-new Camaro. I'm not suggesting we'll see a spike in teenage-inspired flights. But those same kids that dream of it now will be flying in a couple of years. And that . . . that is what we are thinking of."

The room was silent.

Rachel met Jason's gaze.

His slow smile said he approved.

Jason stood by when Rachel handed Glen his requested budget proposal. He flipped through the pages as the conference room emptied out.

"How did you do all of this in a week?" Glen's gaze never left the document in his hand.

"I wanted to make sure Fairchild Charters didn't regret bringing me out here from LA."

Glen glanced up, slapped the file in the palm of his hand. "I don't think that's possible."

Jason felt a bit of pride in his chest, although he didn't own it. Still, for some reason, he took joy in Rachel's success.

"I like how you think," Trent said as he slid a hand behind Monica's back.

"I'm glad," Rachel said.

"I'll meet you in the lobby at noon?" Monica asked.

"I'll be there."

Jealousy that Monica could have an innocent lunch with Rachel when Jason couldn't sat in his chest.

Jason hung back, waited until the last employee had made their way out of the room before he spoke. "Wow."

"Is that a good wow, or . . . ?"

"If even half of what you're presenting worked out, I can see our bottom line increase within six months to a year."

"It's more of a three- to five-year plan."

"Even better." He waved his own stack of papers in his hands. "I'll need you to work with Glen on a bottom-line budget."

"I'll schedule an appointment with his secretary."

Jason was never so happy that Glen was happily married as he was at that moment. His once upon a time player brother would have jumped at someone like Rachel before Mary entered into his life.

He lowered his voice. "How is Owen?"

"Kids bounce. He's okay."

"Good." He couldn't think of any legitimate reason to keep her by his side.

Rachel shifted from one foot to the other. "Well . . ."

"Yeah . . ."

"How is the Christmas party planning?"

God, she was beautiful. "Good, uhm. I think. You're coming, right?"

"Yes, of course."

"What is Owen doing?"

"Staying with friends."

"That's probably for the best. The brokers really party," he told her. They didn't deny people bringing their kids, but . . .

"Just the brokers?"

"No, but they let loose. Most of them used to be Wall Street traders. High stress. We try and minimize that here, but most of them are just wired that way."

Her eyes narrowed. "I had no idea."

"Well . . ." He didn't want to leave.

"Yeah," she said again. "I should get back to work."

"Me too."

Neither of them turned to leave.

"This is awkward, isn't it?" she asked, breaking the tension.

He leaned closer. "It is."

"That's stupid. It shouldn't be."

She gathered her paperwork closer to her chest, smiled. "We'll talk later," she told him.

He stood back and watched her as she left the room. Jason was pretty sure his eyes just violated some kind of sexual harassment clause by the way they lingered on her ass.

Chapter Twelve

Monica had Rachel laughing long before their lunch arrived.

". . . So you call your husband *Barefoot*?"

"From the day we met. If he had his way, he'd walk into the office with flip-flops."

"He's one-third owner, what's stopping him?" Rachel asked.

"Peer pressure from his brothers. He is casual Friday every day of the week, however."

The waiter arrived with lunch and promptly left. Monica picked up her sandwich. "So you're from LA too?"

"Yep. Santa Monica, the last couple of years."

"I lived in the Inland Empire."

"Isn't that hot?" As far as Rachel was concerned, the IE was a place to drive through on your way to Vegas.

"Yeah, I hated it."

"Why were you there?"

Monica shrugged. "Grew up out there. Lived with my older sister while I finished nursing school and eventually found myself in the ER."

The two of them glanced out the window of the small restaurant. New Yorkers were bundled in heavy coats, hats, and boots. "Now we're both here in the cold."

"Yeah," Monica agreed. "It's all good until after Christmas, and then it just gets old."

"Really? I was hoping I'd get used to it."

Monica turned her gaze back to Rachel. "Sorry. I shouldn't make it sound so awful."

Rachel finished chewing her food. "I'd rather the truth than sugar-coated bull any day."

"When I start getting moody, Barefoot takes me to Jamaica."

"The perks of your husband owning planes," Rachel said.

"You'll have to come sometime."

Rachel couldn't imagine taking Monica up on the offer. Chances were the suggestion was her polite way of making conversation, anyway.

"Maybe," she said, knowing she'd never do it. "So let me tell you about my idea of Flying with a Heart."

"Flying with a Heart? Is that a slogan?"

"Yes, which is up for change. But I had to call it something while I outlined my ideas." For the next thirty minutes, Rachel recapped what she thought she knew about Fairchild Charters' involvement with relief efforts from disaster torn regions and let Monica fill in some of the blanks. Borderless Doctors and Borderless Nurses were partnering players, and Monica and Trent were the liaisons between all parties. Fairchild had started a foundation closer to home for organ transplant flights. As Monica pointed out, it wasn't just the rich who needed a liver or heart, and when the cost of flying was taken into the cost of transporting organs, it often meant people in need did without.

They knocked around ideas for finding more backers, putting a heart in all the Fairchild Charters marketing plans to remind everyone who used their service that their support as a customer helped, in a small way, to help others.

By the time they finished their sandwiches, they were both on the same page.

They both bundled up in coats before walking outside. "It smells like snow," Monica said only two feet from the restaurant.

"Does it?"

"Yeah, I should get home before it lets loose. I brought my car instead of taking the train."

Rachel glanced at the gray clouds above the skyscrapers. "I haven't taken the trains yet," she confessed.

"You're kidding."

"No . . . they're so, I don't know."

"Hey, I get it. I'm from LA, too. But driving in the snow and dealing with Manhattan traffic in bad weather isn't worth it. You'll end up in a ditch or worse."

Rachel smiled. "You mean like Jason?"

Monica glanced over as they walked the two blocks back to work. "What do you mean?"

"That's how I met your brother-in-law."

"You ended up in a ditch?"

"No, *he* ended up in a ditch. To be fair, I was probably driving about as fast as a nearsighted ninety-year-old, and he was trying to pass me on a hill. But he's the one that ended up in the ditch."

"You're kidding?" Monica asked, laughing.

"Nope. I gave him a ride to my house, where he waited for someone to give him a ride home. Imagine my surprise when I walked into a meeting last week to see him there. I had no idea he was my boss."

Monica stopped her by placing a hand on her arm. The people behind them just walked around as if they were a rock in a stream and the water needed to move beyond. "He didn't tell you his name?"

"He said Jason. Last names didn't seem needed." Rachel started walking again.

"That's crazy."

"Yeah." Rachel wanted to quiz Monica. Why was someone as together as Jason not married? What kind of women did he date? What did he do when he wasn't at work and wasn't putting up her Christmas lights? Was he a sports guy, or would he rather watch a movie?

"Someone got quiet."

She shook off her train of thought. "Sorry."

Monica chuckled. "It's okay. He's a good-looking man, they all are."

"I-I wasn't thinking about how attractive Jason is."

"Really?"

"No, I was wondering why he isn't married."

"That's easy. He doesn't date."

Rachel hesitated. "Why not?"

Monica opened the massive glass door leading into the high-rise. "I don't know. I ask Barefoot all the time. He tells me his brother is overly dedicated to his job and it would take someone special to pull him away from it. Glen says he hasn't dated, outside a social obligation, for years. Neither of them even know the last time he asked someone out."

Rachel actually snorted.

"What?"

"Nothing," she said a little too quickly. The last thing she needed was Jason's sister-in-law to know he'd asked Rachel out. "I bet he just keeps his private life to himself."

"I thought that, too. Probably for the best. Someone as eligible as him and people will start rumors and predictions. I'm glad Trent and I didn't have society breathing down our necks when we were dating. I didn't know his world, and he had only seen a glimpse of mine. And Mary . . ." Monica pressed the button for the elevator. "That's Glen's wife, she lived on the West Coast when they were dating. Of course, Glen was a playboy, so the rumors were that he was dating some movie star or some such garbage."

"I thought I read that his wife was a therapist."

"She is. Very sweet and always analyzing people."

They moved into the elevator with several other people. Rachel lowered her voice. "So what does she say about"—she looked around, didn't want to use any names—"him not going out?"

Monica leaned in closer, almost whispered, "Something about him being the oldest. Trying to be a role model for his brothers. Taking over for his parents in a weird sort of way."

"That would have to fade at some point. I mean . . ." The elevator door opened and several people got out. "It isn't like your husband is a teenager."

"I know. Believe me, Mary and I have been on a quest to set him up."

They reached their floor, stepped out. "I doubt that would be hard."

"For women, no. But he wants nothing to do with it." Monica leaned in again. "We even have it set up to auction him off in our spring fundraiser if he doesn't show up with a date."

Rachel started to laugh. "Dinner with the CEO millionaire?"

"Yeah, something like that."

"Sounds like a romance novel."

"We hope so. He either brings a date or we set him up. His choice."

The thought of Jason standing on an auction block while women bid on him had her grinning. "This I'd like to see."

"He's a great guy. I just hate to see him solo. I don't even care that he gets married, just go out and enjoy life a little more."

They came to the intersecting hall where Monica would veer off to the higher management offices and Rachel would return to her cubicle.

"I'm glad we had this time to chat," Rachel said.

"Me too. You have a lot of great ideas. I'm sure Jason is happy to have you on the team."

"We'll talk again."

Monica smiled as she walked away.

"Oh. My. God!" The snow held out until sometime in the middle of the night. Then it dumped. There was well over a foot in her driveway, and it was still snowing. From her bedroom window, she could see up and down the street. There were very few tracks in the snow, and almost no activity. After turning on her TV to the local news to catch the weather report, she ran through her room, throwing on clothes. Rachel had lived there long enough to hear the locals talk about nor'easters. From the looks of outside, they weren't exaggerating.

She all but ran past Owen's bedroom, rapped a few times, and kept moving. "Get up!"

Downstairs, she shoved her arms into her heavy coat and pulled on her warm boots.

"What's going on?" Owen's sleepy voice accompanied the look of him in flannel pajamas and tired eyes.

"Snow. Tons of it. I need to shovel the driveway to get out."

Owen moved to the window and smiled. "Is school canceled?"

"How do I know? Do they announce that somewhere?"

"Check your phone. I think the school calls with announcements."

She started back up the stairs, yelled behind her, "I know work isn't canceled, so get dressed and help me shovel."

Sure enough, the school had sent an automessage, informing her that Owen's district was canceled for the day, making sure all parents knew that a day would be tacked on at the end of the year to make up for it.

Owen was back in his room, pulling a sweatshirt over his head.

"One of us gets to play hooky."

"Nice!" Owen beamed with excitement.

Rachel opened the garage door and sighed. "How the hell am I getting to work?" Two feet of snow blanketed everything, and it had blown up against the house, leaving drifts closer to thirty inches. The road hadn't been plowed yet. "Damn, damn, damn. I should have set my alarm an hour early."

She dug in the back of her car and found the chains Jason had given her as a thank-you, and removed them from the bag. There weren't any instructions, just warnings that using the right size chains for your car was imperative for safe driving. In big red letters the bag told her not to exceed thirty miles per hour. "Shit." Getting to a plowed road and removing them would have to happen. "Still gonna be late."

The garage door opened and Owen walked out. "Wow."

She glanced up from where she was laying the chains behind her tires so she could drive onto them before securing them.

Owen had his cell phone in hand. She'd bet money he'd already posted pictures on Instagram.

"Grab a shovel, dude."

The previous owners had left an old, rusty flat shovel, but not one of those broad ones used for snow. Owen picked it up and dug in.

There wasn't enough room to back onto the chains until some of the snow was cleared.

"Why don't you just call in sick?" Owen said after they'd been shoveling for ten minutes. All Rachel had to work with was a pointy-head shovel that didn't move much of anything.

"Because I told them I'd be there."

"Are you going to take the train?" Owen leaned on his shovel and pulled out his cell phone.

"I can make it." She kept shoveling.

"I don't know. This looks pretty bad." He turned the screen toward her and showed her all the red on the freeways.

"I'm sure it's not that bad."

Owen blinked at her a few times, the snow dropping around them in big flakes.

"Why don't you get ready for work, I'll do this," he told her.

She looked down at the jeans she'd tossed on. "Good idea. Thanks."

———

Sitting over a cup of coffee and the newspaper on his tablet, Jason watched the snow from the kitchen window. How he'd loved the first snow of the season as a kid. The land surrounding the house was nothing but a sea of white that screamed for him and his brothers to go and sled, build stupid snowmen . . . bury each other in it. He remembered Shadow, a big black lab that bounced around them during snowball fights, chasing the ammo they tossed at each other.

The ranch had plenty of great memories.

The screen on his phone flashed, and Owen's name popped up. You work in the city, right?

Yup, why?

Two seconds later Owen sent a picture of Rachel's car in her garage, snow piled up around a partially cleared driveway.

Jason left his coffee and grabbed his keys.

On my way. Don't let her leave.

Owen's response was a thumbs-up emoji.

Did Rachel really think she was driving in to work?

When he arrived, she had backed onto the chains and was attempting to secure them around the wheels. The task wasn't easy for a seasoned player; for Rachel, Jason imagined it was nearly impossible. He pulled his Jeep up along her driveway and kept the engine going.

"Hey, you."

Rachel looked up. "What?"

Jason waved, glanced at Owen, and smiled.

She stood and turned to Owen. "Did you call him?"

Owen grinned. "Maybe."

"Need a ride?" Jason walked up the drive, his boots sinking into the snow.

Rachel's cheeks were red from the cold, and the snow caught on the edges of her hair sticking out from the beanie on her head.

She glanced between him and Owen, then at the road beyond.

"We're headed in the same direction, Rachel."

She stared at her car. "Fine."

When she turned to grab her purse, Jason stuck his hand out for Owen to slap.

Rachel paused next to Owen. "Stay warm, have fun, don't get hurt."

"Got it."

Jason walked her to his Jeep and opened the door.

"Hey, Rachel?" Owen called out.

"Yeah?"

"Stay warm, have fun . . . and don't get hurt."

It was good to hear her laugh.

Jason tucked behind the wheel and waved as they pulled away. "He's a great kid."

"I can't believe he called you." She pulled off her gloves and removed her hat. The static in her hair had it going everywhere.

"I can't believe you were going to drive in this."

"I would have made it."

He laughed. "By noon tomorrow. Were you really going to drive all the way in?"

The four-wheel drive ate the snow as they drove through. He couldn't imagine a two-wheel-drive anything doing the same.

"That's what the chains are for, right?"

"Chains will help you around town, to the train station."

Rachel tensed, looked out the window. "We're taking the train?"

"Yup."

He heard her gulp.

"It's gotta happen sometime, hon."

"Oh, geez."

He reached over, patted her hand resting in her lap. "I've got ya covered. Don't worry."

Still, she fidgeted all the way to the station.

By the time they parked, the lot was nearly full. Jason had come to the conclusion that Rachel reacted to anxiety with silence. She'd offered one-word answers to his questions on the drive and flexed her fingers many times, as if easing her tension.

He walked her through the process of buying a pass for the train, not that she couldn't figure it out. But since her eyes were wide and constantly looking around, he felt the need to point everything out.

"There's a lot of people," she said as they waited on the platform.

"Driving in on a day like this isn't smart. Not only would it take you hours, but the chance of someone driving you off the road is too great."

She forced a grin and stepped closer as other people pushed in.

"You'll get used to it," he said when the train rolled up. "And the pickpockets are all sleeping in."

She hesitated.

Jason took her hand and pulled her inside. They were early enough in the run to have open seats, which he took advantage of.

The trains and subways leading into the city had changed over the years, cleaner and safer . . . a place where everyone from street performers to politicians could occupy the same space with the same goals.

With her hands in her lap, she glanced over. "Now what?"

"We have one stop to switch trains once we hit Manhattan in about fifty minutes."

She tapped her fingers. "So what do we do now?"

He looked around. There were already people with their heads back, eyes closed, purses and briefcases held close. There was more than one person with a laptop open, and even more listening to music on their cell phones.

"I'll tell you what we're *not* going to do," he said. "We're not going to honk our horns, or slam on our brakes . . . or sit at a dead stop, watching the time." Not that he watched much of the time. If he was that crunched or due in a meeting that couldn't be rescheduled, he would use the company helicopter that sat in a hangar on the property.

Maybe not on a morning like this, where the sky was too dark and the ceiling too low to fly, but on a normal shitty driving day, he would.

When the train slowed down to stop and pick up more passengers, Rachel sat taller.

He reached over and grabbed her hand. "Is it the people?" he asked.

"It's just new. I think. I'm fine."

No, she wasn't, but he was determined to make sure she was. Across from them a man had fallen asleep, his jaw slacked open. The woman sitting next to him kept looking at him.

"Shall we lay bets on how long before his head bounces on her shoulder?" he asked Rachel.

She smiled and stared until the woman beside the sleeping man looked over.

Rachel looked down and talked over her shoulder. "Five minutes."

"I'm guessing three."

Rachel glanced up briefly. "How will she wake him up? Nudge or noise."

"Both."

For the next four minutes, they took turns watching until the man's head drifted too close to the woman.

She shifted in her seat, and his head bounced back up, eyes open.

Rachel bit her lips together to keep from laughing.

Jason nudged her leg with his, pointed out a kid not much older than Owen, bopping his head to the music he was listening to.

"I'm thinking he's a musician."

"He has the face for theater," she whispered.

For the next fifty minutes they sat while the train filled to standing room only, talking about the people and laying bets on other people's behaviors.

And Rachel stopped fidgeting. Twice Jason found his hand covering hers, and once he looked down to see her hand on top of his.

Once in Manhattan, she followed close behind as they switched trains. He pointed out the trains that went uptown and which ones went downtown. They stood facing each other and holding on to a pole. A couple of times, he held on to her when the train took off or came to a stop. Unlike the first leg, this time she jumped right into talking about anything and everything. When he led her from the subway and onto the snowy streets of Manhattan, she was chatting like she always did.

She glanced at her watch. "I still have twenty minutes."

He started walking toward their building.

Rachel's legs didn't move.

"What?"

"We can't walk in together."

"Why not?"

"People will talk." She looked around.

"About how we were on the subway at the same time?"

"They will assume something else."

He pulled her to the side of a building and away from the mass of people, all trying to get to work on time.

"Which we both know is just an assumption."

She sighed and looked at him as if he had only half a working brain. "Rumors are bad, Jason. I can't deal with that right now. Melissa already thinks I want her job. Julie is starting to look at me funny after every meeting. Gerald just stares." She grasped his hands in hers. "Just wait here two minutes, let me go in first."

"You're serious." He was amused.

"Please." She blinked a few times. The overly animated movement of her eyelashes said she was trying to sway him with a smile.

Which worked.

"This is ridiculous." He shifted on his feet, knowing he wasn't moving for two whole minutes.

"Thank you, Jason."

She leaned forward, kissed his cheek, and then walked away.

Chapter Thirteen

Rachel took great pride when Gerald paused by her desk, thirty minutes past eight, and stared.

"You're late," she told him, teasing. "I hope you don't make this a normal thing when it snows. I mean, we do have snow here in Manhattan."

"What the . . . ?"

She grabbed her coffee cup, looked inside. "I could use a refill. Want one?"

Julie snickered from her cubby.

An hour later she snuck into the break room and texted Jason. Thank you.

He'd been such a sport, letting her walk in without him. She was sure he understood her position, but still, considering how he had gone out of his way to help her through her virginal stint on the train, he took waiting in the cold well.

You're welcome.

Let me know when you're leaving and I'll meet you at the station.

She waited while his dot, dot, dot filled her screen.

You sure you don't want to stagger our departure by ten minutes to avoid wagging tongues?

She'd considered that, actually.

The risk of me missing my stop outweighs the possibility of seeing people I know on the subway.

Ha. I see how this is.

She smiled into her phone. Have a great day.

You, too. Now get to work. I'm not paying you to stand around and flirt.

Rachel tossed her head back. If I were flirting, you'd know it. Okay . . . that bordered on flirting.

Looking forward to it.

She couldn't text fast enough. Someone is cocky.

Someone is fooling herself.

Why was she giddy inside?

Am not!

Are too.

Were they suddenly five years old again?

Two hours later she replied a second time.

Am not!!!

Half his staff were late, a quarter of them didn't even bother showing up at all, and the other quarter kept watching him as he went about his day. Jason didn't care.

Rachel had placed a smile on his face the minute she jumped into his Jeep without argument.

And she was flirting with him.

Good, old-fashioned flirting that resulted in silly smiles and warm, tingling shivers deep inside his chest.

He soared through his day. It helped that two of his outside appointments canceled due to the weather. Audrey kept eyeing him; twice she asked him what had him smiling. Twice he told her he had a lot to smile about.

The hours rolled down to the end of the day. The snow had stopped by noon, leaving three feet on the roads and creating havoc most of the day. The same staff that showed up late left early.

Audrey poked her head into his office by four thirty. "Hey, if you don't mind . . ."

"Go," he encouraged.

"See you in the morning."

He waved her off and picked up his cell phone.

Leaving in twenty minutes. He sent the text to Rachel and waited for her reply.

Street level at the station?

Perfect.

Yep, he had it bad. What was worse, he didn't care.

———

He saw her a block away. How that was possible in a sea of people all rushing to leave the city, he didn't know. But Rachel stood like a beacon for him to find.

She waved when she noticed him. "This is nuts."

The crowd was much thicker on the way home.

"It will thin out on the second train."

She moved beside him down the steps and into the Manhattan subway. On the platform, people stood behind the line, waiting for the train to arrive. Street performers played by the walls, making the already loud space deafening.

Unlike the ride in, Rachel pushed into the car when it arrived and found a pole to hold on to while the train moved. Jason had no choice but to push in close, not that he minded. Rachel smiled when he slid up next to her.

"Did you have a good day?" he asked, not sure how the small talk was going to work out.

"I did. You?"

"The snow slowed things down in the office."

"Is that a bad thing?"

"It made for some trouble with flights, but it all worked out. Safety first and all that."

She shook her head. "Sometimes I forget that there are actual Fairchild planes out there, flying every day and night."

"That's the goal."

The train stopped, people shoved in . . . Jason moved closer.

"Do you like flying?" she asked.

"Love it."

"Do you get up there often?"

He shook his head yes, then no. "No. Glen, Trent, and I force each other to fly with each other at least once a year. I fly more, but it's the transatlantic flight that reminds me why I love it so much."

"Why?"

"I don't know, something about taking the controls and leaving one country and landing in another."

"Why don't you do it more?"

"Work, obligations. There is always so much to do here."

"But you're the boss."

"Which means I'm responsible."

Rachel shook her head.

"For everyone." That felt strange to say aloud. "I'm not even sure how many employees we have right now. Pilots and mechanics all over the world, everyone in this office, the one in London. A lot of households depend on what we do to put food on the table. My father never lost sight of that."

"And you took over for your father when he died."

She was staring at him, a softness in her eyes.

"Firstborn. It was implied."

"It wasn't in writing?"

"My parents left it up to us. Glen, Trent, and I got pissing drunk after their death and decided what was best."

Jason noted the station they were at; they had one more stop before they had to switch trains.

"Did you really want to take over all of it?"

He looked directly into her eyes. "Did you really want to become a mother to a teenager?"

Instead of answering, she slowly smiled with a nod. "Still glad I did."

"Yeah, me too."

Jason was fairly certain that was the first time he'd ever confessed his feelings about taking over for his father.

They switched trains and found a place to sit for the remainder of their commute.

"How is it Owen is so well-adjusted?" he asked.

"Emily." The name apparently answered the question for her. "She was fire and light. There wasn't a thing in this world she was afraid of trying to conquer. I didn't know her when she had Owen, but she replayed enough of that part of her life with me, it felt as if I was there."

"How did you meet?"

"I hadn't left college. I was doing an internship for a high fashion clothing line. Em worked in sales. We hit it off. I think I was one of her only friends who didn't mind doing stuff with Owen. She was older, full of knowledge and spunk. I was just starting out and inspired by her energy."

"And she infused all of that into Owen?" he asked.

"Oh, yeah. He oozed confidence early on. She set rules, told him the consequences, and always followed through. I remember a trip we took to Disneyland. We weren't an hour in and Owen started whining about something. She gave him one warning, told him if he didn't stop, we were leaving. Owen tested her and we left."

"Really?"

"Yeah. And tickets to Disneyland aren't cheap. Owen tested her after that, but she only had to tell him once that they were leaving, the toy would be thrown away . . . whatever, and he snapped out of his fit. Of course, that wasn't quite the way things worked out when he got older. He became quite the negotiator. Emily gave him say in many of her decisions, which is where his confidence comes from. He doesn't take crap from anyone but knows when he needs to keep his trap shut." Rachel sounded like the proud parent herself.

"Does he take authority from you?"

She shrugged. "I haven't really had to come down on him about anything. He does better than okay in school. The kids he hangs out with are respectful and don't seem to be in the wrong crowd. Because I'm not his mother, we get to have a friendship. Losing a parent changes you." She looked up and met Jason's gaze. "But I don't have to tell you that."

"I was older."

"Still."

He was drowning in her smile. If he didn't continue the conversation, he was at serious risk of reaching out to remove fake lint from her hair, or brush his fingers against hers . . . anything to touch her and ignite the flame that burned low in his gut, which he wanted to grow. "Are your parents still around?"

"Yeah. My parents are typical Southern Californians. Love the sun and hate the snow. Which is why they aren't coming around this Christmas. They want to visit in the spring."

"It's nice that time of year."

"Dad still works, so it isn't like he can visit all the time. They're very fiscally responsible."

For the remainder of the ride home, Rachel spoke of her parents and brother. It was obvious that she missed them but wasn't lost without them by her side. Her independence was just one of the things Jason was beginning to admire about her.

Back in the parking lot of the local station, the snow was piled everywhere. The cars that hadn't moved all day held several inches. The slope of the Jeep's windshield made quick work of snow removal, and they were on the road and headed back to Rachel's within a few minutes.

"Wow, the snow seems thicker here."

"It will stick around for a few days. Once it starts to melt and freeze over at night, driving becomes even more difficult."

"Great."

"I'm sure you'll be fine."

She looked at him over her shoulder. "Is that your way of saying I should take the train again tomorrow?"

He drove past the hill that ditched his Audi and made the turn toward her home. "I'll pick you up at six thirty."

Jason caught her grin and noted a lack of denial.

The lights of his Jeep caught the snowman greeting them from Rachel's front yard. The colorful lights glistened on the roof, and the tree inside her house welcomed them.

"Looks like Owen has been busy," she said.

"I used to love snow days."

He pulled into her driveway, left the engine running.

"Thank you, Jason."

"You're welcome."

She jumped down from the Jeep, grabbed her purse. "See you in the morning."

"All right."

He watched her walk to the front door and waited until she turned and waved at him before he pulled away. And he prayed it would snow again before the end of the week.

By Friday the snow had melted to a few inches, and taking the train was no longer a requirement to make it into work on time. And since Rachel had promised Julie she would join her for a girls' night out after work, there wasn't a choice about driving into the city.

"You sure you'll be okay?" she quizzed Owen while he was eating breakfast before she left Friday morning.

"Geez, Rachel. I'm fifteen, not five. I'm going to the football game, just like always. I won't miss you not being here."

She held her little black dress in a garment bag. A small makeup kit was shoved in her purse. "I won't be too late."

"Take your time. It isn't like you ever do this kind of thing."

"Okay." She picked up the boots she would wear out, and filled the back seat of her car with everything she needed.

It was a typical Friday at work, with people peeling away early to get a jump on the weekend.

Gerald told Rachel and Julie to leave early once he got wind of their evening plans. By five fifteen Rachel was standing in Julie's apartment down in the Meatpacking District, pulling her little black dress over her head.

"I heard the apartments in New York were small, but holy cow," Rachel told her friend.

"If I went bigger, I'd need a roommate. Been there, done that, lost my computer and my stash of cash when she moved out."

"Really?"

"Before Tricia, there were four of us in a two-bedroom flat, a big loft that we partitioned off to give us our private space. Damon kept bringing his boyfriend over, and listening to the two of them go at it every night killed it for me. So I live in a glorified closet with a kitchen I never really cook in."

"Sounds reasonable to me."

Rachel adjusted her dress, glanced at her profile in the mirror mounted to the back of the bathroom door. "I honestly don't remember the last time I dressed to go out."

Julie tucked her head around the corner and looked at her. "If I had your boobs, I'd rock that dress every day."

She looked down, wasn't unhappy with her cleavage. "They're not that big."

Julie moved to stand beside her, stuck out her chest. "This is what it's like to be hit with the Korean gene."

"Maybe a push-up bra?" Rachel suggested.

"This *is* a push-up bra."

Oops . . . "How about a boyfriend that will buy you a pair?"

They both laughed. "Someday."

Rachel tucked beside her in the bathroom to fix her hair. She'd given it little thought after winter set in. Wearing a beanie or muffs over her ears had become the norm, which meant teasing her hair to some kind of perfection never happened.

Julie groaned and took the pale pink lipstick out of Rachel's hand. "Tonight is a red night."

"It is?"

"Yep, here." From a never-ending drawer of makeup, Julie unearthed a shade of red Rachel wouldn't have thought to buy. She had to admit, once it was on, it worked.

By six they were headed out the door. "It's early for the nightclubs, but we can hit happy hour, grab some food, and then find some live music."

"All within walking distance?"

"We have dozens of options in a few blocks." Julie tucked her arm around Rachel's. "You're gonna love this city."

The first bar they walked into was just outside Julie's building and across the street. Happy hour was in full Friday night swing, and everyone in the place knew Julie by name. Rachel wasn't sure if that was a good thing or not.

Julie introduced her to half a dozen people before they ordered.

Like many places in Manhattan, the bar was a tight spot with a dozen tables lining the walls around the space. Finding a place to sit wasn't an option, even at their early hour.

"How come we haven't seen you here before?" The bartender had dyed Christmas red hair and a tank top that exposed more flesh than a bikini on the beach in California.

"I live outside the city," Rachel said.

"She's been here four months, and this is her first night out."

The bartender offered wide-eyed disbelief. "Welcome to the crazy."

Rachel sipped her vodka soda. "Thanks, I think." She scanned the bar, not sure what she was searching for.

"See anything you like?" Julie asked her.

Rachel looked again, decided there wasn't anyone of the male variety that tickled an itch. "Everyone looks perfect."

"Everyone in this town is a wannabe actor or model. You have the whole musician crowd, and they all look perfect, too."

It was one of the things Rachel had noticed before the weather went bad. The women had amazing legs, probably because of the amount of walking everyone did in the city. And the men were beautiful. They dressed as if they were one chance meeting away from finding the perfect agent or gig. While she didn't consider herself unworthy, Rachel didn't believe she measured up to a New Yorker her same age.

"I'm not worthy," Rachel teased.

"See why I said 'little black dress'?"

"Jules!"

Julie turned around and beamed. "Mimi."

Mimi had to be six feet tall, but maybe that was the four-inch heels she balanced herself on. Bone thin, with high cheekbones and perfectly black hair. She was stunning.

"Mimi, this is my friend Rachel. Rachel, this is Mimi."

Rachel stuck her hand out, felt a little awkward when Mimi's handshake resembled that of a child. "I'm guessing you're a model."

That had the woman beaming. "Why, thank you."

"Sit." Julie patted the barstool next to them.

"I can't for long, I'm meeting Monique."

Julie's smile dropped. "I thought you two broke it off."

"She's an addiction, what can I say?"

Julie nudged Rachel. "I could never hang with Mimi if she wasn't into girls. I'd never get laid."

The three of them laughed.

For the duration of one drink, the three of them chatted about the men and women walking into the bar. Monique showed up, and the men who were eyeing Mimi abruptly stopped when the bombshell slid her arm around her girlfriend's waist before welcoming her with a kiss.

Rachel and Julie waved them off, settled their bill, and worked their way to a cozy and very filled restaurant a block away.

Once they ordered, Julie brought up work. "You know they are grooming you for management."

"I hope so."

"Which means you'll be my boss. I have to admit, that is gonna suck a little."

"Why?"

"I've been here for three years."

Rachel opted for water since she would be driving later that night. Julie was on her third drink since they'd left her apartment.

"So why not apply for management?"

"I need to finish my degree first."

"Are you taking classes?" Rachel didn't think so, they'd never spoken of it.

"I've thought about it. I don't know. Not sure I want the pressure. It will give me wrinkles."

It wasn't a secret that part of the reason Rachel took the job with Fairchild Charters was because they were looking for leadership in marketing. So far everything was pointing that way.

"So what's happening between you and Jason?"

The question came from nowhere.

Rachel hesitated. "Nothing."

"Uh-huh . . . you do remember the part where you told me the guy you helped that was stranded on the side of the road was killer good-looking."

There wasn't any denying that.

"He *is* killer good-looking."

"They all are," Julie said.

"True."

Julie tapped the edge of her cocktail with a fingernail. "You're seeing him, aren't you?"

"No! Of course not. He's our boss."

"You said that waaaay too fast, girlfriend." Julie lifted her fork and used it as a tool for pointing. "You've been quiet at work. I see you texting more during your day than ever before. Smiling into your phone. I know the signs that there is a guy in a woman's life."

Rachel sighed and offered most of the truth. "We are not dating. I assure you. I told him we couldn't."

"Ha! But he wanted to."

She looked down at her salad. "Yes."

"I knew it. The way he watches you in our meetings is a dead giveaway."

"I'm not going there, Julie. Just because he helped us with the Christmas lights and tree doesn't make us dating. Dating requires dinner and drinks and—"

"He hung up your Christmas lights? Jason Fairchild hung your lights?"

Rachel squeezed her eyes shut. She hadn't meant to say that.

"He offered before I knew he was a Fairchild."

Julie's smile beamed. "That's priceless."

"And no one at work should know about it." Rachel stared. "Promise me you'll keep this between us."

Julie pushed her lips into a thin line and pretended to button them.

Rachel doubted the button would hold.

"What does Owen think of him?"

It was hard not to smile. "Owen likes him, a lot."

Julie stuck her fork in her salad. "I'm guessing he isn't the only one."

Rachel spoke around her food. "Not going there. Fastest way to lose your job is to date your boss."

"Uh-huh . . . I'll remind you of that."

For the next hour they talked about anything and everything outside of Jason Fairchild. By eight thirty, they were standing three deep at a bar just a couple of blocks from where they'd started. Rachel sucked on soda water and kept her eye on her watch.

There was a time when the bar scene was one she enjoyed. The young energy, and the spark between strangers that created conversation and connections. Julie introduced her to many of her friends, or perhaps barroom acquaintances.

Twice Rachel texted Owen to see how his night was going.

Twice he told her she was being a ninny.

The third time, he took a picture of his room, telling her he was tucked into bed and not to worry.

Rachel knew there was no way in hell Owen was in bed before nine.

"Are you texting Jason?" Julie asked, trying to catch a glimpse of her phone.

"Owen."

"Who is Owen?" the guy who'd been attempting to grab Rachel's attention over the last half hour asked.

"My friend's son who lives with me." She really needed a better way to say that.

"You have a kid?"

"He's not my . . ." She stopped. "Yes, kinda."

"I don't do kids." And Pickup Guy was gone.

Julie stepped in and watched him go. "Whatever."

Rachel tucked her phone into her purse and sighed. "I should go. I'm an hour from home and the roads are still slick."

"It's early!" Julie complained.

"I know, but Owen is home alone. I don't want to push it."

Julie pouted.

"This was great, really. I want to do it again." Rachel glanced around them.

"I'll walk you back to my apartment so you can get your things."

"No, no . . . just bring them to work on Monday. You stay. I'll taxi to my car at the office."

"You sure?"

Rachel kissed Julie's cheek. "Thank you for getting me out."

Within twenty minutes, she was in her car and on her way home. Since when did she call an end to a Friday night before nine?

On the bright side, there wasn't any traffic to speak of, and she pulled into her driveway just after ten.

Lights were on in the living room and upstairs. She pulled into the garage and walked around the boxes still piled in the corners.

Once inside, she shook out of her big jacket and left her purse on the kitchen table as she walked through. Voices drew her to the second floor. The temperature dropped as she climbed the stairs. At first she thought Owen had his TV up loud, but then she realized the door to his room was open and no one was inside.

"Owen?" she called his name and walked to her room. The door was closed, and light and noise came from the other side of the door.

Owen's music from bands Rachel couldn't identify reached her ears.

"Dude! You're not very good at this," she heard Owen say.

"You're one to talk, you're wearing more than you're getting on the walls."

Jason?

She sniffed and knew exactly what the guys were up to.

"I have an excuse, I'm fifteen."

"Ha. I have an excuse, I'm old."

Rachel smiled behind her hand before slowly opening the door.

Her bed and dresser were pulled away from the wall, the nightstand sat on her bed, with the lamps plugged in and lighting the room. Plastic tarps covered everything. The paint she'd picked up, which had been sitting in the garage since Halloween, now covered most of her walls.

The window in the room was open, helping to air out the fumes and letting in the cold.

Jason had on a pair of worn jeans and a denim, long-sleeved shirt. Owen was decked in a pair of old shorts and a T-shirt.

Owen saw her first. "Oh, man."

"What?" Jason used a step stool to reach the corners with a brush.

"Jig is up, dude."

"Wow." Rachel stepped in, careful with the splatters of paint.

Jason turned to look at the sound of her voice.

"What are you guys . . . this is fantastic."

"I wanted to surprise you," Owen said, grinning.

"Color me surprised."

"Whoa!" Jason stared at her, his eyes taking their time looking her up and down.

She'd forgotten that she was still in her little black dress and boots that went to her knees. Heat reached her cheeks with his blatant stare. "What are you doing here?"

He sucked in a long-suffering breath. "Owen asked me for help."

"I knew I couldn't get it done in one night by myself."

"You didn't have to—"

"I know. Now get out of here so we can finish. We're almost done."

Rachel put her hands in the air, laughing. "Okay, okay."

She bumped up the thermostat and removed her boots.

Less than thirty minutes later, Owen ran down the stairs to retrieve a large plastic bag from the garage before disappearing back upstairs. When he came back down again, the tarp had been bundled up and shoved in the sack. He opened the front door and placed it on the porch. "Okay, you can see it now."

With her hand through the crook of Owen's arm, Rachel walked with him up the stairs and back into her bedroom. The furniture was still pulled away, but everything was back on the ground. The painter's tape had been stripped from the molding, and the window was still open a crack.

Jason stood in the center of the room, smiling.

"Wow, guys. This is wonderful."

"You might want to sleep on the couch tonight," Jason suggested.

The smell of the room would drive her out. "Good idea."

"Consider it an early Christmas present," Owen said.

She hugged him hard. "I never expected this." The home improvement projects had been hers. Owen had helped when he could, but she hadn't expected him to do any of it on his own.

Owen yawned. "We wanted to have it finished before you got home."

"I didn't think you'd get out of Manhattan before ten," Jason said.

"I'd still be there if Julie had her way."

"I'm gonna shower," Owen announced. "Thanks again for helping," he told Jason.

"Anytime."

The two bumped fists, and then Owen left them alone.

"I don't know what to say," Rachel admitted. Replacing the olive green with this lighter shade brought the space into the current century.

Jason took a few steps toward her, looked above her head. "*Thank you* works."

She turned her back to him, looked at the ceiling. "This is one of the nicest things anyone could have done for me."

"It's paint."

"It's more than just paint. It's a project. A ton of work." She turned back around to find him right beside her. A spot of paint dotted his cheek, and she lifted her thumb to brush it off without thinking. It smeared. "Oops."

"Better?" he asked, grinning.

"The Early American look works well for you."

"Is that right?"

She laughed.

He glanced down. "The sexy black dress works well for you."

"Is that right?" She bounced his words back his way.

He leaned closer.

She didn't back up. Didn't want to.

"Rachel?"

She watched her name on his lips.

"Yes."

Jason slid the backs of his fingertips on her collarbone and onto her neck.

She shivered.

"You didn't say thank you," he whispered.

Rachel licked her lips. "Thank you, Jason."

His eyes found hers, briefly, and his lips moved closer. "You're welcome."

Her chest lifted with short, unsteady breaths, the heat of his lips only a hair away from hers.

"Oh, God," she said before taking the last step and reaching his kiss. His lips were soft, his touch tender. How did he smell so damn good?

This was stupid, on so many levels, but she couldn't stop from touching him any more than she could avoid the smell of fresh paint in the room.

Jason folded her into his arms and arched her back. Everything tingled when his open-mouth kiss deepened and explored. She could drown in his kiss alone, but when his fingers fanned over the small of her back, she melted. When was the last time she'd been held this close, or felt this wanted?

There was no doubt Jason wanted her, and she'd be foolish to think she didn't want more of him. Her fingers clawed at his chest through his shirt, his lips never left hers. She should come up for air but was afraid to break the spell.

Logic would seep in, and she wanted nothing to do with it.

Jason's hand slid past her hip and squeezed.

There were stars . . . hot, desirable stars shooting in her stomach and warming her body for the man touching her. She lifted her leg, her hips pushed forward. She didn't realize her move until she felt him react with a groan.

He pulled back, smoky eyes staring down.

Logic marched forward.

Not yet.

She pulled him back to her lips, didn't stop him when he filled his hand with her breast. Nipples hardened and her body strained for more.

"Hey, Jason . . . I put your keys by the—"

Owen's voice stopped them cold.

"Oops, sorry."

Jason's hand dropped.

Rachel squeezed her eyes closed. When she opened them, Owen had already backed out of the room.

She dropped her forehead on Jason's chest and started to laugh.

"That's a first," Jason said in her hair.

She took stock of how she was holding him, where his hands were on her. Thank God they hadn't removed any clothing.

"Oh, boy."

Jason pulled far away enough to lift her chin with one finger so he could look at her. "Don't overanalyze this," he told her.

"How can I not?"

"Just don't." He had a goofy smile, and the paint smear on his face had her grinning.

"But you're my—"

He shook his head, stopped her words with a finger to her lips. "I'm just a guy, falling for a girl."

"Jason." How could he say that?

"And you're just a girl, falling for a guy."

"You make it sound so easy."

"It doesn't have to be complicated."

But it was, and they both knew it.

He pulled out of her arms and held her hands. "I'm going home. Going to take a very long, cold shower, and try to get some sleep."

She could use the cold shower herself.

At the front door, he kissed her again.

She let him.

"I'll buy you a new dress," he said, looking down.

Rachel followed his gaze.

Splatters of paint dotted her outfit. "Oh no."

He placed a hand on the side of her face. "It was worth it."

Much as she hated to admit it, it was.

Chapter Fourteen

Many corporate businesses housed in the heart of Manhattan all but closed down for the last couple of weeks of the year. Not Fairchild Charters. The private charter business hopped this time of year. Affluent people couldn't always get the commercial flights they wanted, so they sucked up the cost, booked a charter. The other, more frequent flyers booked their planes months in advance to avoid the hassle of busy holiday traffic and delays.

Much like retail worked the day after Thanksgiving to put their businesses in the black, Fairchild did the same, booking more in the month of December than any other two months combined.

Jason made a point not to visit Rachel at work. The weather stayed surprisingly warm, not allowing for the excuse to carpool to the train station. He didn't remember the last time he prayed for snow until that year.

Just because he didn't physically see her at work didn't mean they weren't talking.

He would send a flirty text, much of which centered around the type of dress he wanted to buy her to replace her green-paint-spattered polka-dotted black dress she now had. She'd pretend he wasn't being too personal, and he'd ask her if she always tasted like honey.

The company Christmas party was on a Saturday. As much as he wanted to have Rachel come as his date, he knew she'd never allow it. Instead, he greeted the employees and invited guests and customers. A band played holiday music while the cocktail party progressed. The venue they rented filled quickly, making it hard for him to spot her.

When he did, he forgot to breathe.

"Wow." She wore red, with spiky black heels showing off her legs.

"What?" Glen stood beside him. "Oh, wow indeed."

"You're married," Jason reminded him before walking away from his brother.

Jason mingled with a few guests before making his way to her side.

"Merry Christmas," Julie said when he walked up to the both of them.

"Merry Christmas to you, too."

"The place looks lovely," Rachel told him.

"You'd never guess I had a hand in picking the decorations," he teased.

"Really?" Julie asked. "Most of the guys I know are color-blind."

"I might have had a little help."

Rachel laughed.

He wasn't sure if Julie caught on or was simply thirsty. "I'm grabbing a glass of wine, want one, Rachel?"

"I'm good, thanks."

"Suit yourself."

Jason leaned close, whispered in her ear, "You're killing me in that dress."

She smiled. "I had a black one, but someone painted it green."

He kept a respectful three feet away and wished they'd picked a smaller venue as an excuse to move closer. "Where is Owen tonight?"

"Staying with Ford."

"Any news on Daddy coming to visit?"

She frowned. "Christmas Eve. We're invited to the Colemans' for a perfectly stuffy dinner with tension."

"I'm sorry."

"Me too. I tried to push it off. Owen wants nothing to do with it."

"Don't go."

"I have to, Jason. Tereck assured me there wouldn't be any more bad-mouthing of Emily. And TJ has the right to see his son. We need to try and make this work."

"Hey, Jason." They both turned to the sound of Trent's voice.

"Hello, Rachel." Monica moved between them. "Merry Christmas."

The women hugged.

Jason envied his sister-in-law.

"How are you liking your first New York winter?" Trent asked Rachel.

"It's not as bad as I thought it would be."

"Are you going home for Christmas?" Monica asked.

"No. Owen and I are staying here."

"Just the two of you?"

She nodded. "He'll probably play video games most of the day and only duck his head out of cyberspace long enough to eat."

Monica glanced at Jason and Trent. "You should join us."

Now Jason wanted to hug Monica.

"I couldn't—"

"Why not? We have room. There is already a crowd. Don't you think, Jason?" Monica asked him.

"I think that's a great idea."

Rachel matched his stare.

"I don't know . . ."

"I'm ten minutes down the road. If we're boring, you can go home."

"Hey, speak for yourself, I'm not boring," Trent told his older brother.

"I'll talk to Owen."

"Good, that's settled." Monica pulled Rachel away by her elbow. "Let me introduce you to Mary."

Their voices faded as they walked away.

"Looks like someone has a date for Christmas after all," Trent said.

"Don't let her hear you say that, or she'll back out."

"Why?"

"Because she works for us."

"It doesn't look as if that is going to stop you."

Jason couldn't keep his eyes off her ass. "It's not."

Trent patted him on the back. "C'mon, let me buy you a drink."

"It's an open bar."

"Okay, let me get you a drink . . . and I'll join in."

The Colemans lived forty minutes north of them, and holiday traffic made it worse. "We won't have to deal with this tomorrow," Rachel told Owen as they drove bumper-to-bumper.

"I wish we didn't have to deal with this today."

"It might not be that bad."

"You say that every time."

She gripped the wheel. "That's because I pray every time that it will get better."

"What if it doesn't? What if they continue to be douchebags?"

"I wish I had an easy answer for that, Owen. Maybe TJ will help the situation."

"Or maybe he'll be a superior ass and make it worse."

"Watch your language."

Owen rolled his eyes. "Oh, please. You're thinking it, too."

"Thinking, not saying." She smiled at him.

He grinned back.

"We'll get through this. Play nice. We eat dinner. They will probably give you a present or two."

"I don't want their charity."

"Take it anyway, and smile. Then, when you're ready to go, tell them you're feeling sick, or have a headache or something."

Each home sat on a minimum of two manicured acres. The lawns were covered with leftover snow from two nights before, a pattern that Rachel had noticed since the first flake fell. People had told her it was unusually warm for that time of year and warned her that it wasn't uncommon for snow to come down and stay for quite some time.

It was the second time they'd been to the Colemans' home. The colonial, three-story brick structure was as cold as the people inside.

They stood by the white lights from the front door and waited while the ridiculous chime of their doorbell went through its song.

Owen hummed the death march under his breath, and Rachel started cracking up.

They both stopped laughing when Tereck opened the door.

"Come in, come in . . . Merry Christmas."

There was noise in the house. A lot of noise.

"Are we late?"

"No. You're right on time."

They stepped inside the white stone foyer and took off their coats. Rachel had opted for slacks and a sweater and insisted that Owen wear a button up shirt.

Tereck took their coats and placed them in a very full hall closet.

"Come in. Let me introduce you to everyone."

Owen stuck to her side and whispered, "I thought it was just them and us."

"So did I."

They realized their mistake when they walked into the great room packed with people.

"He's here," Rachel heard a woman say from across the room.

Deyadria approached them, wearing a dress that belonged in a runway fashion show. The floor-length formal made Rachel feel completely underdressed.

"Here is my lovely grandson." Her smile was entirely too wide, her words overly animated. She pulled him away from Rachel's side without so much as a hello. "Let me introduce you to your family."

Rachel scanned the room for TJ and found him in the back, watching his son.

Owen was surrounded by people within seconds.

The hair on Rachel's neck stood on end. They'd been ambushed. No one had said anything about some massive family reunion. Although she should have thought it was a possibility, she didn't see it coming.

Rachel stood out like a red apple in a sea of green. Nearly everyone ignored her, as if she wasn't in the room. A few looked her way and whispered to each other.

"Hi," a voice came from behind. "I'm Selma. You must be Rachel."

Selma had the only kind smile in the room aimed at her. "Hello."

"I'm Deyadria's niece." Somewhere in her early twenties, and owning some of Deyadria's height. "You look shell-shocked."

"We weren't expecting this many people." And from a few feet away, Rachel noticed when Owen's face went blank. He was going through the paces of being nice, but she didn't think it would last.

"Aunt Deyadria always leaves out details."

"Is everyone here family?"

"Mostly."

Rachel had no idea.

She still held the wine she'd brought with her for their small holiday dinner, which they'd planned on skipping out on as soon as they possibly could. From the reception line that stood up to meet Owen, that wasn't going to happen anytime soon.

She watched as TJ walked up to Owen and opened his arms.

Instead of offering a hug, Owen put his hand out to shake. At fifteen, Owen was only a few inches shorter than his father, and there was no mistaking the resemblance. "We're glad you're here, Owen."

Rachel noticed Owen's shoulders stiffen.

She handed the wine to Selma and walked to him without apology.

"Hello, TJ," Owen addressed his father.

Some of the family around them muttered among themselves.

She had to literally push her way to Owen's side. There weren't many times she'd seen Owen vulnerable. A couple of times when they were in the hospital when it became apparent Em wasn't going to make it, and again at her funeral. Right at that moment, Owen glanced around the room, his eyes wide.

"Merry Christmas, TJ." Rachel attempted to disrupt the tension.

"Hello, Rachel."

"Owen and I had no idea your family was so large."

TJ held his arms wide. "Well, we are."

Rachel looked at Deyadria. "A little warning might have been warranted."

"So you could have kept him away from us?"

The room went silent.

"Mom." TJ looked at his son. "We're a lot to take in."

"Wait until Uncle Theo starts drinking," someone in the crowd said.

Several people started laughing.

"You okay?" Rachel asked Owen.

He attempted a smile and a quick nod.

She leaned close so only he could hear her. "Say the word and we're outta here."

For over an hour, introductions were made, a laundry list of names she'd never remember. Selma offered her wine twice, twice Rachel said no. There was no way in hell she wasn't going to be able to bolt out of there if Owen so much as sneezed.

The room was overwhelming for her, and she wasn't the center of everyone's attention.

The dinner table stretched to accommodate the mass of people. If there was a kids' table to be had, Owen would have been the only one at it. Apparently the two cousins in their late twenties who had new families were living out of state.

Owen answered the polite questions about school and adjusting to the move. When he didn't offer more than brief answers, Uncle Theo, who was the obvious drinker in the group, changed the subject to TJ.

"So are you sticking around now?" the older man asked.

TJ glanced at Owen. "That's the plan."

"I thought a photojournalist spent their time in foreign countries, chasing wars," Owen said.

"I'm ready for something new."

"Have you found a job here?" Rachel asked, really wanting to know all the details she could about TJ's sudden change of heart about traveling all over the world.

"I'm working on it."

Deyadria spoke up. "Did you know your father has had his work featured in just about every political magazine and national newspaper in print?"

"No."

"Well he has. He's quite famous in his field."

Rachel couldn't help but wonder if that were true, why it was he didn't have a job with the first place he interviewed.

"I hope the sacrifices you made were worth it," Owen said directly to TJ.

TJ didn't respond. Instead he took a long swig of his cocktail.

Several conversations started around the table, taking the light off them. By the time dinner was done, Owen looked like he'd had enough. Much to Deyadria's and Tereck's distress, Owen said he wasn't feeling well, and Rachel ran with his cue.

While Owen said good-bye, TJ pulled her aside. "I want to start seeing him."

"That really isn't up to me."

"I want a chance with him, Rachel."

She lowered her voice. "Then do yourself a favor and don't pull this kind of crap on him. Ask him what he wants, and respect his response."

"He's just a kid."

"No, that's where you're wrong. He is fifteen going on twenty-five. He has a mind of his own. Don't treat him like a child."

It looked as if TJ wanted to argue.

He didn't.

Owen was silent most of the way home.

Then the floodgates opened. "Where the hell were all those people my entire life?"

"I don't know."

"Some of them had sticks up their ass, just like the weather killers."

"Selma was nice. Theo was real."

"He was drunk."

"It doesn't get more real than that," she said.

He rolled his head back. "What is TJ up to? Since when does he want to be a dad?"

"Did he tell you that?"

"Yes."

"How do you feel about that?"

"Like he's too late. He should have thought about that when I was a kid. I know my mom gave him a choice, never forced him to step up. But that didn't mean he shouldn't have."

Rachel turned off the interstate. "I hear ya, Owen. But before you blow him off, think about what you might be missing the rest of your life if you do."

"Like what?"

"That big family."

"With the hag?"

Rachel grinned. "Every family has at least one hag."

"I bet there isn't one hag at Jason's tomorrow."

That was probably true. "Just think about it. Don't cut people out of your life because of one hag and one deadbeat dad."

She pulled onto their street. "Oh, by the way . . ."

"Oh no, what?"

"About tomorrow."

"Don't tell me it's canceled. Jason promised me a match on *Call of Duty*."

The thought of Jason hashing out a video game with Owen had her smiling. "No, we're going."

"Then what?"

She pressed the button on the remote and pulled into the garage.

There wasn't an easy way to tell him, so she just did. "Jason is my boss."

"What do you mean?"

She cut the engine, opened the door so the dome light lit their faces. "I didn't find out he was my boss until after I picked him up on the side of the road."

"How could you not know he was your boss? Don't you see your boss every day?"

"Okay, he's not my direct boss. He, ah . . . he owns the company."

"You're kidding?"

She let herself out of the car, expecting Owen to follow.

"It was super awkward at first. Still feels strange. Anyway, tomorrow you'll meet his brothers and their wives. I was told there were a handful of other people coming, but nothing like we saw tonight."

Owen shrugged, rather unaffected by the news. "As long as no one claims to be a long-lost uncle or cousin once removed, I'm good."

"No risk of that."

Inside the house, they dumped their coats in the mudroom and turned on the lights.

"Thanks for having my back tonight," Owen said.

"I'm always going to have your back."

He offered a rare one-arm hug and then turned to go to his room.

She watched him go, pride in the man he was becoming filling her chest.

Later, once the light in his room went off, she dug into her closet and played Santa for the first time in her life.

Chapter Fifteen

Nothing could have prepared Rachel or Owen for Jason's home.

With Owen guiding her with the GPS on his phone, they turned into a drive that had a private gate.

"Is this it?" Owen asked. He sat up in his seat, staring out the window.

She glanced at the address, looked at what she'd written down. "Yep."

After ringing the bell, they waited as the gate opened to let them through.

They drove for what felt like five minutes before the tree-lined drive opened up to the house. The sprawling ranch home had to be three stories tall at the highest point but spread the length of six of the houses on her block. The circular cobblestone drive had a massive fountain in the center and a two-story garage to the side.

She gasped. "Holy shit."

Rachel was fairly sure Owen just dropped an f-bomb.

"How big is this company?"

"It's pretty big."

Owen pointed out beyond the house. "Are those horses?"

"I think so." Jason had horses? How did she not know that?

"I've never ridden a horse."

Unlike the night before when they meandered out of the car, today they scrambled a bit quicker, unable to wait to take it all in.

The massive front door opened, and Jason stepped outside.

"Dude!" Owen ran up the stairs. "This is your house?"

Jason received the one-arm hug from a smiling Owen.

"Ridiculous, isn't it?"

"It's epic. Are those your horses?"

"Yup."

"Wow, can I go explore?"

"Go, knock yourself out."

Rachel stopped him. "Don't you wanna say hello first?"

Owen ran off.

"Apparently not," she muttered.

She brought another obligatory bottle of expensive wine and a token host gift.

Jason walked down the steps. "Let me help you."

She handed him the wine and closed the car door. "I should have guessed you lived in a place like this."

"It was my parents' idea of nirvana."

"Not yours?"

"It's okay."

Rachel rolled her eyes. "Okay? Really?" She looked up. "I bet you didn't hang those lights."

"Nope. We brought in a crew."

"That's crazy."

She started walking toward the door.

He stopped her. "Wait."

"What?"

Jason stepped in front and lowered his lips to hers. It was warm, inviting, and way too brief. "Merry Christmas."

Was this what they were now? Greetings with a kiss, butterflies in her stomach, a never-ending smile on her face? "Jason—"

"Don't worry, I won't do that in front of everyone."

She grinned.

"Yet."

She moaned.

"C'mon. Wait till you see the rest of the house. I think you'll like it."

Like was not a word to describe the Fairchild estate: wood and stone, warm colors, and Christmas everywhere. The grand room housed a massive fireplace small children could walk into. Floor to ceiling windows looked out over a lake sprawling beyond a massive span of dormant grass. Jason's Christmas tree, or one of them, from what she could see in just the one room, stood at least fourteen feet tall.

"I'm speechless," she told him.

He helped her out of her coat; his hands lingered on her shoulders. He led her to the windows and pointed beyond the lake. "In the summer, everything is green. My father stocked the lake so we could pretend to fish, although my mother refused to let us kill the things. When she was out with friends, my brothers and I would cook them on an open fire just beyond the trees."

"Defiant kid." She laughed.

"Does Owen fish?"

"He was raised by a woman, I doubt he was given the chance."

"We'll have to change that."

We? They were a we?

"He told me he was going to start the tae kwon do classes in January."

"Yeah. He's excited."

Jason placed a hand on her hip and squeezed. "He's going to be great at it."

The sound of footsteps had Jason dropping his hand.

"I thought I heard voices." Monica walked in and greeted Rachel with a hug. "We're so glad you could come."

"Thank you . . . this is unreal."

"I know, right? You should see it from the air."

Rachel didn't think Monica was kidding.

"Where is Owen?"

"Running around outside," Jason said.

"Can I get you something to drink?"

Rachel sighed. "Sure."

———

She was here, in his house, in his kitchen, with his family. She'd shoot him a look every once in a while, one that asked both questions: *What am I doing here? And is it okay that I am?*

The few women he'd spent time with had never been in his personal world. They never felt right. Bringing them to the estate would have been like asking a woman to meet his parents. Until Rachel, he hadn't wanted to do that.

Then she picked him up on the side of a snowy road, and his world changed.

The sliding back door opened and Nathan stepped inside. "Look who I found wandering around the hangar."

Nathan had his arm around Owen's shoulders. The boy beamed.

"He has an airstrip, Rachel. A friggin' airstrip!"

"We do own a company that flies planes," Glen said.

Jason spoke up. "Owen, this is . . . everyone. Everyone, this is Owen."

A chorus of hellos commenced.

Owen walked up to Trent. "You must be a brother."

Trent hesitated.

"Jason's brother?"

He laughed. "Yes, I am. Trent."

"And I'm Glen."

Owen shook hands and looked around the room. "This is the complete opposite of last night."

"How so?" Jason asked.

"Rachel was the only white woman in the room, and today I'm the token black kid."

"You're black?" Mary asked with a wink.

They laughed.

"Soda's in the fridge, Owen. Help yourself," Monica told him.

Owen didn't need to be told twice. "So is the inside of this place as big as the out?" he asked.

"It's like Narnia," Glen told him. "We'd play hide-and-seek for hours."

"That's because Trent would fall asleep in a closet and we'd get bored trying to find him."

"I'd get lost," Owen said. He twisted at the sound of the train as it passed through the room. "There's a train?"

For a moment, Trent and Glen glanced at Jason, and the three of them shared that first moment again. The one when their father watched their reactions as the train made its way into the room for the first time.

"It just gets better," Owen said, following the path of the train out of the room.

"Makes all the hours putting that thing up worth it," Glen said.

"You have a train moving around your house." Rachel shook her head.

Jason leaned against the counter. "Christmas and trains. What's not to love?"

Hours later, after their neighbor Betty arrived with her yippy Jack Russell and Mary's family joined them, they sat around the living room, watching the rain fall outside the window.

"Five degrees . . . we need five lowly degrees and I could have had my first white Christmas," Owen complained.

"It will happen if you live here long enough," Monica told him. "No more holidays in flip-flops."

"By February, you'll wonder if the sun will ever come out," Mary told him.

Glen pulled his wife close. "And on February second, we'll fly to sunshine to forget the cold."

"Do you all know how to fly?" Owen asked.

Jason nodded, as did his brothers.

Owen sat dumbfounded.

"Have you been in a plane, lad?" Nathan asked.

"My mom told me I was, but I don't remember it."

Jason glanced at Rachel.

"We did the road trip thing when we moved," she said.

Trent leaned forward, filled his glass from the bottle of wine on the table. "Oh, we need to fix that."

Owen grinned.

"I'd taken my first solo flight by the time I was fourteen," Glen told them.

"Bragging rights by two months because I was the firstborn and Mom wouldn't let me go up alone until I was fifteen," Jason added.

Once the laughter faded, Owen sighed. "My mom would have liked you guys."

Rachel was close enough to Owen to reach out and touch his shoulder.

There wasn't a person in the room that didn't become acutely aware that this was the first Christmas Owen had spent without his mother.

"What was she like?" Mary Frances, Mary's adoptive mother, asked.

Owen shrugged, brushed off the tears in his eyes. "I don't know, a mom." He glanced around. "She complained when I left a light on, nagged when my grades weren't great. You know, a mom."

Trent was the first to comment. "I hated school. Mom pissed and moaned about my grades."

"You just didn't like authority," Jason told him.

"Still don't," Glen added.

Owen laughed along with them. "My mom was, ahh . . . she was amazing. We didn't fight over stupid crap. We laughed all the time. She wasn't like a lot of moms that find fault with everything."

"It helped that you're a great kid," Rachel told him.

"Yeah, but Mom didn't stress over the dumb stuff. If we had food, and she had money to pay the bills, we were good."

Silenced filled the space.

Owen looked at the floor, and a single tear fell from his eye.

Jason squeezed his eyes shut.

"You miss her," Mary Frances said.

Owen nodded, shifted into the small space beside Rachel on the sofa.

Rachel hung her arm around him and pulled him close.

"It gets better," Jason told him. "It's been eight years now. I miss them. At first it was every day . . . then life made me forget every once in a while. I felt guilty about that."

Glen moaned. "I hated those moments."

"Then it got better. It's like they're here, but not here," Jason said.

"That will happen for you, Owen. It's just going to take some time," Mary said.

There were tears falling from Owen's eyes, but crying from everyone's heart.

Rachel sat in quiet comfort for the boy, her arm over his shoulders, her head close to his. She choked back her own emotion; Jason saw that on her face.

"To Emily." Jason lifted the glass in his hand and everyone followed.

Owen smiled his thanks.

"I say we open presents," Mary Frances suggested.

The unwrapping began, and laughter soon took over the place of tears.

Mary Frances presented Monica and Mary with gift packs that included prenatal vitamins, pink and blue booties, and copies of a popular pregnancy book. "Yes, this is a hint. I'm not getting any younger."

For Glen and Trent, she bought them boxer shorts. "Because those tight things kill sperm."

Owen ripped into his gift. "Virtual reality headset! This is dope. Ford has this. Oh, man, this is so cool. Thanks, Jason."

"Virtual what?" Nathan asked.

Owen opened the box and moved to Nathan's side to show him what it was all about.

Jason dominated the empty space next to Rachel and handed her a small box.

"What is this?"

"Open it."

Her eyes narrowed. She looked relieved when she pulled out the piece of paper and started to read.

"You've hired a crew to finish my basement?" She looked shocked.

He leaned close, whispered in her ear, "It's a little early for jewelry."

"This is too much."

"Just say thank you," he said.

She placed a hand on his leg, looked in his eyes. "Thank you."

He wanted to kiss her but held back.

"I didn't know what to get you."

"You're here, that's all I wanted."

She stood and handed him two gifts. "This is from Owen, and this is from me."

He opened Owen's first and burst out laughing. *"Basic Survival Guide for Driving in the Snow."*

Owen pointed a finger in Jason's direction. "You did end up in a ditch. I thought you could use a few pointers."

Trent laughed. "You'll fit in just fine, Owen."

Nathan had the virtual reality glasses on, his head moving around, looking at things only he could see, but he added his snark, too. "You're never gonna live that down, lad."

Separate conversations circulated the room while Jason opened Rachel's gift. It was a glass ornament of a man standing on a ladder, hanging Christmas lights on a house. "It's perfect."

"It's silly." Rachel bit her lip.

This time, when the desire to kiss her rolled over him, he didn't hold back. It was brief, but just enough to make her blush. "I'll cherish it."

He settled back into the sofa and casually took her hand. Together they watched the others open gifts and play with Owen's new electronic toy.

As Christmases went, this was one of the best Jason ever had.

"Nathan is going to teach me how to drive!" Owen rattled on and on the second they left the estate.

"Oh?"

"Yeah, he said the airstrip was the perfect place to start for Jason. And since it's private property, there isn't a problem with breaking the law."

Rachel couldn't argue with that.

"And Trent said he's going to take me up in a helicopter."

"Yeah, I heard that . . . I don't know."

"I wonder if they'll teach me to fly. That would be epic."

"They're very busy, Owen."

"Hey, they volunteered. It would have been rude to say no." Owen tilted his head and gave her one of those *you can't argue so don't even try* looks.

"What am I going to do with you?" she teased.

"You can't throw me back," he said.

She laughed and turned onto their street.

As they pulled into the drive, she realized Owen had gone silent. She glanced over to see him staring out the window with a frown.

"What is it?"

"You could throw me back. If you really wanted to."

"Whoa, stop that. No. Owen, that is *never* going to happen." She put the car in park, left it idling. "I told you before Em passed, at the funeral, and every step along the way. You and I . . . this is a thing forever. I can never replace your mom, but I'm here for life. I'm never throwing you back."

He swallowed and tried to smile. "I miss her so much."

Rachel leaned over the seat and pulled him into a hug. He sniffed several times as he cried. She allowed herself a few tears but held out to give Owen the strength he deserved. It wasn't often he'd let loose, but he did now. "She would have loved your friends."

"They would have loved her."

Owen took a few deep breaths and got it together. He sniffed. "She would let me go in the helicopter."

Rachel smiled into his shoulder. "We'll see."

When he pulled away, she wiped his eyes with her thumbs. "You okay?" she asked.

He nodded.

"I think we did all right for our first Christmas."

"We did better than all right."

It was only a three-day workweek between Christmas and New Year's. Most of the city was overtaken by tourists, who would fill Times Square at midnight . . . that is, if they didn't pass out beforehand.

"You should bring Owen and watch the ball drop," Julie told her.

"It sounds like a massive party."

"It is, but there are families that go."

The thought of freezing her butt off and driving home after midnight didn't sound like a good time. Then again, maybe Owen would be interested.

"Maybe." Which really was more like a *probably not.*

The phone on her desk rang and kept her from having to make more excuses. "This is Rachel," she answered.

"I like it when you sound all business."

She tried to hide her grin. "Good to know. What can I do for you?"

Jason moaned. "Now you're trying to turn me on."

Rachel really hoped Julie had gotten busy and wasn't listening to her end of the conversation.

"No, I haven't completed that yet."

Jason laughed.

"Is there anything else?" If she didn't end the call soon, she'd blow her cover and say something that made it crystal clear that Jason was on the phone, flirting with her.

"I actually do have a few questions about your plan," he told her. "Do you have a few minutes to come to my office?"

Phew. "I do."

"Great. See you in five."

Rachel hung up, shook her head, and pushed away from her desk. "Jason has a few things he wants to go over," she told Julie.

"Anything I can help with?"

"I'm not sure."

Julie went back to her computer. "You know where I am."

Rachel took her working file and walked to the opposite end of the building.

Audrey looked up when she approached. "Go on in, he's expecting you."

"Thanks."

Rachel had seen Jason's office when she was given the tour of the place but had never been inside. Like any CEO of a company as large as Fairchild Charters, Jason took a corner of the building with breath-taking views of Manhattan. With a palette of gray and purple, which fit the logo of the company, the lines inside the office were modern without feeling cold.

Jason glanced up as she walked in, the look on his face all business. "That was fast," he said.

"You said five minutes." She set the papers down.

He walked around his desk and behind her to close his office door. Before she could turn around and sit, his hands were on her waist and he twisted her into his arms, his lips on hers.

She was stunned, and excited. Her arms fanned up his chest and around his neck. Lips opened, and their kiss became very indecent very quickly. They didn't come up for air, just kissed as if they were learning how.

He slowed down, his breath heated against hers. "I had to see you."

Rachel nodded with her eyes closed. "I can tell."

"Do you think anyone will notice if we have daily meetings right before lunch?"

"Yes. I do." She opened her eyes and drowned in his. "Is this why you called me in here?"

"Guilty."

"Jason!"

He held her face with both his hands, kissed her again, and made her forget she should be mad at him.

This time when he pulled away, he sat on the edge of his desk and pulled her between his legs. He tucked a strand of hair behind her ear and looked her straight in the eye. "Thursday," he started.

"New Year's Eve?"

"I'm picking you up at six."

"Is that right?"

"Wear something nice."

"Are you asking me out?"

Jason grinned, his eyes dancing. "Oh, no. I'm not giving you the chance to say no."

"You're serious."

"Yep. Owen is hanging out with Nathan. They'll probably play video games until midnight."

"I hope Nathan knows what he's getting into."

Jason squeezed her hips. "Six."

Chapter Sixteen

Rachel took advantage of New York's shopping experience in an effort to find a last-minute New Year's dress. As long as you had money, you could find it in Manhattan. Although she wasn't hurting, she had a hard time swallowing the average price tag on a glittery party dress.

Having spent more than she wanted to, Rachel looked at the dress on the hanger in her room.

"I like him, Em. He's such a great man. And he adores Owen. They talk all the time. Owen will text him a stupid joke just because he knows Jason will respond."

Rachel moved around the room, carefully picking out her bra and panties. In truth, the dress didn't allow for much in the way of a bra. With a grin, she closed that drawer and picked out a thong.

"I haven't had sex since Lyle. Remember Lyle?" The memory of the man made her shiver. "You warned me. I didn't listen."

Rachel wiggled into her thong and moved to her bathroom. She looked at herself sideways in the mirror, sucked in her stomach. "What if he doesn't like what he sees?"

Deep inside, Rachel heard Em's voice. *If he doesn't like it, screw him. He doesn't deserve you. And if he does like it, screw him.*

They'd laughed at that one for hours.

Only, the desire to hook up for the sake of hooking up hadn't been on Rachel's radar for well over a year.

Even now, knowing damn well that if she spent any alone time with Jason, they'd end up naked, that wasn't the single-minded desire with him. There was something else there that scared the hell out of her. She was thirty-one . . . the dream of finding Prince Charming ended when she watched her best friend die without a perfect man by her side. Nothing in this life was promised. Yet Jason offered hope of a relationship Rachel hadn't thought was possible.

"He isn't Prince Charming," Rachel said to the air. Then she smiled. Okay, he was kinda charming enough . . . and if clout and money made a man a prince, Jason qualified.

She shook the negative thoughts from her head . . . the ones that reminded her that she was dependent on him for her job. That if the two of them didn't work out, and most relationships didn't work, she'd be out of a job.

Oh, God.

She stared at her reflection in the mirror. Her makeup was perfect, her hair suitable for the dress she spent entirely too much money on.

The doorbell rang.

Rachel jumped. Looked at the time.

Damn it. Son of a . . .

She scrambled around her room. "Owen?"

No response.

"Owen!" This time her voice penetrated the clouds.

"I got it!"

She sighed and put on her dress. The high heels had no place on her feet with the sleet covering the ground outside, but boots didn't work with the outfit.

The purse she chose held her ID, a cell phone, and a tampon, not that she needed one today . . . thank God.

Nerves shook her before she opened the door of her bedroom and walked downstairs.

Jason's, Nathan's, and Owen's voices met her before she saw them.

Jason stopped talking first.

Owen turned.

"Don't I wish I were twenty years younger," Nathan said.

She knew she didn't look half bad, but the expression on his face was one for the movies.

Owen broke the spell. "You clean up pretty good."

Rachel rolled her eyes as she met the bottom step.

Jason had yet to speak.

Owen handed her a coat she had by the front door.

"You two kids make good choices."

Jason shoved Owen's shoulder.

"You're pushing your luck, lad."

"Wow," Jason finally said.

Rachel's belly filled with heat. He dominated the room simply standing in it. Under his long, wool coat he wore a tux. Bow tie, vest . . . the whole nine yards.

She brushed invisible lint from his jacket. "You don't look half bad yourself."

He took her hand, kissed the backs of her fingers.

"Okay, I'm out." Owen tossed his hands in the air and turned around.

Nathan laughed. "I hope you like pizza, lad. I'm not a cook."

"Neither am I."

Jason helped her with her coat and led her out the door while Nathan and Owen settled in for the night.

He drove the Audi.

"Should I be worried I'm in heels?" she asked.

"It's not snowing."

"I'll remember that."

To her surprise, they headed toward his house, the opposite direction of the highway. He followed his expansive fence line around the property and opened a wooden gate that hid everything beyond it.

A patch of trees opened to a clearing. "This must be the airstrip Owen talked about."

Security lights went on automatically as he approached.

The lights fell on a helicopter.

She panicked. "Are you . . . are we . . ."

Jason cut the engine of the Audi and twisted in his seat. "Do you trust me?"

Rachel pointed out the window. "That's a helicopter."

"It is."

"Oh, boy." She turned to look at him.

"C'mon. I'm going to have fun buckling you in."

With shaky legs, she held on to Jason's arm to keep from falling. He opened the door and took the liberty of hoisting her into her seat. She numbly sat back while he fiddled with her belt and ran his hands over her stomach and chest as if he needed to smooth out the surface.

"Was it good for you?" Rachel asked when he completed the job.

"Safety is important," he teased. He handed her a headset. "This might mess up your hair a little. You can fix it when we get there."

She shivered.

He closed her door and moved around the chopper, checking things as he went.

"I'm in a helicopter," she whispered to herself.

Jason swung into his seat, winked, and appeared to do another systems check by switching a few levers and buttons. "Ready?" he asked.

She shook her head no, much to his amusement, and followed his lead when he put on his headset.

Then he turned the helicopter on.

He leaned over and lowered a microphone, and the sound of his voice was directly in her ear. "Just breathe."

"This isn't . . . this is crazy, Jason."

"Not quite crazy. Not for me, anyway."

The inside of the chopper warmed up slowly. And within a few short minutes, Jason said, "Here we go."

Rachel held the edge of the door and clutched her seat belt when they lifted into the air.

Like a deer in the headlights, Rachel stared at the ground as it pushed away.

"Take a look." Jason pointed toward the house. The Christmas lights were still up, the yard around the home illuminated everywhere.

"Whoa." It was pretty spectacular in the dark; she could only imagine what it would look like in the day.

"Do your neighbors complain about the noise?"

"Look around. We don't have close neighbors."

From the ground, it was hard to see the property lines. She did see two homes close by. "What about them?"

Jason pointed to the largest one. "That's the guesthouse Nathan occupies, and the other is for my housekeeper."

"Oh."

"They don't complain."

"I would think not."

He lifted the chopper higher and headed north. "How are you feeling?" he asked.

"I'm okay, just don't let it get too warm in here."

"No real risk in that. It's a short flight." He pointed down. "It's hard to see, but your house is below us."

"It is?" She looked out the window, couldn't make out the details of the street. "There is no way I'm keeping Owen out of this thing now."

Jason laughed.

Within minutes the lights of Manhattan spread out everywhere.

"Wow."

"It's a beautiful city."

"From up here especially," she said.

They made a big circle and followed the Hudson until Jason turned toward their building.

She shouldn't have been surprised, but still was when he landed the thing on the giant X at their work.

"This is quite the parking spot you have here, Mr. Fairchild."

He turned everything off, and the propeller slowly came to a stop. When he took off his headset, so did she.

"Now you see how I get here when the weather is awful."

"I'm surprised you ever drive in."

"There are other businesses in the building that use the landing pad, although Fairchild Charters owns the lease on it."

"I would think you'd need to own the building to have that," Rachel said.

"Fifty-one percent. We own sixty."

She had no idea. "But you only occupy one floor."

"And we rent out the rest. But that is a conversation for another day. No more business tonight."

He jumped down from the chopper, ran around, and helped her out. The winds at the top of the skyscraper cut right through her coat and messed with her hair. Jason hustled her out of the cold and into the building.

He took the elevator to their floor, and the two of them walked through the abandoned space and to the office across the hall from his. "Mary and Monica equipped Glen's bathroom with everything a woman needs to fix the mess we make by flying you in," Jason told her.

Glen's office was a mirror of Jason's, only a tad bit smaller. As he said, she found everything she could need to force her hair into submission. When she emerged, Jason was leaning on Glen's desk, waiting.

"Feel better?" he asked.

"We just flew into Manhattan and landed on the roof. That isn't a normal way to start a first date."

"We can fly back and I can drive you in, if that will make you feel better."

She walked up and straightened out his tie. "That would be silly. Not to mention a waste of fuel. Which I'm guessing isn't cheap."

"You're worth it."

The man had all the right lines.

"What's on our agenda?"

"Dinner . . . because a proper first date has to have food."

She rested her hands on his shoulders, took comfort in his hands, which held her waist.

"Then there is a cocktail party I'm going to show you off at."

That made her a little nervous. Although keeping their dating to themselves seemed impossible if she was flying in with him in a personal helicopter.

"There will be fireworks."

She licked her lips. "What's not to love about fireworks?"

His hand slipped around her back, his fingers playing with the edges of her dress that dipped low in the back. "Lick your lips like that again and we will start with the fireworks."

She was half tempted to call him on that. "In your brother's office?"

Jason pulled her forward and kissed the space between her breasts. "Our first time will not be in any office," he told her.

"What about our second?" she asked.

"Highly possible."

He forcibly moved her away, held her in place, and grabbed her coat. "Let's go before I change my mind," he said.

The French restaurant was as quiet as any establishment could be on New Year's Eve in Manhattan. The table for two had high-back seats, offering some privacy for an intimate conversation.

They talked about Owen, and about Jason's family. Jason wanted to know even more about her parents and brother.

He held her hand across the table, and Rachel found herself guilty of playing with her hair close to the dip in the front of her dress just to watch his eyes follow her movement.

"You're doing that on purpose," he said after nearly spilling his wine.

"You are a very perceptive man, Mr. Fairchild."

"What ever happened to your concern about dating me?"

She wasn't sure. "It's a bit late for that, isn't it?"

He lifted her hand from the table, kissed her fingertips. "From the minute Owen walked out of the kitchen with a butcher knife."

Laughing felt so good.

He was a walking hard-on. Thank God it was subfreezing outside and every time they walked out of a building his body was forced to settle down.

That dress! His eyes lingered on the opening of her coat and the way the neckline plunged. What was she wearing under there anyway? It couldn't be much.

The car he hired took them to their next destination, their final one before the morning, if he was reading Rachel right. The way she slid up next to him in the back of the car, ignoring the seat belt. Not that you needed much of one when traffic crawled at under five miles per hour.

He placed a hand on her thigh, as if he'd already laid claim to the space. Touching her was fast becoming an addiction. Just as talking with her, texting her . . . spending as much time as he could with her had become. He found a tender space on the inside of her knee and heard her pull in a sharp breath. Jason leaned close so the driver couldn't hear his words.

"Have the fireworks already started?"

She shifted in her seat, brushed her hand across his lap. He felt himself harden again.

"It's going to be a long night," she muttered.

They pulled into a turnaround, and the driver let them out.

Rachel walked alongside him, his hand urging her forward on the small of her back. They walked past the reception desk and straight to a bank of elevators.

New Year's Eve party banners with a sticker saying the event was sold out told Rachel where they were going before they reached the top floor of the hotel.

They heard the music before the doors opened.

Jason helped her out of her coat, told his body to shut up and behave before he led her in.

"Wow," she exclaimed. "This looks like quite the party."

The two-story hall at the top of The Morrison had a balcony that stretched along one whole side of the building.

"You light up the place."

"That was a cheesy line," she cautioned him.

"I'll work on it." With that, he led her deeper into the room. Before stopping at any familiar faces, he first wanted to say hello to his host.

"I have someone I want to introduce you to," Jason told Rachel.

"A client or friend?"

"Friend first, he has his own planes, but his business does often charter from us."

It was hard to miss the tall Texan, and if on the off chance you didn't see the man, you heard him from half a room away.

Jason moved around the entourage surrounding the man and waited to be noticed. "Jason!"

He accepted the strong handshake and one-arm man-hug.

"I see you're charming *all* the women, Gaylord." And there were several women, much younger than the silver haired single billionaire standing in front of him.

"It's the accent," Gaylord boasted. "And who is this filly?"

Jason placed a possessive arm around Rachel for the introduction. "Gaylord Morrison, this is Rachel Price."

Rachel's carefree smile twisted. "Morrison? As in . . ." She looked around the room. "Morrison?"

He pushed his chest out and winked. "If hotels impress you more than airplanes, let me buy you dinner."

She laughed and shook his hand. "I'm full, but thank you."

"Sassy. I like her, Jason."

"She's taken."

"Oh, *is* she?" Rachel turned her head Jason's way.

He squeezed her waist. "Yes. *She* is!"

The glow on her cheeks empowered him. "Did Jack and Jessie make it in?"

Gaylord looked over their heads. "They're around here somewhere. So when am I going to see you out at the ranch?"

"I should have some time in February."

"Good. Make it happen." Gaylord was a demanding man. "You work too hard."

"You're one to talk," Jason said.

"Not as much these days. My grandkids need me."

"I'm sure they do." It was nice to know the man was slowing down.

"Now go find my son so I can concentrate on finding my next Mrs. Morrison." Two of the women standing by him glanced at him with his announcement.

"It was a pleasure, Mr. Morrison."

"It's Gaylord, darlin'. Now go along, you're crampin' my style."

Rachel was laughing as they walked away. "That guy is a riot."

"He's quite the character."

A waiter stopped and handed them each a glass of champagne. "Who is Jack?"

"That would be Gaylord's son. Jessie is his wife and Monica's sister."

Rachel hesitated. "How do I not know this?"

"You do now."

When he found Jack, he also found Monica and Trent.

Monica greeted Rachel with a hug. "I was hoping Jason would bring you."

"He flew us over in a helicopter. Who does that?"

Trent laughed.

"Don't get me started," Monica said. "This one wouldn't own a car if he could get away with it."

Jason watched as Rachel settled into a conversation with Jessie and Monica about dating a man with a plane.

"You brought her out in public," Trent said low enough to avoid Rachel catching his words.

"Is that some kind of issue?" Jack asked.

"She works for us," Trent told him.

"In marketing."

Jack glanced at the women. "How are the other employees taking it?"

"They don't know yet." And Jason didn't care what people said.

Someone close by snapped a picture of the three women.

Trent patted him on the back. "That's about to change."

"Jealousy runs thick, my friend. Watch her back," Jack said.

Jason's gaze ran over the back of her dress, what there was of it. "I plan on it."

A few minutes later, the band switched tempo, and Jason decided to find out if Rachel liked to dance.

He took the glass from her hand and put it down on a nearby table. "Excuse us, ladies," Jason told Monica and Jessie. "Rachel promised me a dance."

Rachel looked at him. "I did?"

He pulled her onto the dance floor and wrapped an arm around her waist. "I haven't touched you for ten minutes, I was having withdrawals."

She leaned her forehead into his shoulder and giggled. "I think there are at least three people from the management team at this party," she said. "Everyone is going to be talking on Monday."

"Let 'em. I don't care."

He could tell she was thinking too much about it.

He spoke in her ear. "I will never let you and Owen down."

She rested more comfortably in his arms as he moved them around the dance floor. When the music changed, he kept on dancing, swinging her around, making sure she was breathless. Twice he saw her adjust her dress so she wouldn't fall out of it.

The outside air instantly cooled them off after they stopped dancing. The patio was full of people, some smoking in a far corner, others taking in the view. He took his jacket off and put it around her shoulders.

"Look at the streets."

There were shoulder to shoulder people, the noise from the party below echoed up every building. A distant firework cracked with someone celebrating the new year a little early.

"This is a different view than when I went out with Julie," she told him.

"We can grab our jackets and go down there if you like."

She leaned back and let him hold her. "No. I like it up here."

"Are you glad you moved here?" he asked.

"I am. Two months ago I would have given you a different answer."

"What changed your mind?" he asked, fishing.

She held his arms, which wrapped around her, and kept her gaze on the skyline. "I started to get into the pace at work. Owen met a few kids he hangs out with . . ."

"Oh."

"I met this guy. A little cocky. Pushy, even."

"Is that right?"

She laughed. "Yeah, but he's cute, so I'll give it a try."

He leaned down and kissed the side of her neck.

Rachel shivered.

"Jason?"

"Yeah?" he whispered in her ear.

"What are the chances of us getting a room in this hotel tonight?"

He hummed in her ear. "I already have one."

She smiled up at him. "I suddenly have the desire to lie down."

"Was it the helicopter ride?" he asked, knowing it wasn't.

"No. It's the fireworks."

Chapter Seventeen

They didn't make excuses, they simply slipped away.

Rachel kept expecting nerves to rush to the surface, but they didn't.

Jason directed the elevator down two floors and walked her to a room. The corner suite offered a similar view as the party going on upstairs. The room itself was composed of a separate bedroom, a sitting area that included a dining table, and a complete minibar. A bottle of champagne was chilling on a coffee table, along with a snack tray with cheese, nuts, and fruit.

"Someone has been planning this," she said.

"Since the night we met," he confessed. "The hotel was a last-minute choice."

"Last minute?" She set her coat down and turned to smile at him.

"Okay, last week."

She gathered her purse. "I'm going to use the restroom."

Taking a moment to herself, Rachel offered herself an out. Pros and cons of sleeping with the boss.

Pros . . . those were obvious. The sighworthy man treated her well. She assumed the sex would be worth every breath she took. He wanted her in a way she didn't think she'd experienced before. He was gorgeous, and Rachel needed his touch more than she needed to eat.

Cons . . . her job. But it was too late for that even without intimacy. Feelings were already involved, so the damage was done. She'd come to that conclusion the night she'd found him in her bedroom, painting it.

Rachel turned to the mirror and messed with her hair.

When she finished with the bathroom, she took a fortifying breath and opened the door to her destiny.

Jason had taken off his jacket and tie and opened the bottle of champagne.

Her stomach fluttered.

He crossed the room and handed her a glass. "Nervous?" he asked.

"A little, I guess."

"We don't—"

"Speak for yourself."

Jason smiled, clicked his glass to hers. "To us."

She watched him over her glass as she drank.

He reached out and touched a strand of her hair. "I want to say something profound, but all I can think of is how beautiful you are and how lucky I am that you're here."

Rachel set her glass down and reached to take his. "Show me."

Jason didn't need any more encouragement. He reached for the back of her head and ran his thumb along her lips. He watched his slow, methodical movements.

The rough texture of his thumb pulled her bottom lip down the slightest bit, her tongue touched the tip, and her breath caught.

"I dream of these lips."

He moved closer but didn't take the step to kiss her. "Have you dreamt of me?"

She nodded, not trusting herself to speak.

"Tell me," he said, his mouth close to hers, his hands firmly on her face, holding her.

She dared to look in his eyes, the heat in them matching the fire he was provoking in her stomach.

"Do you want me to kiss you, Rachel?"

Again, she nodded.

"Then tell me your fantasy."

She licked her lips, found her voice. "We were in your office."

Jason trailed one hand down her neck and over her shoulder.

"What were we doing in my office?"

"I was wearing a skirt."

He trailed his hand down her back and over her hip. "Like this dress?"

"No. It was different. Office attire."

"What was I doing with your skirt?" His fingers slowly crawled over the edges of the material she wore, gently pulling it up.

She attempted to kiss him, but he pulled back slightly.

"What was I doing?"

"Reaching under it."

"I wasn't taking it off?"

"No. We kept our clothes on."

The coolness of the air brushed against her thighs as Jason did the things she described.

"Was I inside of you in this dream?" His voice was low, the image he brought to mind shot fire into her belly.

"Yes."

"On my desk?"

She looked him straight in the eye. "On your desk. Against the wall. In your chair."

The smile on his face fell, his nose flared.

"I fantasized about what I shouldn't want."

He dropped the material, rounded his palm over her ass, and pulled her close. "Now I'm going to picture you in my office every day I'm in there."

There was a whole lot of satisfaction in his statement.

"Jason," she said, moving closer.

"Yes?"

"Stop. Talking."

He kissed her with an open mouth, a hungry kiss she returned with the same fervor.

Fire already burned hot with every sweep of his hands over her body, like she'd only dreamt about. And she touched everywhere, his broad shoulders and strong arms. The dress shirt he wore was soft under her hands, but she needed skin and pulled at his clothing to find it. It wasn't fair that she was standing in a dress that had about the same amount of material as a pillowcase and he was fully dressed from head to toe.

She lost her train of thought when he slid his hand into her dress and cupped her breast. Delightful shivers coursed through her body.

Jason's tongue disengaged from hers, his lips reaching for the place his hand had been.

With her head leaning back, the heat of his breath brushed the edge of her nipple long before he tasted it. She was breathless before he stopped.

"This dress should be illegal." He moved to the other side.

When her knees buckled, he caught her in his arms and lifted her off her feet.

She kicked off her pumps as he walked them into the bedroom.

The city offered the only light in the room. The occasional thump of music from the party going on upstairs managed to permeate her senses. Otherwise it was only Jason in her thoughts as he lowered her onto the bed.

She loved the way he was touching her, the whispering of things he wanted to do to her . . . with her. Every word was a level of foreplay Rachel couldn't remember ever having.

She gave up on the buttons of his shirt and pulled it over his head. The feel of him over her made her squirm. The stiffness of the erection still held tight in his clothing pushed against her, making her gasp.

Jason lowered the sleeves of her dress and reached around to take down the zipper. "I'll make love to you in my office with your clothes on, but tonight I want to see all of you."

She lifted her hips when he pulled her dress away. "We'll get caught in your office."

Her dress hit the floor.

"That's what makes it hot."

He leaned over and kissed her from nipple to belly button, his fingers playing with the edges of her thong. Rachel knew she was wet, his touch firing every nerve in her being. But when he touched her, that slickness welcomed him.

"So beautiful," he whispered as he kissed the inside of her thigh.

She opened, wanting . . . hoping . . . waiting.

He moved the strap of clothing aside, and he found her with his mouth and tongue.

"Oh, God." She arched closer, her heels dug into the bed, her hands clasping the bedspread.

The hard tip of his tongue found the perfect spot. She rose to meet his every touch, and the slow burn lit a fuse. He pulled away and returned more times than she could count. "You're killing me."

"Not yet."

She tried to hold his head in place, keep him where she needed him to orgasm. He teased her until she demanded.

"Jason!"

He chuckled against her and buried his head.

Her body exploded, the teasing made everything more powerful as she rode out the pleasure in crashing waves.

It was a very good thing there was a party going on and not people sleeping all around them, or she wouldn't have been able to show her face outside the room in the morning.

He took one more pass with his tongue and she jumped.

"Now *that* is what I fantasized about," he whispered.

"I like your fantasy better."

He crawled up her body, lowered himself between her legs. "We'll make all the dreams come true," he told her.

She smiled into his eyes and wrapped one leg around his. "We're going to have to get you out of these pants before we do that."

He wiped his mouth with the back of his hand and rolled off the bed.

Rachel tossed her damp panties on the floor and made room for him when he returned.

"You look entirely too relaxed," he said when he pulled her back into his arms.

"All your fault." She ran her fingernails over his hip and down his thigh. For a man who sat in an office every day, he sure felt as if he spent most of it at the gym.

He positioned his knee between her legs and kissed her briefly. "I have to confess . . . I love long fingernails."

She scraped him again just to see his eyes widen in the dark.

"And dresses that barely cover a thing."

"Less material to gather paint," she said.

"And high heels. I love your legs in high heels."

Rachel ran her fingernails up his leg and around the front of him. His cock reached forward for her touch. She brushed against him twice, teasing him.

"I'll see about adding more shoes to my bedroom collection."

"You do that."

She ran a nail along the length of him.

Jason shuddered as if he wasn't able to control himself.

With her thumb, she played with the head of his penis, thankful for the size she felt in her hand.

His hips thrust forward, searching, before he kissed her again.

Legs tangled and hands searched out forgotten places.

Rachel rolled on top of him, let her hair fall forward to cradle their kiss. He searched the core of her.

"Condom," she whispered.

He moaned, let his hand hang over the bed. "In my wallet."

Reaching over, she found his pants and handed them over.

Fumbling, he tossed what he didn't need away and ripped into the prophylactic before handing it to her.

Rachel took her time securing it in position, let her hands play with all the soft and especially all the hard places. Two could play at teasing, and she wanted him to know she could step up to the plate to make him squirm.

When he couldn't take it any longer, he removed her hands from his erection before lifting her hips over his. She leaned over him, her breasts brushing against his chest, her lips hovering over his as she slowly sank down on him.

He filled her so completely it took her breath away.

Both of them paused, the moment seeping deep into their systems. "So good," she told him.

"Perfect," he agreed.

He kissed her, soft and tender as his hips started to move against hers.

She might have been on top, but it was Jason making love to her. He used his knees, his hips . . . guided her with his hands. Everything inside her opened for the length and girth of him. The deeper he went, the harder it was to stay calm.

At some point they both stopped being polite in their quest for completion, and that made everything even better.

She clawed.

He pinched.

She felt a bite that might leave a mark, but didn't care.

Soon the edge of the cliff rushed toward her, and with one last leap, she was falling into pieces, calling Jason's name.

His thrusts came harder, his hands gripped firm, and he, too, moaned until his body stilled with his release.

The muscles inside her squeezed him hard, she felt him jump within her with one last surge. Only then did she collapse on top of him and welcome the calm.

Breathless, they said nothing.

And then the sky outside lit up with a crash and pop.

They both looked out the hotel window to see the fireworks signifying the start of a new year.

Rachel couldn't help it; she started to laugh. "Two more minutes and our timing would have been perfect."

Jason reached up, caressed the side of her face with the palm of his hand. "We'll have it down by next year."

Was it possible they could last that long?

She hoped so.

"Happy new year, Jason."

"Happy new year, love."

He kissed her again, then slipped away from her and tucked her into his side.

Together they watched the show out the window after taking in all the fireworks inside.

—

They made love again, ate the fruit in bed, and sipped from the bottle of champagne.

And Jason knew he was gone. Throw away the phone numbers that came before her. Rachel was the real deal.

They laughed at the fireworks and shared sexual fantasies until she fell asleep.

How was it possible he'd fallen so completely in such a short time? He didn't know, didn't really want to question it. Jason also cautioned himself against revealing everything in his head. She'd tossed aside her concerns about him to get to this point. Now he needed to prove himself outside of the bedroom.

As he fell asleep holding her, he let his mind wander to all the things they could share.

The phone in the room shook him awake long before dawn.

Rachel bolted from the bed. "Owen?"

Jason fiddled with the phone and turned on the light. "Hello?"

"Jason, lad."

"Is Owen okay?" Rachel was practically in his lap, asking the question.

Nathan must have heard her question. "Tell the lass Owen is perfectly fine. Sleeping."

Jason placed a hand on her shoulder. "He's fine."

Some relief washed over her.

"What's going on?" Because no one woke you up at five in the morning for a good reason.

"A plane went down."

Jason was wide awake now.

"Where?"

"Costa Rica."

"Who was on it?"

Nathan hesitated.

"The Lamberts."

Jason waited for the other shoe to drop as he pictured the couple the last time he saw them.

"Wendy didn't make it. Ron is in critical but stable condition."

Jason squeezed his eyes shut. "The kids?"

"They weren't on the plane."

Jason's head fell forward. "Thank God."

Rachel placed a hand on his forearm, looked at him with concern.

"What about my crew?"

"The copilot isn't looking too good."

"And the others?"

"The pilot was in surgery when they called, the flight attendant walked away, but there is a problem."

More than losing a client on one of his flights? "Tell me."

"There is already talk of substance abuse with the pilot."

"That's hardly unexpected." Every initial report wanted to blame the pilot, and drugs weren't ruled out for hours.

"I don't know, Jason. There is a lot of talk already on this one."

"When did the plane go down?"

Rachel's eyes opened wide.

"Hours ago. Glen has been trying to call, he finally obtained Rachel's number from Gerald and called her house to find me."

Jason needed to get ahold of his brother. "Wake Owen, take him to the house. We're on our way."

"How bad is it?" Rachel asked the second he hung up the phone.

"It's not good. We need to get dressed."

———

Wearing rumpled formal attire at five in the morning took the walk of shame to a new level, although Rachel was fairly certain Jason couldn't care less.

A Morrison Hotel car was at the curb when they walked outside.

They pulled up to the Fairchild building to find a few men with cameras waiting for them.

"Mr. Fairchild, do you have anything to say about the fatal crash?"

He walked past them as if he didn't see them.

"Mr. Fairchild?"

Panic rose inside her. This was a PR nightmare in the making. Without thinking twice, Rachel paused, making Jason slow down. She turned to the media and smiled. "Mr. Fairchild has no comment at the moment. He needs to assess the situation and comfort the family before a formal statement can be made."

"Is it true the pilot was under the influence of cocaine?"

"Again, a formal statement will come soon. Thank you." Rachel turned and let Jason lead her into the building.

Inside, a security guard opened the door and locked it behind them. "Thank you, Gunther."

"Mr. Fairchild. The helicopter is fueled and ready."

Rachel smiled at the man she'd never given a name to and rode the elevator beside Jason.

He kissed the top of her head. "Thank you."

"Just doing my job."

He squeezed her hand. "You're not my public relations manager."

"No, she's in London for the next week, or until you can locate her and drag her back." All information she'd heard over the water cooler and kept tucked inside her head.

The elevator stopped at the top of the building, they stepped out, and Jason addressed a man who stood just inside the door leading to the roof. "She ready?"

"Checked her myself."

Jason shook the man's hand. "No flights in or out until I return."

"Of course, Mr. Fairchild."

Rachel ran to keep up, not easy in four-inch heels that were meant for a cocktail party and not running across a rooftop.

She jumped into the passenger seat and reached for her seat belt.

Jason looked over the aircraft, only faster than he had the first time they got in one together. Inside, he put his headset on and immediately started the propeller spinning.

"Are you okay?" she asked.

He looked over, grasped her hand. "You're here, right?"

"Yes."

"Then I'm fine."

She wasn't completely sure what to make of that. In the car over, he'd told her about the crash, about the couple inside the plane. He'd known the Lamberts since before his parents died. Big clients of Fairchild Charters, the couple and the Lambert company used their jets nearly every month.

Jason lifted the helicopter into the air, speaking into the mic. "You worked in public relations before you went into marketing, right?"

"My last job, they were one and the same."

He pointed the chopper in the direction of home. "I need you to come with me and handle the media until I can get Phyllis on board."

She hesitated. "What about Owen? I can't leave him—"

"We bring him with us. He's out of school until the second week in January, right?"

Could she do that? "He is."

"Does he have a passport?"

"Yeah. Emily thought she might find new treatments for her cancer overseas and made us all get one." Unfortunately there wasn't anything that they could have flown toward to save her.

"Then it's settled, he stays at the hotel while we deal with this issue. It will be a vacation for him and work for us."

"Alone in a hotel in Costa Rica?"

"Nathan can come along. I'll need him to go over the FAA reports as they come in, anyway."

Costa Rica.

"I need you, Rachel."

She grasped his free hand. "What should I pack?"

Chapter Eighteen

Owen thought it was an epic adventure, Jason was on the phone even at thirty thousand feet, and Rachel scrambled to write press releases and statements to reflect every scenario they might come across, all while flying in Jason's personal jet. Nathan acted as copilot.

Three hours into their five-and-a-half-hour flight, Jason stepped away from his computer and to her side.

Owen sat in a leather reclined seat, watching a Marvel action flick while continually looking out the window and making comments about the landscape below.

"This is not how I pictured you in this plane for the first time."

"I can beat that. I never pictured me here."

He snuggled her neck. "Well, get used to it."

Her heart kicked hard against her rib cage.

Before she could say a word, he kissed her cheek and moved behind Owen. "What are you watching?"

The two of them spoke over the movie, and Rachel looked around the cabin.

This wasn't just a jet. It was a private jet of an owner of a massive company that flew jets. It didn't boast a few seats; there were a minimum of a dozen, and two bedrooms . . . it was massive. Jason had apologized for the lack of an attendant, as if they needed one. Rachel was fairly certain the only thing different from Jason Fairchild's private plane and that of the president was the cabinet of people inside.

How did I end up here, Em? the voice inside asked her friend, who couldn't answer.

Owen laughed at something Jason said, the two of them watching grown men act like superheroes.

She glanced at her notes, reread what she'd written for Jason to say. *Do your job,* she cautioned herself.

She knew he'd asked her to come along as his support, but he'd also mentioned her abilities at her job. Letting him down, the company down, wasn't an option.

Without anything else to do, and with fatigue already biting at her head, she sat back and closed her eyes.

———

Costa Rica was hot and wet. The sun was still up as they shuffled through customs and into a waiting car. Nathan and Owen took a separate car to the hotel so Jason and Rachel could go directly to the hospital.

Jason's first priority was the people on the plane.

Jason had never met either pilot. On the flight over, he pulled up their employee files and directed his US based staff to expedite transportation for their families to travel to be with them.

In Jason's time as CEO, he'd only had to go to a crash scene two other times. Both were free of fatalities, both were issues with takeoff. The airplanes in both situations sustained some damage but were by no means a complete loss.

According to the early pictures Jason received in flight, that wasn't the case with the Costa Rica crash.

The hospital was like nothing they'd seen in the States. Less than six stories tall, with walls that appeared to be crumbling and unsuitable for occupancy on the outside, it had a surprising amount of technology inside.

It took a little time to find the right person to speak to, one who spoke English enough to get the information they needed.

The staff allowed both Jason and Rachel into the large room where both the pilots were being treated.

Neither man was conscious.

Both of them looked like they'd been run over with a truck. Or fallen out of the sky, as it stood.

One of the doctors came to the room when he heard there were visitors for the survivors.

"How bad are they?" Jason asked after Dr. Salvador introduced himself.

"Mr. Hyde should recover without complication. He suffered a spleen injury and some damage to his intestines."

Jason looked at the other man. "And my copilot?"

"Mr. Berglund is more complicated. There is swelling in his brain and several broken bones. We assumed he wasn't wearing the safety belts required for flight. There weren't any abrasions along his pelvis like that which we found on Mr. Hyde."

Jason shook his head. "I haven't been to the crash site, or received any information from ICAO or the local agency yet."

"I understand a flight attendant survived with minimal injuries. Perhaps she can help with the facts."

Rachel placed a hand on Jason's arm. "Weren't you told Ron was in critical but stable condition?"

Jason did a quick scan of the unit. "Where is Mr. Lambert?"

"Ah, yes, the passenger. He was transferred to a lower unit."

"Lower?" Jason asked.

"His injuries are not life threatening. He is down one floor."

There was some relief in that.

After the doctor walked away, Jason and Rachel moved to a small waiting room outside the unit.

"I guess they don't worry about HIPAA laws here," she said.

"Thank God."

They took a flight of stairs and found the nurse caring for Ron.

Through the broken English of one of the staff, they were told Ron was heavily medicated and shouldn't be disturbed for a few hours. Jason was relieved to have a few more hours before he was forced to speak to the man who just lost his wife.

"What now?" Rachel asked once they left the floor.

Any other staff member, and Jason wouldn't hesitate, but because he was speaking with Rachel, Jason cringed. "I need you here while I go to the crash site. Try and find the flight attendant and get some information from her. If any of the family shows up, they need to see us on-site. We should have more reinforcements by morning."

If Rachel was concerned, it didn't show. "That's why I'm here," she told him.

"You have your phone and a charger?"

She patted her briefcase.

"Money?"

"I have a credit card. I'm fine."

"Okay." His gut squeezed. "You're sure you're—"

"Jason! I'm a grown woman. Go. Do your job." She smiled.

He pulled her close and kissed her. "Be safe," he said before he walked out the door.

Several hours later, Rachel had given up on finding the flight attendant. She called around to the local hotels, many of which had people on staff who spoke English, and none said they had the attendant's name in their registry.

The only hospital information was that she was treated for a few lacerations and a broken wrist and sent away. No one had seen her since. Rachel hoped it wasn't an omen and was simply a case of not looking in the right places to find her.

Rachel sent several texts to Owen while she sat in the hospital waiting room. As expected, he was overly excited about being in a foreign country and was vowing to do better in his Spanish class when they returned to school later that month. On that, they both agreed.

Jason wasn't on the radar. Then again, he was traveling to a clearing in a dense forest that probably didn't have a cell tower for miles.

Around ten, she wondered if she should stick around or make her way to the hotel. She'd give herself till midnight, or until someone on the staff kicked her out. So far, there didn't seem to be anyone playing police to visiting hours.

Doing everything in her power to keep from falling asleep . . . and only a few minutes from her midnight deadline, two Americans wearing pullover shirts with the Fairchild Charters logo walked into the lobby.

She stopped them before they found the elevators.

"Hello?"

The woman was probably in her fifties, not more than five feet three inches tall. The man looked to be in his early forties and had to spend five hours a day in the gym working out. They turned at her voice and smiled.

"You must be Rachel Price."

"I am. It's nice to hear a familiar language."

"Mr. Fairchild told us you'd be here. I'm Louis, and this is Isa. We're part of the crisis team. Are there any changes?"

"No. Not really. We have a crisis team? I didn't think we had a need."

"It's new. Part of the relief effort sector."

Isa offered a soft smile. "I'm a clinical psychologist and fluent in four languages."

Rachel was impressed.

"And I'm big and scary and double as a bodyguard."

"I don't know what to say to that." And she didn't.

He grinned. "I'm here for Isa. But Mr. Fairchild wanted me to see you to the car so you could go back to the hotel and rest."

"I was just about to take that trip alone. The last thing I want to do is fall asleep in the lobby."

They said their good-byes, and Rachel left the noise and smell of the hospital.

Once on the road, Rachel was grateful that San José, Costa Rica, had private drivers in relatively normal cars. But as the city passed by, she noticed people driving around in cars that would have been found in abandoned alleys without a license plate back in the States. She had felt safer driving into the city with Jason by her side than she did now, alone in a strange car.

Still, it didn't take long for the driver to pull into a hotel turn-around and open the door for her.

It was a Morrison, which after the previous evening didn't surprise her. At the desk, she gave them her name, and they handed her a key.

An attendant swiped her key inside the elevator and escorted her to the top floor.

There were only three doors in the short hall. She found the one with her number and quietly opened it.

She didn't need to act like a mouse.

It was a penthouse suite with everything one would expect in the US.

She heard snoring coming from one of the rooms and poked her head inside. Nathan lay on his back, his mouth slack with sleep.

After a little more investigation she found Owen curled up on his side in another bedroom, the curtains open and the lights from the city drifting in.

The master bedroom held a king-size bed that called her name. The suitcase she'd packed, along with the one Jason had tossed together, sat in the corner of the room.

Instead of jumping right in bed, she made use of the minifridge and snack basket.

Before sliding under the covers, she sent Jason one more text, telling him she'd made it to the hotel.

Attempting to stay awake for Jason proved impossible, and she gave in to the night.

Sometime, very early in the morning, Rachel felt Jason's arm around her waist.

For a brief moment, she wondered if he'd just gotten in . . . but then she realized he was already sound asleep, his deep, even breath brushing against her neck in quiet comfort.

She smiled at the thought of him beside her. She was acutely aware of how comfortable she felt. In a foreign country, sleeping in a bed with her boss . . . these things should put an itch under her skin. They didn't.

Closing her eyes, she allowed sleep to find her again. Only this time, Rachel found a dream worth remembering when she woke the next day. The two of them were in his jet, she wore white, and he was in a tux. The taste of champagne sat on her tongue and warmth filled her heart. She lifted her heavy hand, noticed a shimmer on her left ring finger, and then the jet began to plunge from the sky.

Rachel woke with a start, her heart pulsing against her chest.

Costa Rica.

Jason in bed beside her.

Noise from the other side of the bedroom door.

Owen's laughter.

She closed her eyes and forced her heartbeat to slow. But the memories of her dream lingered long into her day.

It took two days for Jason and his team to gather the truth behind the events leading up to the crash, and another two for the preliminary report from the International Civil Aviation Organization.

Rachel stood beside Jason as he spoke to the press. After thanking the media for coming and for displaying patience while they determined the exact reason Fairchild Charters flight 262 went down, Jason delivered all the information he could.

"First, we want to extended our deepest sympathy to the Lambert family. Wendy and Ron have been close friends for many years, and Wendy will be missed by everyone. Ron has already flown home, and we hope the press will grant him and his children their privacy as they work through the loss of a wife and mother."

Rachel kept her face void of emotion, never letting the media see the thoughts she had inside.

"Toxicology reports have removed the chance of any drug or alcohol use as a reason for this unfortunate accident." Jason lifted his chin slightly. "A combination of pilot error and passenger interference with the flight crew has been recorded as the cause of this accident. Fairchild Charters will increase our training safety procedures upon landing and takeoff as a result of this accident."

Three men holding recording devices started to speak at once, all of them asking about the passenger interference part of Jason's statement.

Jason held up a hand. "Every passenger on every flight, whether it's with a private company or on a jet with five hundred other people, has a certain code of propriety that must be maintained for their own safety and the safety of others."

"What safety procedure did the Lamberts ignore?" one overly large and loud reporter asked.

The others reached forward with their recording devices to wait for the answer.

Rachel saw Jason's struggle with his reply. She knew he wanted to blurt out the facts but had to hold them in.

"It will all be in the written ICAO report."

"Is it true that Wendy Lambert stormed the cockpit door?"

Jason spoke into the microphone one last time. "Thank you."

Rachel scurried beside Jason as they were escorted away from the media. Another part of Jason's team stepped up to the microphone to answer some, but not all, of the questions the media sought.

"Well done." Glen patted Jason's back once they were away from the crowd.

"I said a whole lot and a bunch of nothing." Jason rolled his tired eyes.

"You told them what they needed to hear. The rest is in the report. Taking the heat off Fairchild Charters and displaying sympathy for the family was all we needed to do," Glen said.

"I still can't believe Wendy went off the way they said she did."

"Telling your wife that you're sleeping with the nanny while a plane is taking off wasn't the wisest choice on Ron's part."

"Sleeping with the nanny trumps telling the wife," Rachel said.

"Let's hope for all involved that some of the facts never get revealed. Wendy going postal inside the jet is one thing, the copilot opening the door to determine what the threat was is on us." From there, Wendy physically fought the man and then stormed the cockpit. According to the flight attendant, everything happened fast at that point. The plane lost altitude, and because they weren't even at ten thousand feet, they dropped quickly.

"Any word on Albin's condition?"

"No news from the neurosurgeon in Dallas," Rachel told Glen. "And Roger is flying home tomorrow."

"Then we're just about done here," Glen said. "If you want to go home now, I'll stay and mop up the rest of this."

Jason smiled at her. "I think it would be better if we stayed and cleaned up and if you went back to the office to determine what we're returning to. I'd like any heat deflected off Rachel before we come back."

Glen eyed them both. "You sure you just don't want to soak up the warmth for a couple more days?"

Rachel wanted to deny Glen's allegation, but Jason beat her to it. "A couple days of sunshine and rest sounds like a better start to the new year than we've had."

Glen patted Jason on the back. "I have ya covered, brother." He hugged Rachel. "We'll see you back in New York."

"Fly safe," she told him.

Jason watched his brother leave before turning her way. "I hope you don't mind me kidnapping you for a few more days."

"As long as we can sleep in tomorrow, I won't complain." They'd been running since the moment they arrived in San José, while Nathan tutored Owen on the finer points of picking up women.

"No more room service. No more hospitals."

She put her arm through his as they walked out the door. "Do you think Ron is going to be okay?"

"I don't know. He's going to have to live with Wendy's death, knowing it was him who put her over the edge."

"How old is the nanny?" Rachel asked as they got into the rental car.

"Not old enough," Jason moaned. "Legal, but . . . no."

"She's out of a job now." Rachel realized for the first time that the nanny was sleeping with her boss, and look how that worked out.

"Stop that," Jason said from the driver's seat.

"Stop what?"

"Where your mind went just now. I don't care if you sleep with the nanny, you'll never be without a job."

Rachel couldn't help but smirk. "I have no desire to sleep with Nathan."

Jason huffed out a short laugh. "That's quite an image."

Halfway back to the hotel, she brought up the office. "You know they're all talking about us."

"I imagine they are."

"It probably isn't good."

He glanced over briefly, then watched the road. "If I made a habit of sleeping with my secretarial assistants, perhaps you'd have a point. Not only have I never done that, I've never introduced a woman as a girlfriend. I will accept some noise over the situation, but I expect a certain degree of respect. Neither of us deserves any less."

She blinked.

"You lost me at 'girlfriend.'"

He didn't bother looking her way. "Well . . . catch up."

Smiling, she watched the rest of the miles melt away as they turned to the fun part of their working vacation.

Jason took them to the coast. He rented a house on the sand that came with a chef and a housekeeper. Before they arrived, he'd forced Rachel to pick out a few things to wear on the beach, telling her he owed her a dress after the splattered paint incident. Now they were even.

For the next three days he laughed, ate, soaked up the sunshine he knew would be absent when they returned to New York . . . and he fell even harder. It wasn't going to be easy letting her return to her own bed now that he'd had her in his. Returning to work was going to prove difficult, which was a big reason as to why he opted to stay in Costa Rica a little longer.

Glen had sent him a message letting him know the office gossip was running wild, and that it probably wouldn't die until they returned to squelch it.

"Someone looks comfortable." He heard Rachel's voice above him.

He opened his eyes in the hammock he'd managed to get into without dumping his butt on the ground. "I need to get one of these."

"The hammock or the house in Central America?" she teased.

"Both."

Her smile dropped.

He winked.

"I never know when to take you seriously about those things."

"Gotta keep it a little mysterious, or you'll start sleeping with the nanny."

"Nah, the accent does nothing for me."

"The accent does something for everyone in a skirt," he told her.

She looked down at her bikini. "I'm not wearing one."

His eyes traveled down her frame as he remembered the tiny mole she had on her left hip, which was barely covered by the material she wore. "I see that."

"If I didn't know better, I'd say you just undressed me in your mind."

His eyes stopped at a particularly warm spot between her thighs. "Guilty."

She shuffled from one foot to the other.

Jason patted his side. "Come here."

"In the hammock."

"Yeah." He scooted over a tiny bit.

"You're nuts. We'll both dump on the sand."

"I have great balance."

Rachel approached gently and set her butt on the net.

"Now just lie back."

The second she leaned back, the net twisted. Jason tried to right them but ended up on the ground, on his back, with Rachel on top of him.

"You okay?" she asked, laughing.

"It hurts." He scowled.

"Aww, poor baby."

He grabbed her butt with both hands and squeezed.

She laughed before leaning over to kiss his lips.

He was hard instantly, the pain in his back from the stick that he landed on forgotten.

Rachel wedged her knee between his thighs and took full advantage of her position. Jason liked her like this, raw and real. The care of work and responsibility had left them the moment they'd left the city of San José, and the woman on top of him had turned into a playful minx he wanted to enjoy all day and night.

Sand stuck to their bodies as their kiss turned more heated and determined.

"Where is Owen?" he asked, having zero desire to have the kid walk up on them.

"Back at the house." She moved her lips to his ear, bit the lobe. "Nathan said they were having a poker tournament."

"Sounds like it will take a while," he said against her ear as his hand slid to the knot tying her swimsuit.

Her hand slid into his shorts, the sand she brought with her grating against the soft skin of his cock. He imagined she would be just as raw if they finished this where they were.

"Sand."

She shifted her hips. "I don't like it either."

He looked at the turquoise water and private beach. "I have a better idea."

Lifting her off him, he stood to his feet and swept her off hers.

The water was bathtub warm, the gentle waves nothing more than a lap pool without a current. He waited until he was waist high before letting her stand. Salt water replaced sand, but felt much better against his skin when she touched him.

"Is this gonna work?" she asked, hopping up and wrapping her legs around his waist.

His cock pushed against their clothing. "We won't know until we try." And boy, did he want to try. Their weightlessness in the water made it easier for him to reach between them and pet the folds of her sex.

She whimpered and kissed him, riding his hand until he couldn't take it anymore.

With her hands wrapped around his neck, he adjusted their clothing while she kissed him. He teased her with his cock and then pushed deep inside her with a gasp.

Or was that her?

Rachel dropped her forehead onto his shoulder. "I like this."

So did he.

She used her hips, and he guided her with the palms of his hands.

And they made out like teenage kids on summer break. Their bodies became one in the water, the feeling prolonged by the unique and unfamiliar position. But as they always did, they found a rhythm that worked for both of them.

Rachel clawed at his back as she found her release, and he buried his head in her chest when he found his.

"You're habit-forming," she told him.

"Like chocolate?" he laughed.

"Without the calories."

She looked at him, her eyes warm and sated.

When he slipped out of her, she pouted.

"We aren't leaving until the morning."

She grinned again. "And we can sleep on the plane."

The look in her eyes told him they wouldn't be sleeping that night.

"I don't want to leave at all," she said. "I could homeschool Owen."

"You're proficient in chemistry?"

She dropped her head onto his shoulder again. "That won't work."

"We'll come back," he promised.

Rachel kissed him again, and Jason wondered if the owners of the house would be interested in selling. A weekend a month on this beach would be worth whatever price they wanted.

Chapter Nineteen

Returning to the cold was like a slap in the face. To make it harder, there were three inches of snow on the ground.

"You sure I can't stay the night?" Jason asked one last time as he said good-bye at her door.

"We agreed to weekends," she told him again.

"You suggested weekends . . . I said every day that ends in *y*."

"I will *see* you every day that ends in *y* and *sleep over* on the weekends."

It was a compromise Rachel knew he didn't want but agreed to anyway.

Besides, what he was suggesting sounded a whole lot like moving in together. And that was moving at warp speed and not something she'd ever done in her life. There was Owen to consider first. And the two of them hadn't had a private conversation since before the new year.

"Am I picking you up in the morning?" he asked.

"Are you taking the train?"

"I'm thinking I'll fly in."

She shook her head. "I'll take the train."

"Why? Everyone knows you and I were together in Central America."

"Fine, but I'm not ready to rub it in."

He narrowed his eyes. "Are you always going to be this stubborn?"

"Probably."

He turned to leave. "I've been warned."

"Hey."

"Yeah?"

"No kiss good-bye?"

He hooked an arm around her waist, pulled her in. "Stubborn and demanding."

"Get used to it."

He kissed her, hard, and then slapped her butt with his free hand. "See you tomorrow."

When he walked out the door, she leaned against it and wrapped her arms around her waist with a grin. She glanced at the pile of mail that could wait until morning, and walked upstairs to chat with Owen.

Rachel felt a kinship to Moses as she walked into work the next morning. The sea of colleagues parted as she walked by, some ducked their heads and spoke to each other, some shifted their eyes away. When she made it to her desk, she'd felt the daggers from every angle of the building.

"Nice tan!" Julie hovered over her, extending a hand holding a cup of coffee.

"Thank God for coffee."

Julie sat, wheeled her chair close. "You know everyone is talking."

They weren't within earshot of anyone, but they still kept their voices low.

"It isn't what everyone is thinking."

"Oh?"

"It's different, Julie."

Julie looked unconvinced. "Uh-huh."

"It is!"

Julie slid her sleek black hair behind an ear. "We're friends, right?"

"I like to think so."

She glanced up, determined she could say more, and did. "What would you say to me if I told you I was sleeping with Gerald?"

"I'd remind you he's married."

"And if he wasn't?"

"That he's too old for you."

Julie swatted her arm. "And if he wasn't?"

Rachel didn't like the advice swimming in her head.

"You'd remind me he was my boss!" came Julie's horse whisper.

"I know . . . I know. But it isn't like that. I assure you."

Julie shook her head. "What is the company name on your check?"

"I know." And she did.

"You might know, but you've forgotten. Be careful, Rachel."

And Julie swiveled back to her cube and clicked away on her computer.

Then her voice interrupted Rachel's self-argument. "So how was Costa Rica?"

"Spectacular. Once the investigation was over."

Julie moaned. "I hate you a little right now."

Rachel smiled, knowing they'd be just fine.

She attempted to stay at her desk most of the morning, but nature called, and she needed to stretch her legs. Silence followed her everywhere, and after ten minutes, she walked back to her desk.

Beside it, Gerald stood with two of New York's finest and a woman she'd never seen before.

"Here she is now."

Everyone turned to stare in Rachel's direction. "What's going on?"

"This is Ms. Brenner from the Department of Children and Families."

Rachel's heart plunged. "Is Owen okay?" She searched the faces of the police officers and didn't see pity.

"Owen is fine," Ms. Brenner told her.

As soon as the feeling of dread left, one of anxiety took over. "So what's this about?"

Ms. Brenner wasn't a lot older than Rachel, much shorter and wider, without a bit of kindness in her face. She stepped back, and the officers stepped forward.

"We'd like to have a talk with you, Miss Price."

Rachel stepped back. "About what?"

"You took Owen Moreau out of the country, is that right?" Ms. Brenner asked.

"Yes. We just returned last night, why?"

"You've been specifically ordered not to take Owen out of the country or the immediate area of your residence and employment. Violation of that order could result in kidnapping charges, fines, and possible imprisonment," Ms. Brenner said.

Air left her lungs. "What are you talking about? What order?"

"Do you really want to do this here, Miss Price?"

Rachel followed the gaze of Ms. Brenner to find a dozen coworkers watching.

She swiveled back to her accuser. "I have legal guardianship over Owen."

The taller of the two police officers stepped forward. "Why don't we talk about this at the station."

Rachel was seeing stars. "Am I being arrested?"

"Kidnapping is a felony," Ms. Brenner announced, louder than she needed to.

"I didn't kidnap Owen!"

"Let's talk at the station."

Rachel stepped back again. "And if I refuse?"

The officer placed a hand on her shoulder.

She glanced at his badge. Officer Paton. "We're not asking, Miss Price."

This isn't happening.

He turned her around, the other officer flanked her other side, and they started down the corridor that had parted a path for her only a few hours before.

Before they reached the elevator, Jason and Glen ran toward them, putting the police officers on guard.

"What the hell is going on here?"

Rachel wanted to run to him, let him make this all go away. "They're saying I kidnapped Owen."

"What the fu—"

"Sir, you're going to have to stand back."

"Rachel didn't kidnap her own kid."

"Owen is not Miss Price's biological child."

Jason turned his glare on Ms. Brenner. "Who are you?"

The officers nudged Rachel into the elevator when it opened.

Jason started toward her again, Glen held him back. "I'll be there with an attorney," he told her as her eyes swelled with unshed tears. "Don't say a thing."

Once they were alone in the elevator, Officer Paton read her her rights.

———

Rachel sat in a room she'd only seen in the movies. A large, dark window screamed a single view from the opposite side, cameras pointed at her, and a heavy door kept her inside. The only saving grace was that she had yet to be fingerprinted or placed in handcuffs.

The police officers informed her that they would be forced to restrain her if she didn't cooperate.

So many raw emotions coursed through her minute by minute. Disbelief came first, then crashing concern for Owen. Where was he? Was he okay? This had the Colemans written all over it. She wasn't even given the chance to retrieve her purse and cell phone before they pulled her out of the office. Calling home to see if Owen was there wasn't possible.

Taking Jason's advice, she waited in the interrogation room while the social worker questioned her repeatedly. The only thing Rachel offered was the honest truth.

"I have not seen any paperwork from the court, any court, telling me I have restrictions on where I can take Owen. This is all a misunderstanding."

"The Colemans believe you're a flight risk, which mandates the court stop you from traveling more than a hundred miles until the matter can be solved."

Rachel glared at the social worker while talking with the investigating officer. His name, she'd already forgotten. "Which I would have followed had I been told."

"You were informed," Ms. Brenner said from the corner of the room.

"Where is Owen?" Rachel asked.

"He's safe."

Rachel clutched her hands into tiny fists and kept them hidden in her lap.

"Why did you take Owen to Costa Rica?"

They were trying to catch her on something they could use against her. That was the point behind being told her Miranda rights. *Anything you say can and will be used against you in a court of law.*

"I'd like to speak to a lawyer."

The investigator sucked in a deep breath.

"It's a simple question, Miss Price," Ms. Brenner said.

"I have the right to an attorney, Ms. Brenner." Being bullied by a social worker was not something Rachel was going to stand for.

"You took Owen out of the country to hide him from his father, knowing he will gain custody."

Rachel's jaw dropped. "I thought social workers were neutral parties that didn't take sides."

"Owen is my priority."

Rachel lifted from her seat. "No. Owen is *my* priority!"

The officer stood, placed a hand in the air. "Ladies!" He turned to the social worker. "Miss Price has requested a lawyer, we will continue this when she's obtained one."

Once Ms. Brenner left the room, Rachel lowered her head to the table.

Alone in the room, adrenaline oozed from her system and left her in tears.

When the door opened again, the investigator entered, this time with a woman in uniform. "We're moving you into holding."

"Am I being charged?" Rachel asked.

"Not yet," the woman told her.

Rachel knew enough to understand that was a good thing.

She was led to a phone, where she made her call. Unfortunately, she hadn't memorized Jason's number and she'd been told not to contact Owen. That left her with work. The direct line to Gerald's office went unanswered, so she tried Julie.

"Julie."

"Holy shit. What is going on?"

"I don't know."

"Are you in jail?"

"I have one call, Julie. I don't have Jason's cell memorized. Can you get ahold of him?"

"Everyone left here the second they took you away."

"Talk to his secretary. I need a lawyer."

"I think that's what he was screaming about. The legal team here is scrambling."

"I can't believe this is happening." Rachel voiced her thoughts, looked around. "I've been told not to get ahold of Owen. I need to know he's okay."

"What's his number?"

Rachel gave it to her. And then questioned if that was the right thing to do. "He needs to know I'm okay."

"Are you?"

No! "I'm fine."

"You don't sound fine."

"Tell him I'm fine. This is all a huge misunderstanding that we will get worked out soon."

"I will. Be careful in there."

"Like I have a choice."

A holding cell in the heart of New York was not where Rachel thought she'd be when she woke up that morning. For a Tuesday, the place was surprisingly packed. It wasn't like it was the middle of the night or a weekend. The small cell closed behind her with a resounding click.

Two bone-thin women at the opposite end of the cell both eyed her up and down. Neither of them looked older than thirty, but both wore clothes much too skimpy for winter with worn-out high heel shoes.

"Miss Fancy Pants," someone cackled.

"I bet you ain't never been in here before." The woman who spoke looked homeless.

Rachel looked around for a place to sit and decided standing was a better idea.

"What's a matter, honey? Ain't got nothin' to say?"

Talk about being tossed into a den of snakes. "I'm having a shit day," Rachel said to anyone listening.

Several women burst out laughing. "Ain't we all, honey . . . ain't we all!"

"Let me guess," one of the skinny, worn women in the back said. "It's all a misunderstanding and you ain't guilty."

That brought laughter a second time.

Telling this crowd she was guilty of taking Owen to Costa Rica for a week probably wouldn't earn her any respect.

Instead of saying anything back, Rachel leaned against the bars of the holding cell and prayed Jason would arrive soon.

Chapter Twenty

This was a first.

Jason's experience with the legal system was only on the level of corporate paper pushing and covering one's ass. As his attorneys quickly informed him, they weren't proficient at criminal representation but had a handful of high profile attorneys who would jump.

Clive Redshaw walked alongside Jason's attorney up the steps of the police station.

After introductions were out of the way, Clive jumped right into his questions.

"I have no idea what they could possibly be holding her on. We went to Costa Rica following the downing of one of my planes. She took Owen since I needed her with me."

"Owen is the child she has legal guardianship over."

"He is fifteen, but yes."

"That's all you know?"

Jason hesitated. "I know Owen's grandparents have been rattling on about Owen staying with them."

"Where are the parents?"

"Mom is dead. Dad hasn't been in the picture."

Clive looked him straight in the eye. "Anything else?"

"I have nothing."

"All right, then. I need to talk with the investigating officer and then Rachel."

"Can I see her?"

"Not yet. Hold on." Clive smiled and walked away.

Jason's phone rang and Owen's face lit up his screen.

He tried his calm voice when he answered. "Hey, buddy."

"What the fuck is going on?" Owen's shaky voice brought all of Jason's nerves on edge.

"Are you okay?"

"No. I'm not okay. I was home, sleeping, when the police pounded on the door."

"Take a deep breath."

"Rachel isn't answering my calls or my texts."

Jason looked up at the facade of the police station, and then to his lawyer, who was watching him.

"She can't talk to you right now."

"They told me I have to go to my grandparents' house. I'm not going. I need to talk to Rachel."

"Owen, calm down."

"I'm not going to the hag's house," he yelled.

"Is there someone there now?"

"Some social worker and a cop."

"Let me talk to them."

He heard a few more colorful expletives from Owen's lips before an unfamiliar voice got on the phone.

"Mr. Fairchild?"

"That's right, who is this?"

"My name is Benjamin White, I'm with child services. I've been called in to relocate Owen to his grandparents' home until this matter is resolved."

Jason's back teeth hurt with the pressure he was placing upon them. "And how is that working for you, Mr. White?"

"Seems Owen is refusing."

"You would, too, if you didn't trust your grandparents."

"Well, we can't leave him here unattended. He is a minor."

"He is fifteen. That's hardly a child."

"Regardless, we need to place him in the care of a home until we can determine custody."

"A home? I have a home, he can stay with me."

"I doubt that is an option in this situation, Mr. Fairchild. Our understanding is that you've been named as a possible accomplice in taking Owen out of the country after an order was given to keep him here."

The desire to reach through the phone and grab a neck gripped him hard.

"Then what are our options, Mr. White?"

"We will need to take Owen to a temporary foster care home until a more permanent solution can be found."

Something told Jason that wouldn't fly for long either.

"Fine. Let me talk to him."

Owen exploded the minute he was back on the phone. "Fuck foster care."

"Whoa, calm down."

"Jason?"

"Close your mouth and listen to me, okay?"

A long-drawn-out breath pulled Jason into the phone.

"Rachel and I need you to stay calm."

"Where is she?"

Owen already knew the answer; Jason could hear it in his voice.

"The authorities are questioning her."

Owen hissed. "In jail?"

"Questioning her, Owen. Nothing I can't handle. Do you trust me?"

"Yes."

"Then stay calm. I have my phone on me. You have Nathan's number if I don't answer. Let them take you to the foster care house."

"Jason—"

"It's temporary, Owen. I promise you."

"Why can't I just stay here?" Owen's voice started to break. Having the kid cussing mad was a hell of a lot easier than hearing him cry.

"We will figure this out."

"I hate them."

Who *them* was didn't need to be explained.

———

Clive Redshaw was in his late forties; his suit mirrored the type Jason wore. There wasn't a hair out of place on his head and his smile looked fake.

"Attorney-client privilege plainly means that you can tell me anything and I cannot reveal this conversation to a judge or the police . . . anyone."

"Is that your way of asking if I kidnapped Owen?"

He looked her straight in the eye. "Did you?"

"No!"

"Great, now that we have that out of the way, let's get started."

He removed a large legal pad from his briefcase and looked through his notes. "The charges they are racking up right now have little legal footing until they can determine if you were given proper notice of the Colemans' intent to obtain custody of Owen. Did you receive a certified letter from the child custody courts?"

"No. Not since Emily died and California granted me guardianship over Owen."

"Nothing in New York or Connecticut?"

"Nothing. Certified means I would have had to sign for it, right?"

"Exactly."

"I would have remembered signing for a court hearing. Do we know when they sent it?" she asked.

"I was told after Christmas. It's recorded as received, which is why you're here. I'm waiting on a clerk at the county office to pull the tracking and see the signature."

"How long is that going to take?"

He didn't look hopeful. "It's the county. They don't move fast."

"They can't prove I received something I didn't. So once that is determined, this all goes away, right?"

"Maybe."

Rachel glared.

"You took Owen out of the country."

"I have legal guardianship."

"You have the means to take him out again."

"It's not my plane," she argued.

"It's your boyfriend's. So the answer is yes. The court will look at you and Owen as a flight risk and ground you until custody is determined. And they won't likely allow you guardianship until that is figured out."

"I thought I had to be deemed unfit and that Owen's life and well-being are in danger in order for anyone to take Owen away."

Clive thumbed through a few papers, pulled out one, and started to read from it.

"It says here that you have exposed Owen to harsh chemicals resulting in illness."

Rachel's jaw was going to have to be surgically removed from her chest at this rate. "What?"

"You've been remodeling an old house with lead paint, containing possible asbestos, and not taking the necessary safety precautions."

"What a crock of garbage that is. Owen has had a few colds, most likely due to the change in weather neither of us are used to."

"Does your house have lead paint?"

"I don't know. It's an old house."

"Asbestos?"

"I would think the home inspector would have said something if there was."

Clive folded his hands on his notepad. "All of this will have to be determined."

"So let me get this straight. The Colemans are claiming I'm a danger to Owen, unfit as his guardian, and the court is willing to take him away based on an unsubstantiated claim?"

"The court has taken him away. The emergency injunction was filed two days ago because it was discovered that Owen was out of the country."

"So what were they doing? Watching the airport for our return?"

"I doubt they had to do that. Does Owen have an Instagram account?"

"He's fifteen, he has all that stuff."

"Then chances are he posted when he came home, which is why you're here today."

"So where is Owen now?"

"I don't have that answer. Right now I'm working on getting you out of here."

She sat taller in her seat. Once she was out of there, she'd find Owen herself. "I didn't kidnap Owen. If I did, then I'm the most unintelligent criminal on the planet, since I returned home with him. And if the court has taken him away, I can't possibly leave with him again, now can I?"

"All sound arguments I will use."

"Then use them, please. The thought of sleeping here makes me ill."

Clive looked around the small room. "I believe that is the point, Miss Price."

He stood to leave. "I have to caution you . . ."

"I'm listening."

"When I do get you out of here, don't contact Owen. Let others talk for you. Don't meet him without a social worker present and with permission."

"I've already asked a friend to check on him."

"Which shows concern, but from this moment on, do not speak to the boy alone."

She wanted to cry. "He's going to be scared."

"He will be cared for."

She shook her head. "No one cares more for that child than I do."

This time, when they led her back to the holding cell, Rachel didn't care that she sat on a sticky bench that could result in an unnamed disease. She leaned her head back against the cold stone wall and closed her eyes until her name was called again.

She'd aged five years in six hours.

Jason pulled his jacket from his shoulders and folded her into it as he shuffled her out of the station.

"How is he?" she asked before they made it to the waiting car.

"Angry."

"Please tell me he isn't at the Colemans'. He'll run away the first chance he gets."

"They placed him in foster care." He shuffled her into the back of the waiting car, and the driver pulled away from the curb.

"Strangers."

"He has my number and is texting constantly."

Rachel blinked several times. "The lawyer told me not to contact him."

His lawyer had told him the same thing. Not that Jason was listening. "I told him not to tell me where he is unless he feels threatened. That way no one can accuse us of plotting to take him away."

She made a grabby motion with her hands. "Tell him I'm out and that I love him."

Jason's heart bucked a little with the conviction of her words. He removed his phone and typed in her request word for word.

Within seconds, his phone rang.

"We can't answer it. The police can subpoena the phone records and see we talked to him. We're better off texting."

Can't talk on the phone.

This is bullshit.

"I told you he's angry."

Our attorney is demanding immediate action on releasing you to Rachel.

Tonight?

Jason glanced at Rachel. "Clive said thirty-six hours at the earliest."

"If you tell him that, he's gonna bolt." She glanced out the window. "It's cold outside."

He hated skirting around the truth. **Probably tomorrow.** Jason showed Rachel the text before he hit "Send." With her nod, he did.

School starts tomorrow.

Then go and get your mind off all this. With any luck you'll be home tomorrow night.

It took Owen a few seconds to reply. **This is screwed up. We came** here to the battle ax and her wimpy husband to avoid this crap.

"He needs to vent," Rachel said. "He gets chatty when he's nervous. Talking calms him down."

"How about Nathan?"

"Good idea."

Jason switched contacts and called. After a few seconds, Nathan let him know he was chatting with Owen and letting him bitch.

Only once Rachel was convinced that Owen was taken care of did she collapse into Jason's side.

"What's going through your mind?" he asked, his arm holding her close as the driver maneuvered the car out of Manhattan and onto the freeway.

"I don't think I've skipped one emotion today. Fear, anger, disbelief. Part of me wished we'd stayed in Central America."

He kissed the top of her head. "I thought that more than once today."

She shifted in her seat to look at him. "I don't know what I would have done without you."

"You would have found a lawyer."

"No, not that. I mean, yes, I need someone like Clive, but I mean talking with Owen. I'm all he has. Knowing you've been talking to him makes it a whole lot easier that I was stuck in that dirty holding cell . . ." She closed her eyes and shook her head.

"I'm sorry I couldn't get you out faster."

"I didn't do anything wrong and yet my freedom was taken away, Owen is spending the night with strangers. I have a burning desire to drive over to the Colemans' and scream at them. They're trying to say I'm unfit because of lead paint in the walls of my house. How is any of that possible? How many people live in homes with old paint?" Her shoulders started to shake and her eyes swelled. "Worse, I didn't keep my promise to Emily. I said I'd never let Owen feel alone after she died."

Jason pulled her into his chest. "Come here."

"This isn't fair."

"I know, hon. We're going to make this right."

She cried in his arms until her tears ran out. They drove directly to his home, and he led her to his room. The bathtub in the master suite hadn't been used in years. He drew her a bath and left her alone.

"How is she?" Nathan asked when he found Jason in the kitchen.

"A mess."

"Poor lass."

"Is Owen settled for the night?"

"He is. But I don't think the lad will stay where he is long, Jason. He's strong willed, that one."

"He's fifteen, confused, and angry."

"I'll keep talkin' to him. Let him know to call me before doing anything stupid." Nathan turned to leave the room. "Oh, and Mary stopped by, left a casserole. Said to call if you needed her."

Glen's wife had quickly become a rock in the foundation of their family. "Thanks."

Nathan nodded and left out the back door and across the yard to his home on the property.

After following Mary's instructions and heating up dinner, Jason brought a large plate and two forks up to his bedroom. Two steps into the room and he found Rachel in his bed, curled up into a ball and sound asleep.

As much as he wanted to marvel at the image of her in his space, he couldn't help but mourn the reason why she was there.

He set the plate of food down, took a bite, and walked into his closet to shed his clothes. After a quick shower, he dimmed the lights of the room and crawled into bed beside Rachel.

Chapter Twenty-One

Owen wasn't in a shelter, but the accommodations were uncomfortably close. The room he was given had four beds, two of which were taken, outside of his. And that was for the boys . . . another room housed three beds, with one girl curled up and talking to herself.

"Dude, you gonna eat that?" The kid asking was named Chris. The sixteen-year-old had made it clear he was in charge the second Owen was shown his bed.

Owen glanced at the cold burrito and decided it wasn't worth fighting for . . . even if he thought he'd probably eat it later. The "family" he'd been placed with ate at five thirty whether you were hungry or not. The woman, Mrs. Sims, hadn't missed a meal since birth, her husband was the polar opposite. They both smiled at him when the social worker dropped Owen off. While they didn't completely drop the act when the door shut, it was apparent the couple who took in temporary foster children didn't do it for the love of kids.

"Have it." Owen pushed his plate Chris's way.

The older kid didn't have to be told twice. "Why are you here?" he asked with a mouth full of food.

Owen wasn't even sure how to answer that. "Why are you here?" he asked instead.

"My dad got tossed back in . . . beat up some chick stealing from him."

"Oh, man . . . I'm sorry."

Chris shrugged, took another bite. "Whatever. Better her than me."

Owen swallowed. "What about your mom?"

"No clue. But if I ever find her, I'll beat her myself. Fucking leave me with that asshole."

Owen looked around the barren walls. "Have you been here long?"

"They don't keep you here more than a few days. Gotta find you a couple willing to put up with your drama."

"Sounds like you've done this a lot."

Chris dropped half the burrito on the plate and wiped his mouth with the back of his hand. "Not much longer. I've got some friends hooking me up with a job."

Owen glanced at Chris's drawn eyes and pale skin and couldn't help but wonder what kind of job he thought he'd actually be able to get.

"Yep, get a job . . . make some serious money and get the hell out of dives like this."

"It's not that bad." They both turned to Alex, the other kid in the room. He couldn't have been older than eleven.

"What do you know?" Chris demanded, his shoulders tensed.

"Better than the streets."

Owen's jaw dropped. "You were on the street?"

"Last summer."

"How old are you?"

"Twelve."

He didn't look twelve.

"So what's your story?" Owen's fascination with these kids' lives started to take away some of his own anxiety about the situation.

"My mom is sick."

"Your mom's crazy."

"Shut up! She's sick." For a twelve-year-old, Alex had some bite in him.

Chris decided he was the authority on Alex's life. "I heard old man Sims talkin', said your mom is bouncing around a rubber room with white coats keeping her from jumpin' off a bridge."

Alex was on his feet and across the room in a heartbeat.

Owen stood up and found himself between the two boys. "Knock it off," he yelled at Chris.

Chris looked around Owen and poked his words even deeper. "Crazy and rockin' in a corner, talkin' to herself."

Alex pulled back his small fist and lunged. Unfortunately Owen didn't move fast enough and caught the misguided punch with his lip.

Chris doubled over, laughing, which just made Alex try harder.

Alex pushed past Owen and tried to tackle Chris. He wasn't a match. Chris outweighed Alex by a good fifty pounds and two feet.

"You wanna piece of me, little shit?"

"Knock it off!"

All three of them stilled when the door to the room swung open.

"What's going on in here?" Mr. Sims filled the height of the doorway, his dark stare keeping them silent.

Owen wiped his mouth with the back of his hand, tasted his own blood.

"We were wrestling," Chris announced.

Owen stood speechless.

"Wrestling?"

Alex blinked a few times, then nodded.

Mr. Sims turned his stare toward Owen. "Is that right?"

Not trusting his voice, he nodded.

Sims didn't buy it, but he wasn't concerned enough about their welfare to question further. Sims pointed to Owen's mouth. "Keep it off the face." He closed the door, and Chris shoved Alex one last time.

Jason woke with his heart in his throat. His hand reached out to find Rachel gone from his side. His eyes shot open and the room came into focus. Fog shaded the windows, casting gray light into the room.

Noise from the shower in the master bathroom was music to his ears.

Rachel.

She hadn't left in the middle of the night. The dream he had right before opening his eyes floated in his memory. He was walking around Rachel's home to find all of her personal belongings gone . . . no clothes or pictures on the wall, Owen's room was bare except his bed and a schoolbook on his desk. They simply vanished, and even though Jason was vaguely aware he was in the center of a dream, panic rose in his heart.

The water in the shower turned off, and the sound of the shower door opening and closing had him envisioning the woman inside. Jason's body responded to the image. He closed his eyes and told himself to calm down. Exploring new positions would be the last thing Rachel would be interested in doing now.

"You're up."

Just when his dick started to calm, he caught sight of her. She was in one of his dress shirts, the buttons not completely done all the way up. It stopped at the tops of her smooth thighs and swished around her legs as she walked toward him. Rachel was drying her hair with a towel, her face fresh from the shower.

Jason squirmed on the bed and hoped she didn't notice his discomfort or reaction. They had other things to do. "You look rested."

"I am, surprisingly." She planted herself on the edge of the bed and smiled down at him. "I hope you don't mind about the shirt. It's all you have in there."

"Mind? I'll never wear that shirt again without thinking of you in it." She was smiling brighter now.

He liked having that effect on her.

"I've been thinking," she started.

"Owen?"

"Of course." She tossed the towel aside and leaned over him on the bed. "I need to find a contractor. One who can determine if there is lead in the walls of the house, or any other dangers the Colemans are accusing me of."

Jason rested his hands behind his head. "If he finds something, it will substantiate their claim."

"*If* they find something, then I need to know that and address it like any concerned parent would once something has been brought to their attention. I'm not a licensed environmental health professional, or a contractor. I'm a new homeowner without a reason to question the health of my house. If they don't find anything, we're good."

"Do you think there is an issue?"

"I think the Colemans accused me of neglect and the court jumped first and asked questions later." She rested a hand on his chest. "If there is an issue with lead, then I would guess it would come up in my blood-work. Which brings me to my next question . . ."

"Who is my doctor?"

Rachel leaned forward, kissed his chest. "You're so smart."

He reached for her when she pulled back. "You're sexy."

She moved into his kiss and let her lips linger. Jason was the one who kept the good morning kiss from becoming more. "I'm happy to see you smiling."

"Yesterday I was stuck in a cell. Today I'm free and have the ability to do something about this situation. Until Clive calls with a time for the emergency hearing he is requesting, we can't do a legal thing to get Owen back."

"*Legal* being the key word."

She searched his eyes. "I would never ask you to do something illegal."

"But . . ."

After a deep breath, she said, "That doesn't mean I won't. I'll play by the rules as long as there is hope that this is all going to go away. But if they try and take Owen against his will, I'm keeping my promise to him and Emily."

And his dream will have been a premonition. "Then we'll just have to keep that from happening."

———

They started with Jason's doctor, who brought her in for a physical and the requested blood test. They would have the results by late afternoon, which gave them the rest of the morning to find and hire a contractor.

Rachel walked into her cold, dark house and went directly to Owen's room, even though she knew he wasn't there.

Jason stood silently behind her. "You okay?"

She shrugged. "He's at school. Or should be, in any case . . . not that I'm allowed to text him to find out."

"This can't last."

She wasn't so sure of that. "And I shouldn't have met a half a dozen hookers from the streets of New York, but I have." Rachel turned toward her bedroom and Jason followed. "If there is one lesson I've learned in the past year, it's that anything can happen. And with my luck lately, I would go on to say that if that *anything* is something bad, it will happen."

"Hey, what about me?" Jason smiled as he asked the question.

"Not you . . . although it might have been better if you worked in the pizza joint across the street from the office."

"You wouldn't have noticed me if I made pizzas for a living."

She paused. "I like pizza."

"Hmmm, pizza. Now I'm hungry."

Rachel pushed him toward the door. "Then pop something in the oven. I need to change."

She was still wearing his shirt and her pants from the day before, since she didn't have clothes at his house.

"I don't cook," he complained.

"Follow the instructions on the box."

"But . . ."

"You fly planes and run a zillion-dollar business. I'm sure you can cook a pizza from the freezer."

"You're bossy when you're on a mission."

She pushed him all the way out her door and closed it behind him.

The contractor arrived about the same time the pizza was delivered. Apparently Jason was allergic to turning on an oven.

The contractor called himself T. Just T. Rachel waited for him to clarify his name with something along the lines of T is for Tanner, Travis, Tom . . . but no. Just T.

"Well, T. What I need is an environmental report on this house."

"Specifically lead paint and asbestos," Jason said.

"But test for anything considered toxic."

"Are you trying to find a problem for insurance or something?"

"Oh, no . . . nothing like that. It's personal."

"Have you been sick?"

"Nope."

T looked confused.

"Check for mold, anything that can make you ill."

He gave the living room a once-over. "Fresh paint?"

"Yeah, I've painted almost every room in the place."

"I'm going to have to dig into some of it for testing."

"Whatever you have to do. If you can do it close to the floor or away from where the eye looks and not skew the test results, that would be great."

"Okay, ma'am. You're the boss."

He went back out to his truck, and Jason said in her ear, "You're kinda sexy when you're bossy."

"Ha." She opened the pizza box, and her stomach reminded her they'd skipped breakfast. "You woke up horny."

"Did not."

She tilted her head, offered her best *don't lie to me* stare.

"Okay, maybe a little."

Rachel lowered her head.

"I blame the image of you in my shirt." He grabbed a piece of pizza and shoved it in his mouth.

She thrust a napkin into his free hand and sat down.

Two hours later T walked into the living room to let them know he was finished.

"Anything you can tell us now?"

"I scraped the walls, and my kit doesn't show lead."

Rachel grasped Jason's hand, hope filling her chest.

"But that's not to say there isn't lead in there. I have to send it to a testing center to make sure the coat of paint over it isn't messing up the chemistry."

"How long will that take?"

"Three days."

"Can we rush it?" Jason asked.

"That is rushing."

"Anything else?" Rachel asked.

"There isn't any evidence of asbestos. But if there was at some point, and it wasn't removed properly, you might find some in the insulation in the attic."

Rachel frowned. "Let me guess, you're sending it out for testing?"

"I would suggest that isn't necessary, but you said you wanted everything I question tested. It is an old house, and back when this was built, we didn't know much about what made us sick."

"Okay."

"There is mold down in the basement."

"Oh no."

T smiled. "You and everyone else on this block. It's not black mold, but I did treat the area with the bleach you had by your laundry supplies."

"So it's not a problem?"

"It's smelly but not toxic."

"Does it need to be sent off to a lab?" Jason asked.

"Nope."

"That's all?"

"You wanted to know about hidden dangers, right?"

Rachel wondered what she had missed that they haven't covered. "Anything."

"Well, those stairs leading down into your basement should be removed and replaced."

She released a long breath. "Stairs?" All he had was old stairs?

"It's a decent size space, but I wouldn't want to be lugging my laundry down there. Cold and damp draws lots of insects. I'm not a fan of spiders."

Rachel glanced at Jason, then back at T. "Spiders . . . stairs and spiders is all you found?"

"You sound disappointed." He tore off the sheet he'd been working with and handed her a copy.

"Not at all. Please contact me as soon as you know about the lab results."

"You got it."

Jason shook the man's hand, and they watched him walk away.

Rachel leaned against the door with a smile. "Nothing. He didn't find anything."

"He didn't seem too concerned the lab would disagree with him."

"We need to call Clive."

By two, Rachel was given a clean bill of health, not a speck of lead in her blood. Much like T, the doctor explained that there was always a chance that another person in the house would test positive, and that she should have Owen tested as soon as possible if in fact there was lead detected in the old paint in the house.

Clive called just after three, telling them the hearing was scheduled for eight in the morning the following day. Which for Rachel wasn't good news.

"Owen is stuck in the foster home for another night." She glanced at her cell phone, wishing desperately to contact him.

"I'll call Nathan, have him talk to Owen and make sure he's okay."

Even though the day had been a success, Rachel sat on her couch, her eyes blankly staring at the wall in front of her.

Jason came back into the room and sat beside her. "Nathan is calling him."

She leaned her head on Jason's shoulder.

"Hey, what happened to your smile?"

"I've done all I can. It's not up to me anymore. This is going to come down to my word against the Colemans'. My lack of family ties. How can I prove I didn't flee the country just to see if I could if I needed to?"

Jason tightened his arm around her. "Let's see . . . you didn't hijack a plane. You didn't cause the plane in Costa Rica to crash. I'm the one that suggested Owen come with us. And we all came back. This is all going to work out."

"They are his blood relatives. TJ is Owen's dad. It's nearly impossible for me to stop the man from taking custody of his son." The argument ran through her brain like a mantra.

Jason kissed the side of her head. "Why don't you pack a bag and stay with me until all this blows over."

Her eyes fell on the empty space where the Christmas tree had been up until the end of December. They hadn't pushed the furniture back in place before they'd flown off to Central America. "Sitting here is just going to depress me."

He helped her off the couch. "Go and pack. I'll take the trash out."

When she was done filling a small suitcase with some essentials, she stopped by the pile of bills she'd neglected. She opened a side pocket of her bag and shoved it all inside. Her laptop became part of the overnight bag with the intention of making sure they had a house to come back to once Owen was home.

She left the porch light on, closed the shades, and locked the door on their way out.

Chapter Twenty-Two

"I'm not going back there." Owen pocketed his cell phone after he finished talking with Nathan.

Ford and Lionel sat with him in the high school gym, offering teenage advice.

"You can stay with one of us," Ford said.

"My mom would be okay with you staying the night."

"They'll just come get me from your place, Lionel. No, I need to disappear."

They both looked at him like he was crazy.

"And go where?"

Owen had been thinking about that all day long. In his mind, he had a couple of options. Both were places no one would ever think they'd find him. "The police will question you both, and I don't need you ratting me out."

"We'd never do that."

"The cops always get to the truth. And if you don't know it, you can't tell it."

"What are you going to do about school?" Ford asked.

Owen shrugged. "School will be there when all this goes away."

Lionel and Ford exchanged glances. "And what if it doesn't? What if the court sides with your grandparents?"

"Then school won't matter, because I'm not living with them. I'll really run away then." He'd get word to Rachel and she'd flee with him. That was the pact they'd made over his mother's grave, and he was going to keep her to it.

His cell phone buzzed in his pocket. "Oh, man."

"What?"

"It's Mr. Sims."

Lionel glanced at the screen on his phone. "The dude that let the other kid punch you?"

"Yeah." Owen texted the man, said he was in the library finishing up a project. "I gotta go."

"So you aren't going to run away?"

Owen shook his head and handed Ford his phone. "The last time you saw me was in the library. When you looked, you found my cell phone in your backpack."

"Don't you need your phone?"

"So they can trace it? C'mon, man, think."

Lionel's eyes were wide. "You're really going to run."

"I'm *really* not going back to that place."

They all stood.

"Are you going to be okay?"

"I'll be fine. And when Rachel talks to you guys, get her alone and tell her my mother didn't raise a fool and that I said I'd be okay." Owen hated that he was going to worry her, but he couldn't exactly tell her where he was going without getting her in trouble. "Wait."

He took his cell phone back and turned the camera on himself and hit "Video."

"Hey, Rachel. I know you're gonna be pissed and worried. I'm sorry for that. But I can't go back to that place. And I'm not living with the hag and her chubby sidekick. And if my dad is behind all of this, well, fuck him. This wasn't right. Once all the adults start acting like adults,

I'll be back. And if they can't . . ." He paused. "Well, my mom didn't raise a fool. I love you."

He turned his phone off and handed it back.

"Stall them if you can." He calculated how long it would take to get where he was going and decided to throw everyone off his trail. "I can be in the city in a couple of hours."

"Dude!" Ford yelled after him.

Owen ran out of the gym without looking back.

—⋅—

Jason and Rachel walked through the door of his home and were greeted with the scent of food filling the kitchen.

Rachel turned to him. "Do you have a cook?"

He shook his head no while saying, "Sometimes."

Several voices drew them in to the center of the home. Jason was never so happy to see his brothers and, even more, their wives.

Monica wrapped Rachel in a warm embrace. "How are you holding up?"

Rachel was an instant water fountain of tears.

Mary flanked her other side, and the three of them walked out of the kitchen.

Mary turned to Glen. "Don't let that burn," she told him, pointing toward the stove.

"It's boiling water," Glen said.

She glared.

"Well, I guess that answered the question about how Rachel is doing," Trent said. He pushed Glen out of the way and stepped in wherever Mary had left off cooking.

"Is it bad?" Glen asked.

Jason looked at the backs of the women as they talked quietly to Rachel. "She's held it together really well most of the day."

"Any word?"

"It's like watching grass grow. The only one talking to Owen is Nathan. The lawyer is moving things along, but we won't know any more until after tomorrow's hearing."

"And the house?" Trent asked.

"Clear. I knew it would be. We won't have those official papers for a couple of days."

The three of them shook their heads in silence.

The back door opened, and Nathan walked in with a nod. "Hello, gentlemen. I smelled food."

Trent turned back to the stove and added dry pasta to the boiling water.

"Hey," Jason greeted his friend. "How is he?"

Nathan found the women with his eyes and lowered his voice. "He's not happy. Had a little scuffle last night with the other boys at the home he's at."

"What?"

Nathan lifted a hand in the air. "Settle, it sounded like a simple pissing match to see who wore the bigger boots. Nothing you three didn't do, I'm sure. He's more upset about not being able to talk to Rachel. But he cares too much for her well-being to risk the phone call."

"You told him she was in jail."

Nathan looked directly in Jason's eyes. "He already guessed."

"Can you imagine what we would have done if someone put our mom in jail?" Glen asked.

Jason shook his head. "Yeah, but Owen's smarter than we were."

"Let's hope so," Trent said.

The women returned to the kitchen. All of them had been crying.

Jason felt his system short-circuiting. He could hardly handle one tear-filled woman. Three was way out of his wheelhouse.

Apparently with age came understanding. Nathan came to the rescue. "Do you all feel better now?"

The three of them looked at one another and offered silent nods, and then jumped in to finish fixing dinner.

"Have you spoken to your parents?" Mary asked Rachel during dinner.

She pushed the food around on her plate as she talked. "No. I'm not sure how to tell them I was in jail."

"It really is unbelievable," Monica said.

"I doubt any parent wants to hear their kid is in jail. Besides, they told me from the beginning that the Colemans weren't going to blend into the background, regardless of where I lived."

"What do you mean?" Glen asked.

Rachel didn't hear the question.

"Rachel took the job with us to move closer to try and appease Owen's grandparents and avoid a custody battle."

Rachel glanced up and caught up on the conversation. "I didn't realize how screwed up they'd be."

Mary placed her hand over Rachel's. "You tried to do the right thing."

"Lotta good that did. I should have beelined to the border and learned Spanish."

"What did Emily tell you about them?"

Rachel gave up on trying to eat and left her fork in her food. "She didn't know them. TJ had told her that they were controlling parents that didn't give him the opportunity to live. Which is why Em refused to tie him down. She saw how he fled when he had the chance, and didn't want Owen to become dependent on him and then have him disappear."

The phone in the house shot two short rings.

"Expecting anyone?" Glen asked Jason.

Jason shook his head and got up to answer it.

"Hello?"

"What is that?" Rachel asked.

"The gate at the entrance of the house," Mary told her.

Jason glanced around the room, his gaze stopping at Rachel.

Her heart kicked hard in her chest.

"Come on in."

Jason pressed a button on the phone before hanging it up.

"Who is it?" Glen asked.

"Local police."

Rachel started to shake. Her breath caught high in her throat.

They walked to the door and watched while Jason opened it.

Mary stood at Rachel's right, Monica to her left.

The squad car drove up, and two uniformed officers stepped out.

A radio squealed from one of their shoulders, their belts clicked as they approached. "Good evening."

Rachel heard a chorus of polite hellos.

"Which one of you is Rachel Price?"

Did everyone just move closer to her, or was the universe sucking air from her lungs?

"What's this about?" Jason asked.

The officer speaking introduced himself and kept scanning the lot of them. His eyes fell on her. "It appears Owen has run away," he said without preamble.

If not for the women at her side, there was a strong possibility that Rachel would have fallen over.

"Run where?" she cried.

Both officers focused their gazes on her.

"We were hoping you might know."

"Oh, God." *Owen!*

"I don't know where he went," Ford told them. They stood in Ford's home with the boy's father at his side.

"But you knew he was leaving?" the police officer asked.

Rachel had a strong desire to shake the kid. He knew something he wasn't telling them.

"He said he wasn't going back to that place."

"What place?" Rachel asked.

"The foster home. He had a fat lip," Ford announced. "The kids there talk with their fists."

Rachel squeezed her eyes closed. "Owen doesn't fight."

"Yeah, that's why he had a fat lip." Ford glared at the cops as if they were to blame. "If everyone just left him where he was, none of this would have happened."

Rachel pushed the dread in her heart away and tried to focus. "Did he leave any clue as to where he went?"

Ford shuffled from foot to foot.

He knew something.

"Ford? He's fifteen and it's winter. Please. He might think he's all tough, but we're from California. It's supposed to be in the teens tonight," Rachel told him.

Jason placed an arm around her shoulders.

"He, a . . . he said something about the city."

"New York?"

Ford shook his head. "Might be. He didn't say much. Just that he could be there in a couple of hours."

Rachel turned to Jason. "He could have taken the train."

"And gone where, hon? The city might only be five miles long, but you know how vast it is."

The thought of him alone in the city had her close to tears. "We have to look."

Jason placed his hands on her face. "We'll look."

She nodded a couple of times.

"Is there anything else?" the officer asked.

"Yeah." Ford removed a phone from his pocket. "I found Owen's cell phone in my backpack."

The police had given her hope that they'd be able to trace a call from his number the moment he used it. Now that hope was gone.

Rachel took it from Ford's fingertips and started to scan his recent texts. Many were back and forth from his friends, and a few were from Nathan. She scanned through recent calls while the officers questioned Ford.

She opened his pictures to see if maybe he'd taken a selfie at the home he was in. Anything to give her a clue. The first thing she saw was an image of Owen's bruised face. She pressed the triangle to see the video he'd taken.

Hey, Rachel. Owen's voice caught her throat with emotion. The room went silent, and everyone turned to her. Jason placed his hand under hers when she started to shake. *I know you're gonna be pissed and worried. I'm sorry for that. But I can't go back to that place. And I'm not living with the hag and her sidekick. And if my dad is behind all of this, well, fuck him. This wasn't right. Once all the adults start acting like adults, I'll be back. And if they can't . . . well, my mom didn't raise a fool. I love you.*

The screen stilled.

"Was that Owen?" one of the officers asked.

She nodded and turned the phone his way and watched the video again.

"Does any of that mean anything to you?"

"The hag is how he refers to his grandmother, the sidekick is the grandfather."

Jason glanced at the officer. "Needless to say, he isn't interested in living with them."

"And the fat lip, that's from the kids at the foster home?" the cop asked Ford.

"That's what he told us," Ford told them.

"Can't blame the kid for not wanting to go back," Ford's father added. "He could have stayed with us."

"I told him that," said Ford. "But he thought the cops would just take him back there."

The lead officer shook his head. "Not if there is evidence of abuse."

"There wasn't any abuse at Rachel's house," Ford argued.

"I hear ya, kid. I don't always like my job." He turned to Rachel. "Is there anything else in this that offers any clue?"

They watched the video twice more. "No." She wished there was.

The officers thanked Ford and his family and asked them to call if they heard from Owen, and then the family walked out onto the frozen sidewalk.

"Now what?" Rachel asked the officers.

"We'll give Owen's picture to the local police and NYPD and have him taken in if they see him."

She waited for an *and*. When her stare was met with silence, she said it herself. "And?"

"He's a runaway."

"What does that mean?" Jason asked.

"Teenage runaways aren't anything new. We put them in the database, pick them up when we find them, and return them home."

"But you don't look for them?" Outrage rested behind Rachel's question.

"Miss Price, have you seen the streets of Manhattan? They are filled with teenage runaways from all over this country. I'm sorry. You seem like a nice lady, you obviously care about this boy."

"I'm the only family he knows."

"We understand. But there really isn't anything we can do at this point. If he contacts you, tell him to come home."

"He was forced to leave my home."

"Let him know that if Ford's parents are okay with him staying there for a while, until your custody matters are resolved, most of the time the social workers will approve. Especially in light of the physical abuse he seems to have suffered from the foster care facility."

Jason held her close. "And in the meantime?"

"You might try searching his social media or search his Internet history. He might have looked at places to go before giving up his phone. And pray Owen was speaking the truth in his video about his mother not raising a fool."

The officers gave her their contact information before pulling out of Ford's driveway.

Rachel shivered, realizing for the first time that it had started to snow.

"Let's go back to my house," Jason suggested.

"I'm going into the city to look for him."

Jason stood in front of her. "Let's go back to my house and strategize. See if we can pinpoint where Owen might have gone. Officer Bailey was right. Owen might have looked something up on the Internet that can clue us in. We'll get some help and go search for him together and cover more ground than what the two of us can do alone."

Her teeth chattered. Much as she wanted to leave right then, what Jason said made sense.

Jason forced her into a hotel after two in the morning.

Nathan stayed behind at the estate and checked Rachel's house twice just in case Owen went home. Glen and Trent took the uptown and downtown subways, searching the stations. Mary and Monica spent their time on the phone, calling shelters and hospitals, although Jason wasn't about to tell Rachel about the hospital search. Yet when Mary mentioned doing it, he agreed. The inch of snow they'd gotten overnight wasn't something anyone should be sleeping in. He liked to think Owen would be more resourceful; Jason reminded himself that the kid was only fifteen. Underestimating the power of a cold New York winter would certainly put just about any of them in a hospital emergency room.

They managed less than five hours of sleep before they were up and at it again. Searching the streets for one child may have been difficult in the dark, but in the sea of people walking around in the morning, it was impossible.

They stopped their search at eight in the morning so they could meet Clive at the courthouse for the emergency hearing he'd managed to have placed on the calendar the day before.

Clive took one look at Rachel's disheveled state and frowned. "It's always better to show up in court looking your best," he told her.

She stepped toward him, her lips in a straight line. "We have been searching for Owen from the minute he went missing. Wearing a skirt and a smile isn't my priority."

Clive held up his hands, lowered his head. "I'm sorry. I know. I just want you to win this so there is no reason to return here."

Jason grasped her hand in his and felt her squeeze. "How is this going to go?" he asked Clive.

"There are eight cases being heard today."

"What number are we?" Rachel asked.

"Six."

"When will we be called?"

"I can't predict that. The cases could go quickly, if in fact the families before us have come to some agreement and the judge signs and pushes papers, or there could be witness calling procedures that push us until the afternoon."

"So I have to wait here while Owen is out there somewhere?"

Clive looked to both of them. "That's the way this works."

Rachel released Jason's hand and started to walk in circles.

"Hey, hey," he said, trying to calm her down. "Glen and Trent are still out there. Glen found a private investigator who is an expert on teenage runaways. Ford's parents are joining the search once school is out." She looked away, and he ducked to make her meet his eyes. "We're going to find him."

She held it together and leaned her head on his shoulder.

Jason folded her into his arms and listened to her strangled breathing. He was grateful that she didn't start crying again.

Clive sighed. "Okay, I'm going to speak with the Colemans' attorney. I need you two to stay close."

The mention of the Colemans' name had Rachel's head off Jason's shoulder and searching the lobby.

Although Jason had never met the Colemans, they were easy to spot when Rachel's hatred landed on the couple.

Owen described them perfectly. The hag had pretentiousness written all over her, and the husband looked embarrassed to be there.

Jason had to physically hold Rachel back.

"That is only going to make things worse."

He turned her in the opposite direction and listened to her mutter under her breath about the couple while he grabbed them both a cup of coffee.

Thirty minutes later Clive joined them again.

"Well?"

Clive shook his head. "They won't see reason. Mr. Yanez told me they believe you know exactly where Owen is and this is all an orchestrated plot to convince the court to leave him with you."

"Orchestrated . . ." Rachel pounded her fist on the cafeteria table. "How dare they."

"That's outrageous," Jason said.

"Outrageous or not, we will have to prove they're wrong."

"I thought the law was centered around being innocent until proven guilty."

Jason was pretty sure Clive laughed.

"You said you had a video?"

Rachel produced Owen's phone. Clive watched the video and wrote a few notes on his legal pad. He asked questions about the night before and the discussions with Lionel and Ford. There was some relief because those stories could be substantiated by a third and fourth party and therefore wouldn't be thrown out.

Clive left them alone for a few minutes so that he could check the courtroom to see the progression of the other cases. When he returned he announced they were still on the second case.

"Can all of this go away today?" Jason asked him.

"It could." He didn't sound hopeful.

"Tell us the possible outcomes."

Clive made a strange face. "I doubt this will all go away today. If the father was here, and Owen was present to state his desires . . . maybe. But Tereck Junior is out of the country, according to his parents, and unreachable because he's shooting pictures in the Middle East somewhere."

"But they can't testify for him," Jason said.

"No, but the court will most likely delay any permanent ruling until TJ can be found and come in."

"So what can we expect today?"

"My ultimate goal is to have Owen placed back in your home."

That sounded good. "And charges against Rachel for not following a court order she never received?"

Jason's mention of that information prompted Clive to start digging in his files. He removed a piece of paper and turned it toward Rachel.

"Is that your signature?"

Her face went white. "No."

Clive pointed to it again. "That isn't you?"

She shook her head.

"What is it?" Jason asked.

"It's Owen's."

Clive turned the paper around. "You're sure?"

"Yep." She turned to Jason. "Why would he not tell me about this?"

"I don't know, hon. Maybe he was scared."

Clive put the paper back in his briefcase. "Okay, so when I ask you if the signature is yours in front of the judge, you're going to say no. You are *not* going to reveal whose it is."

Rachel blinked. "You want me to lie?"

"I'm telling you to avoid offering that information."

"And if Yanez asks?"

"If he asks directly if it is Owen's . . ." Clive waved a hand in the air as if he were on the fence as to his advice.

Rachel lowered her voice. "You want me to lie."

"I would never suggest you lie, just hold some truth back without perjuring yourself. If the court thinks Owen received the certified letter, then they will believe you saw it. At that point you defied a court order by taking Owen out of the country, and you're now at risk of charges for doing so."

"I never saw a letter."

"I believe you. But me believing you isn't going to help in there." He waved at the bank of windows that led to the courtroom they'd be heard in.

"Wow."

Clive sat back in his chair, sipped his coffee. "Don't be so surprised. These walls were built on lies. Only half the people in here are telling the truth, the other half are not."

"I thought there were laws against that."

"There are. You spent half a day in New York's Finest's locked unit. My guess is you didn't see anyone in there on a perjury charge."

Chapter Twenty-Three

Rachel ran her hand through her hair for the thousandth time. It was past lunch, and the court was just about to be called back in session. There was only one case in front of them. She leaned against Jason on a bench outside the courtroom.

"It just dawned on me that I haven't called in to work for two days."

Jason's shoulders shook with mirth. "I've got ya covered."

"But you're not my immediate supervisor. I should have spoken with Gerald."

He kissed the side of her head. "I told him he can expect to see you when he sees me."

She laced her fingers through his. The thought of going through all of this alone made her physically ill. Did he feel obligated? Every move he'd made felt sincere, but how could she really know? He'd fallen into her drama the moment she was taken away in his office building. She'd leaned on him like a crutch, a life preserver in a tsunami. "I'm keeping you from your life," she said aloud.

"Whoa . . . hey." He pulled away far enough to look at her. "You didn't bring any of this on yourself."

"I'm invested in Owen. You're not."

His smile fell. "I'm going to forget you said that."

She placed a hand on the side of his face. "I feel guilty for taking you away from your life."

"Stop."

She closed her lips and held her breath.

"From the moment we met, I became invested in you. Owen is a part of you. So stop feeling guilty."

Rachel pushed back the tears in her eyes. "I don't think I could have done this without you, Jason."

"You don't have to." He kissed her briefly.

She sniffled and pulled back the waterworks.

"Where is he, Jason? Is he hungry? Cold?"

Jason didn't seem as concerned as she was. "I can't help but think we're looking in the wrong place."

They didn't get a chance to talk more before Clive walked up.

"We're on."

Rachel filled her lungs and let it all out in a rush.

"I won't let anything happen to him, Em. I promise you."

The smell of antiseptic and sickness filled each fiber of Rachel's being. She knew every name of every employee on the oncology floor of the hospital. Unlike the doctors, the nurses had told her that Emily wouldn't make it through the night.

The light in Em's eyes had gone out two days before, and Rachel and Owen kept a constant presence in the room. She wouldn't die alone, it was a vow the two of them had made when they knew there was no saving her. Rachel and Owen had cried every moment they found themselves alone.

But when in Emily's room, they held it together. When one of them felt the need to break down, they would leave her side.

Rachel had an understanding with the nurses that when Owen needed to step away, one of them was by his side. And if he needed to be alone, they kept their distance, but there was always one eye on him.

But at this moment, the second time Rachel promised Emily she'd take care of Owen as if he were her own, Rachel was alone, and the tears silently fell. "He will be my son from this day forward. I will be there for him when you pass. I will be there for him when he graduates from high school. I will send him to college and welcome his wife into our lives. Your grandchildren will be mine. I will do everything in my power to be there for him. For you." Rachel held Emily's frail hand. The difference between the two of them was more than black and white. It was healthy and deathly thin . . . alive and on one's last breath of life. "I know you're in pain. I know you're holding on. Let go, Em. I've got him. I promise you."

Within the hour Emily was gone.

Rachel swallowed her memory and the pain it punched in her heart. She'd already broken her promise, and it hadn't yet been a year.

With her chin high, she entered the courtroom and sat on the side opposite the Colemans.

Clive sat beside her and whispered, "Don't look at them. Don't show emotion toward them. Don't say a thing until I have you on that stand."

She swallowed with a nod.

Looking behind her, she saw Jason on the other side of the wooden rail.

He offered a supportive nod.

The bailiff called the room to order, and the judge walked in. Rachel thought they were going to make everyone stand, but they didn't. Thrown off, all Rachel saw was the color of the judge's skin.

She was black. An African American woman who earned her place in a robe, laying judgment on others' lives. Never before in Rachel's life had she looked upon the skin of someone else and felt dread.

Rachel couldn't help it. Would race play a significant role in this? Would the judge's decision be swayed because Owen was black?

She wanted to cry.

"Oh, God." The Colemans looked smug.

"Don't look at them."

Her eyes found the city crest and focused on it.

Without hearing, Rachel recognized that her counsel and that of the Colemans introduced themselves for the purpose of the court reporter.

Judge Sherman looked at both parties and started by speaking to the Colemans. "I've read the argument for custody of Owen Moreau from Mr. and Mrs. Coleman." She turned her eyes on Rachel. "And that from the counsel of Miss Price. "I have to admit, I have more questions than answers. Have the parties come to any agreement?"

Mr. Yanez spoke first. "No, Your Honor. We have not."

Judge Sherman looked at Clive.

"We have not, Your Honor."

"All right, then," the judge said with a sigh. "Let's proceed."

Clive stayed standing while Mr. Yanez and the Colemans sat. "Your Honor, before we move on, you need to know that the child in the case, Owen Moreau, has fled the foster care system and is unaccounted for right now."

The judge looked at both parties. "I assume the authorities are notified."

"Yes. My client was with them most of the night and all morning searching for him."

Rachel clenched her fists.

"Let's see how quickly we can move through this."

Clive sat down, seemingly happy with the judge's comments.

Rachel listened while Mr. Yanez opened the Colemans' case and entered a plea that the judge offer them temporary custody of Owen until TJ returned from Syria. Yanez stated that she was a flight risk, as demonstrated by the documentation already presented into evidence regarding her recent flight to Central America with Owen the previous week.

Clive leaned over and whispered, "They have the burden of proof now."

She kept silent and tried to keep her face emotionless as they spoke.

Yanez called Deyadria to the stand.

Rachel tried not to stare as the woman walked by. She stated her name and swore an oath that she would tell the truth.

But the first statement out of her mouth was a lie.

"We didn't know we had a grandson until after his mother had passed."

Rachel bit her tongue.

"And what did you do when you found out?" Mr. Yanez asked.

"We contacted Rachel Price immediately."

At least that part was true.

"We told her we would lovingly take Owen with us."

"What happened then?"

Deyadria looked everywhere but at Rachel. "Nothing. We heard nothing."

"Miss Price took a job on the East Coast, is that right?"

"Yes. A job that gave her access to international travel on a moment's notice."

"Was this concerning to you?"

"Of course. She threatened to leave the country if we pursued custody of Owen."

Rachel grabbed Clive's hand. "That's a lie. I never said that to them." He shushed her.

"What happened after Miss Price moved here?"

"Well, she made it look like she was trying to allow a relationship between Owen and us. But she never allowed us time alone with him."

Rachel leaned over. "He didn't want me to leave him alone."

Clive held a hand in the air and made a note on his pad.

"You've stated in your complaint that Miss Price is not providing a safe environment for your grandson."

Mrs. Coleman shook her head. "The home she's in is falling down. The paint on the walls is peeling. Owen has complained about a headache every time we have seen him."

"Are you concerned for his health?"

"I am. So is his father."

"Objection," Clive argued.

"Sustained. Mrs. Coleman, you cannot testify on your son's opinion," Judge Sherman announced.

Yanez took a breath and asked the question another way. "Did your son express concern about his son's health?"

"Yes."

Yanez paused and then moved on. "Can you tell us the events leading up to your plea for the court to remove Owen from Miss Price's home?"

"My husband and I have been trying to establish a relationship with our grandson since we learned of him. Our son, TJ—Tereck Junior—Owen's father, returned for Christmas and told us he wanted custody of his son. When we told Miss Price our intentions, she became irate and refused to answer our calls after that."

All lies. Rachel looked at the faces of the others in the courtroom to find several people buying the fabricated story.

"What happened then?" Mr. Yanez stood behind his desk and asked questions while Clive listened and scribbled notes.

"She threatened to leave the country and told us we would never see our grandson again."

Rachel shook her head.

Clive placed a hand over hers and offered a curt nod in warning.

Her eyes pleaded with him. She grabbed the pen from his hand and wrote on his pad with a heavy hand:

Not true!

"Is that when you went to the courts and petitioned for custody?"

"Yes," Deyadria said.

"When did you become aware that Miss Price and Owen had left the country?"

"I saw a broadcast of Rachel speaking on behalf of the company she works for when they were in Costa Rica."

"Is that part of her job?" Yanez asked.

"Objection," Clive shouted out.

"Sustained."

Mr. Yanez redirected. "Where was Owen while Miss Price was in Costa Rica?"

"In Costa Rica with her."

"How did you determine that?"

"Owen has a social media thing, Instagram. He posted a picture of a beach."

Mr. Yanez lifted a picture snapped from a phone and handed it to the bailiff. "What does Owen say along with this image?"

Rachel's eyes followed the picture as it traveled to the judge. She glanced at it and then put it aside, no emotion on her face.

"It says, 'The next time I come back here, I'm staying.'"

"What did that mean to you, Mrs. Coleman?"

The woman's lip started to quiver and she glanced at the judge. "It meant I would never see my grandson again."

"Thank you, Mrs. Coleman." Mr. Yanez sat, and all eyes moved to Clive.

"Good afternoon, Mrs. Coleman."

Her quivering lip disappeared, and nerves in the form of a single tapping finger instantly started to show.

"Good afternoon."

Clive smiled. "You have testified, under oath, that you didn't know you had a grandson until after Owen's mother had passed away."

She nodded.

Judge Sherman spoke. "You have to answer with a yes or no, Mrs. Coleman. The court reporter cannot write down that you nodded."

"Yes," Deyadria lied.

"How did you find out about Owen?"

"My son told us."

"TJ?"

"That's right."

"Did your son tell you about your grandson before or after Emily Moreau's funeral?"

"After."

"How do you know it was after?"

"Because he attended Miss Moreau's services."

"So your son had been in contact with Miss Moreau?"

Deyadria looked at her lawyer. "I'm not sure."

"Objection."

The judge didn't rule quickly, so Mr. Yanez continued his argument. "How can Mrs. Coleman speculate on her son's knowledge?"

"Sustained."

"Where is your son now?" Clive asked.

"The last I heard he was in Syria. For work."

"Does your son travel a lot?"

"He is a photojournalist. Traveling to places most of us avoid is his job."

"You sound very proud of your son." Clive smiled.

"I am."

"How long has your son traveled for work?"

"Ever since he graduated from college. Almost twenty years."

"Would you say Syria is a safe country?"

Mrs. Coleman shook her head. "No. I pray for his safety every night."

"Probably not a place he'd take his son."

"No. TJ would never put Owen in danger."

Clive smiled and turned to the judge. "No further questions."

Rachel sighed when Clive sat down.

"Any other witnesses?" Judge Sherman asked Mr. Yanez.

"No, Your Honor."

"Mr. Redshaw, you have our attention."

He patted Rachel's hand and stood before calling her to the stand.

The vulnerable short stride to the bench, where she sat behind a microphone, was the longest walk she'd ever taken. She vowed to tell the truth and then took her seat.

Clive walked around the desk and tilted his head with a smile. "You look like you've had a long night," he began.

"I have."

"Why?"

"I . . . we have been searching the streets of New York ever since Owen went missing."

Clive looked around the room. "Who is *we?*"

"The Fairchilds, myself." She looked at the clock. "By now Owen's friends are out of school, and their families have joined the search."

"Is it hard for you to be in this courtroom right now?"

She nodded. "We should be out there looking for him and not in here fighting over him."

"Objection, Your Honor. If Mr. Redshaw felt the need to postpone this hearing, he could have asked at the beginning."

Clive looked at the judge. "Leaving Owen in the foster care system longer than necessary will prompt the boy to flee again once he's found. Which I will establish during this testimony."

"Overruled," Judge Sherman said.

Mr. Yanez sat down.

"Miss Price, tell me about your relationship with Owen."

"I've known Owen since he was five. His mother and I became best friends shortly after we met."

"Can you describe Emily Moreau for the court?"

Rachel couldn't help the emotion that caught in her throat. "Em was, uhm . . . kind, loving. Very down-to-earth."

"A saint?"

"No, of course not. She was very real and didn't sugarcoat life just to please others."

"What can you tell us about her relationship with TJ?"

"Objection," Mr. Yanez shouted.

"Sustained."

Clive didn't miss a beat. "When did you meet TJ?"

"Owen was in first grade. I remember that because Emily and I were making thirty paper pioneer hats for his class. TJ came over to Emily and Owen's home to see his son."

"So TJ knew he had a son?"

"Yes, since his birth. I saw TJ once more when Owen was maybe ten, and then again at Emily's funeral."

"Would you say that Emily and TJ had a friendly relationship?"

Rachel smiled. "Yes. They were very adult about Owen. Emily never pressed TJ to be a full-time father, and from what I saw, he never tried."

Rachel held her breath, thinking Mr. Yanez was going to object. He didn't.

"Did Owen know TJ was his father?" Clive asked.

"Yes," Rachel said.

"Did Owen ever talk about his father?"

"No. Not really. Not until Emily got sick."

"Let's talk about that. You were living in California at the time of Emily's passing?"

"Yes."

"Why did you move to the East Coast?"

She looked at Jason, smiled. "To avoid this."

"What do you mean?"

"The Colemans did contact me, within a month of Emily's death. They told me they wanted to take Owen in."

"How did that make you feel?"

"Anxious. Worried they would fight for custody. So Owen and I talked about our options and decided to move."

"Just like that?"

"Yes. Honestly, I thought it would be good for Owen to know his grandparents."

Rachel's comment brought a gasp and rolling of the eyes from Deyadria.

"Why?" Clive asked.

"Watching your best friend die at a young age has a way of making you look at your own mortality. I knew if something happened to me, Owen would truly be alone. At least for Emily, she knew she had me. We worked out custody arrangements the month we found out she had cancer."

Clive tapped his hand on the banister. "So you uprooted your life, found a position in Manhattan, and set down roots here."

"That's right. I bought a house, enrolled Owen in the high school."

"How was your reception from the Colemans?"

Rachel looked first at Deyadria, then to Tereck. "Strained."

"How so?"

"I felt they were trying to find fault in everything I did."

"Was it comfortable to be around them?"

"No."

"Have you kept Owen from seeing them?"

"No. We've seen them several times since we moved here."

"Mrs. Coleman testified that you're keeping Owen away," Clive stated.

"If she is referring to the time she asked us to dinner and Owen had to work on a group project at school, then yes. We didn't go."

Deyadria was having a hard time sitting still.

"Or the time I had strep throat and had to cancel."

"Could Owen go alone?"

"If he wanted to. He didn't. I wasn't about to force him."

Clive walked back to his papers, looked at his notes. "On the petition for custody, the Colemans state they believe your home is full of toxins that are making their grandson ill."

"It's an old home, like many in the suburbs. But instead of guessing, I hired a contractor to test every corner of my house for anything toxic."

Clive handed a piece of paper to the judge. "This is the preliminary report on the home inspection, along with blood work testing Miss Price for lead poisoning."

"Has the opposing counsel seen this?" Judge Sherman asked.

"We have, Your Honor."

She looked at the document in silence. "The full report won't be ready for two days."

"That's right," Clive told her.

Clive switched gears again.

"How did you end up in Costa Rica?"

Jason smiled her way, his eyes soft.

"I was with Mr. Fairchild when he learned of one of the company planes crashing. He needed to fly to the wreckage site and asked me to come."

"As a friend?"

"And as an employee. It was New Year's Day. Most of the employees were off on holiday."

"So you grabbed Owen and left?"

She nodded. "Right. I didn't want to leave Owen alone, with me being so far away. He stayed in the hotel with one of Jason's friends while we worked."

"Did you talk about staying in Central America?"

"We talked about coming back to visit. It's beautiful there. Warm. I'm not used to New York winters."

"I've lived here my whole life and I don't like them," Clive said, looking around the courtroom.

Laughter filled the room.

"When did you first hear from the courts about the Colemans' petition for custody?"

Rachel's brief joy vanished with his question. "When the police escorted me out of my office at work."

"Why did they do that?"

"They told me I had violated a court order and they needed to question me."

"But you never saw the court order."

"I didn't." Rachel looked directly at the judge. "I swear to God I never saw any letter."

Once again, Deyadria rolled her eyes and this time muttered something to her lawyer.

Clive handed another paper to the judge. "This is in your packet."

The judge handed it back with a nod. "This is the paper from the service that sent you notice of the Colemans' case. Have you seen it before today?"

"No."

"Is that your signature?"

"No."

Clive walked back to his stack of papers. "I'd like to bring into evidence signature cards from Rachel's bank as evidence that this is not her signature." He handed the paper to Mr. Yanez.

"Any objection, Mr. Yanez?" Judge Sherman asked.

"No."

The judge addressed the court reporter, giving the evidence a number.

"We're almost done here, Rachel. Do you know where Owen is right now?"

"No." She wanted to cry.

"When was the last time you spoke with him?"

"The morning he was taken to the foster home. You advised me not to contact him without permission from the court."

"And did you follow that advice?"

"I have."

"Do you know why he ran away?"

"Yes."

Clive turned back to the judge. "I'd like to submit a recording of Owen from his personal cell phone into evidence."

"Objection."

Clive didn't wait for a ruling. "Your Honor. Owen left a video recording the afternoon of his disappearance. It will show his state of mind and offer some light as to his relationship with the petitioning party."

"Objection overruled." She lifted her hand out.

The courtroom sat in silence as Judge Sherman listened to Owen's message.

Clive ended his questioning.

Chapter Twenty-Four

Jason noticed the moment when Rachel put a rod through her spine to face cross-examination. So far, he thought they were doing really well. He couldn't read the judge, but it didn't seem as if the Colemans had any real evidence against Rachel.

"Good afternoon," Mr. Yanez addressed Rachel.

"Good afternoon."

The pleasantries were making Jason ill.

"I'll be brief, Miss Price."

She glanced at Jason, tried to smile.

"You testified that you took a job in Manhattan."

"Yes."

"What is your position?"

"I'm in marketing at Fairchild Charters."

"Marketing. How did marketing play into your need to go to Costa Rica? Wouldn't risk management or public relations be better suited for damage control?"

Rachel looked at Jason again. "Yes. But—"

"Let me guess, you volunteered to jump on a plane and leave the country."

"Jason asked me to go with him."

"Jason? That would be Jason Fairchild, the CEO and co-owner of the company?"

Jason lifted his chin as the attention in the courtroom centered on him.

"Yes."

"At what time did you learn about the ill-fated Fairchild jet that went down?"

"It was early, five thirty, six in the morning."

"How is it you and your boss were together that early in the morning on a holiday?"

Rachel swallowed. "Jason and I share a personal relationship."

"You're lovers?"

"Objection, Your Honor. This is irrelevant."

"I disagree, Your Honor. Showing Miss Price's ability and intent to leave the country is incredibly relevant to this case."

"Overruled. Answer the question, Miss Price."

Jason kept his eyes on Rachel's.

"Yes. Jason and I are lovers."

"And you work for him?"

"I am an employee of Fairchild Charters."

"Mr. Fairchild is a pilot, is that right?"

"Yes," she said.

"Has he flown you anywhere?"

Rachel's eyes started to lose focus. "Yes."

"Would you say he has the freedom and ability to fly anywhere in the world at a moment's notice?"

Rachel took her eyes off Jason and stared at Yanez. "He owns a company that charters private jets, of course he has them at his disposal."

"And with you as his girlfriend, they are at yours as well, isn't that right?"

She shook her head. "No. It's not like that."

"What is it like, Miss Price?"

"I would never ask Jason to fly me anywhere."

"But you could."

"Objection. Does counsel have a question?"

"Sustained. Ask a question, Mr. Yanez."

"Did you fly a lot before moving to New York?"

"No."

"And Owen, has he been on many planes?"

"No. We drove to New York with the move."

"How is it, then, that you both have passports?"

The direction Yanez was going became apparent. "We got them before Emily died."

"So you could leave the country if the Colemans sought custody?"

"No. It wasn't like that."

"Why would you need a passport, if not to leave the country?"

Rachel sat forward. "Emily thought there might be a treatment for her overseas. She made sure Owen had his passport in case a cure was found."

"That's convenient, since Emily isn't here to tell us otherwise."

Rachel winced.

"Objection!"

Jason wanted to object with his fist.

"Mr. Yanez, skip the comments and ask the questions," the judge warned.

"Miss Price, do you like the Colemans?"

Her gaze moved to the couple. "No. I don't."

"How do you propose to 'foster a relationship' with them for Owen's sake when you don't care for them?"

"The same way I tolerate my Uncle Barry. We don't have to like our family to be around them."

Some spectators chuckled.

"You said you believed Owen should know his biological family."

"I did."

"Do you still feel that way?"

She was torn, Jason could see it in her eyes. "Not at the risk of Owen's safety."

"Have Mr. and Mrs. Coleman raised a hand to Owen?"

"No."

"Have they threatened him?"

"No. Not that I know of," she said.

"Is there anything you wouldn't do to keep Owen safe?" Mr. Yanez asked.

"No."

"Would you take a bullet for him?"

"Yes. I love him as if he were my own son."

Mr. Yanez smiled as if he'd caught her. Jason felt the rabbit hole closing in. "Would you leave the country in order to keep Owen safe?"

Her breathing became a staccato that the entire courtroom heard.

"Objection, Your Honor. Leading the witness."

"Sustained."

Mr. Yanez held up his hand. "One more question, Your Honor." He removed the paper with Owen's signature on it and held it in front of Rachel. "This isn't your signature?"

"No."

"This is your address, correct?"

"Yes."

"Whose signature is it?"

She blinked, twice. "I'm not sure."

"Really? Look again. That signature isn't familiar at all?"

Rachel looked Jason's way again.

Without words, he tried to tell her everything would work out.

She studied the paper again. "It could be Owen's."

Deyadria pounded the table with her hand and said, "Ha."

The people in the courtroom watching and waiting for their turn started to talk among themselves.

"Could be? Or is? You've known Owen since he was five, helped in his primary school classroom. Don't you know his handwriting?"

She looked at Yanez. "It is his."

The lawyer smiled. "Thank you, Miss Price."

———

Rachel sat through closing arguments in a haze. Mr. Yanez painted her as a woman who purposely fostered a relationship with a man capable of taking her anywhere in the world and as a significant flight risk. He argued that she knew about the court order and ignored it. He asked that the court give the Colemans time to locate their son and bring him back before granting her permanent guardianship back.

Clive ended with a plea that the judge recognize the love between Rachel and Owen and the proof of her intentions of doing the right thing by moving there and opening up their lives to the Colemans. He requested the court grant her full guardianship.

Now they all sat in the courtroom while the judge retired to her chambers to review the case.

"Any word on Owen?"

"Nothing." Jason looked at the screen on his phone.

"It's going to be dark soon."

"We'll find him."

"You sound so confident."

"Owen's a smart kid. He isn't sitting out in the cold."

She hoped Jason was right.

The bailiff called the room to order and Rachel turned to face the judge.

"Be seated," she told them.

"I've looked at all the evidence and the statements given by the social workers assigned to this case. Most of the time I can find a clear right or a clear wrong that helps my decision. This isn't the case here," Judge Sherman said.

"Mr. and Mrs. Coleman. You have not shown clear and convincing evidence that Miss Price is unfit as a guardian for your grandson. However, there is still some question as to the state of her home, and the court has no choice but to wait for more information. I'm putting in my order that as soon as Owen Moreau is found, he see a doctor for a physical to rule out any toxicity in regards to Miss Price's home. It is evident your son, TJ, knew of Owen and did not step into the role of father. For reasons unknown. But as Miss Price has pointed out, it is only fair Owen be given the opportunity to know his family . . . all of you. That is going to be a bumpy road, Mr. and Mrs. Coleman, as it seems Owen's trust in you has already been broken."

Deyadria opened her mouth, and Yanez hushed her.

"Miss Price. It is overwhelmingly evident that you will do anything for Owen. I am the mother of two, and I know I would do anything, and I do mean anything, to keep my children safe. Because I know that in my heart, I have no choice but to assume you would as well. I look at this signature card and can't help but wonder if Owen saw and disregarded the paper. I question if you saw it. There really is no evidence outside of the fact the order did indeed end up in your home on . . ." She looked at the paper. "December twenty-seventh of last year. It is clear that you believe the Colemans are a threat. From Owen's words on his video, he feels they are, too. And keeping him from that threat may very well mean leaving the country to do so."

Oh, God. She is going to take him away.

"However, you took him away and brought him back, which points to you telling the truth about not seeing the court order. You don't strike me as an unintelligent woman."

Please, please . . .

"So this is what I'm going to do. Much as I'd love to put this matter to rest today, I cannot. I request Miss Price and Owen Moreau surrender their passports until a final ruling can be made. I want to revisit this matter once all the reports on Miss Price's home are completed, Owen is found and can be questioned, and more importantly, Tereck Coleman Junior, otherwise known as TJ, can be brought in to testify. You see, I do believe a son deserves to know his father. That said, I'm not going to give TJ an unlimited time to make his intentions known. If TJ has any intention of taking custody, temporary or jointly, he will need to report to this court in three weeks. In the meantime, Owen Moreau will be considered a ward of the court and placed in the care of Miss Price. I will not mandate any visitation by the Colemans at this time."

Sparks of joy exploded in Rachel's chest.

"I will encourage Miss Price and the Colemans to come to some peace, for Owen's sake."

"But we're his family," Deyadria pleaded.

Judge Sherman focused on her. "That is where you're wrong. DNA does not dictate family. Both of my children are adopted. One from Vietnam, the other from South Africa. Love dictates family. So, out of the mouths of babes . . . when the adults can 'start acting like adults' again, this matter can be solved. This case is to be brought back to me three weeks from today."

She dropped the gavel, and Rachel turned and threw her arms around Jason.

For the next two days, Jason's home became a field office in their search for Owen.

A map of the city and the trains leading into and out of it that Owen could have taken were drawn out. The shelters had red dots on them, those that had been contacted and/or visited had green dots.

"The problem is, Owen doesn't want to be found," Nathan told Jason and Glen. "If the lad knows he can come home, he will probably just show up."

Ford and Lionel returned from their local search. "We looked at all our hangouts. No one has seen him."

"I can't help but think he isn't in the city," Nathan said.

"Why?" Glen asked.

"Because that would be foolish! There's half a foot of snow on the ground."

Jason looked at the vaulted ceiling of his childhood home, and his brain started to itch. "Oh, shit."

"What?" Glen paused, his pen midair, en route to mark off something on the map.

"This place is Narnia. We got lost in it. Hide-and-go-seek."

Glen caught on and looked around them. "No way."

"It's a big place." And hadn't they sat around that very room, talking about not finding each other as children?

Jason called everyone into the room.

"You seriously think Owen is hiding here?" Rachel asked.

"We haven't looked, have we?"

"That would be crazy," Ford said.

"That would be smart."

For the first time in three days, Rachel had hope in her eyes. They'd been searching on adrenaline and coffee without any sign of Owen.

Jason assigned everyone a section of the house, placed Nathan and Owen's friends on the outside buildings.

He guided Rachel up, into the attic, where his childhood sat in dusty boxes.

The house was suddenly filled with everyone calling out Owen's name.

"Owen?" Rachel called to the vast attic.

Jason found a switch and turned on a long string of fluorescent lights. The entire space lit up like it was noon instead of nine o'clock at night.

"Wow, this space is huge. I could get lost in here."

"Or you could hide in here." He looked around and started walking toward the east end of the house. "Owen?"

"Hey," Rachel said, catching his attention. "The dust is a mess over here."

Jason looked and patted her on the back. "We had some of the Christmas decorations up here."

Her shoulders folded in disappointment.

"Owen?" she called out. "The court said you can come back home with me."

Silence.

They ducked behind every box, looked in every corner. Dusty and more than a little cold, they exhausted the attic search and moved down one floor. Each room and every closet was poked into and overturned. When Jason and Rachel would meet up with another group, they'd take another direction. Finally they all ended up back in the living room.

"Nothing," Trent reported.

Jason looked out the window. "Okay, bundle up."

Their barns and loft were empty, the tack room and storage rooms showed nothing. Rachel checked each stall. Because the space was enclosed and heated, it would make sense for Owen to hang out there.

He wasn't there.

The report from the hangar was the same.

They searched Nathan's house, and the housekeeper's. A separate guesthouse on the far side of the lake was empty and cold.

It was close to midnight by the time they suspended their search.

Rachel held her head in her hands. "Damn it. I thought you were onto something."

Jason did, too. "Tomorrow we put a billboard in the middle of town and another one at his school. I'll have our team work on getting one to place over the side of our high-rise, letting Owen know he can come home."

"We're going to go," Ford told them.

"Thanks, guys," Rachel said, opening her arms to hug them. "If you hear anything."

"We know."

Glen approached them. "Mary and I are going to bunk here."

"Of course," Jason said.

"We're headed out. The dogs are probably eating the furniture," Trent said as he helped Monica with her coat.

"We'll be back tomorrow," Monica said.

The room emptied out.

"I should probably go home," Rachel said quietly. "In case Owen shows up there."

"Okay. Let me grab a few things."

She stopped him before he turned to head up to his bedroom.

"You don't have to come."

He gave his best *you've got to be kidding me* look. "I'm not leaving you alone until we find him. And even then, there's a pretty big chance I won't leave you alone. I'll go pack some things."

She followed him to his room and filled the suitcase she'd brought over a few days before.

Jason filled a small duffel bag with a few essentials.

Out of the corner of his eye, he noticed Rachel looking through some papers.

"What's that?" he asked, closing the door to his closet.

"My bills. I'll be shocked if the electricity is still on when I get home. I've ignored all this since right after Christmas." She kept scanning each envelope, then gasped.

"What?"

She dropped the stack onto the bed and waved one of the envelopes in her hand. "Here it is."

He stopped what he was doing and moved to her side. "Here what is?"

"The court order."

The unopened envelope stared at them.

"Ten bucks says Owen signed for it, tossed it in the stack, and forgot all about it," Jason said.

"I'd bet a hundred."

He turned back to his bag and placed the strap over his shoulder before grabbing hers. "Let's go."

———

Jason stepped out of Rachel's room after taking a shower and found her sitting on Owen's bed. They were going on four days without a sign from him. Jason was fairly certain Rachel had lost five pounds in that time.

"Hey." She tried to smile when she saw him watching her.

"You okay?"

"I think I'm numb."

"You're tired and underfed."

She patted the side of the bed, and he happily sat beside her. "When I decided to give us a shot, I never saw any of this."

He smiled. "You mean when I wore you down and you realized there was no resisting my charm?"

He missed her smile. "I thought our biggest challenge would be work. Never in a million years did I think you'd be pulled into a custody debate with the Colemans or that we'd be keeping our eyes open with toothpicks, searching for Owen."

"Life has a way of throwing curveballs. The fact we can't quite predict everything makes life interesting."

"Makes it crazy."

"Maybe. But I like it. I didn't see you coming, but I wouldn't have it any other way," he told her.

She melted. "You always know the perfect things to say."

"It's easy when you're telling the truth."

"See, perfect." Her smile reached her eyes, and Jason leaned in to seal his words with a kiss.

She released a small moan and leaned into his arms. With her leading the way, he deepened his kiss and hoped she wouldn't pull away. While they had been sleeping in the same bed since Costa Rica, they hadn't made love for days. He missed her soft and pliant in his arms. He missed the way she was touching him right then, her hands on his chest, her legs crawling into his lap.

His body forgot the fact they were sitting on Owen's bed, or that he was still missing. From the way Rachel was searching for his tonsils with the tip of her tongue, she'd forgotten, too.

He didn't resist when she pushed him on his back and pressed her hips against his. With both hands, he held her against him, his erection searching for a break in their clothing.

Her breath caught, and she rode against him, finding pleasure without him being inside of her. If she kept doing it for long, he'd lose it in his pants, and he hadn't done that since high school.

"Yes," she whispered in his ear, her hips moving faster.

He thought of cold water, icebergs . . . anything to keep his erection.

With a quick shift of her hips, she moved in the opposite direction and moaned long and deep in his ear.

His cock twitched in anger at being denied release when she stopped stimulating him.

She started laughing with her head buried in his shoulder. "I think I just violated you."

"Violate me anytime you want, hon."

She lifted her head to look at him. "This should not have happened in Owen's room."

"We still have our clothes on."

"I came."

"Two seconds more and I would have, too."

She smiled and he noticed guilt set in. "This is bad. Owen is missing and I'm . . ."

"You're stressed. You needed relief. Don't kick yourself." He wanted relief, too. But he wasn't going to pressure her.

"C'mon," she said. "Let's go to bed."

She rolled off him and he stood.

With a look of guilt, she smoothed the edges of Owen's bedspread. "So bad."

Jason placed a hand on her waist to tug her away.

With the movement, the bedspread untucked from the foot of the bed, and Rachel stood perfectly still. "Wait."

"What?"

She shoved the blanket aside and then ripped it off the bed altogether.

"What is it?"

"Owen has an electric blanket. It's not here."

"Are you sure it was on his bed the last time he was here?"

"It's always on his bed. As soon as the temperature dropped under fifty."

She pulled his pillow away to unveil his backpack. "He came home."

They both stared at each other.

"We were looking in the wrong house," Jason said quietly.

Rachel flew across the room and tossed open Owen's closet.

Jason ran down the hall, searched closets, down the stairs, the coat closet, the garage . . .

They both stood in the kitchen, and their gazes landed on the door leading to the basement.

"He wouldn't."

Jason had to laugh. "Hide in the one place you would never look for him? Yeah, he would."

They opened the door slowly and started down the stairs.

Behind a stack of boxes, in a makeshift tent, Owen was curled up on his side, the electric blanket working double time in the cold space . . . snoring.

Rachel started to weep before she fell to her knees and grabbed a sleepy Owen in her arms.

"Hey," he said with one eye open.

"I'm going to kill you," Rachel told him. From the strength she was using to hug him, it might be possible he wouldn't make it out of the basement alive.

"You found me."

She pulled away, grasped his face in her hands. "Never do that again. You hear me?"

"I didn't want you to go to jail."

"Never! You don't get to leave. We will figure it out together. But you don't get to leave. Got it?"

"'Kay."

And the hugging began again.

"I'm okay," he told her.

"Yeah, well . . . I'm not."

Owen looked over Rachel's shoulder at Jason, smiled, and then wrapped his arms around her.

Chapter Twenty-Five

"Nice of you to join us, Mr. Moreau."

Judge Sherman held humor in her voice.

Rachel stood beside Owen, both of them properly dressed for a day in court. Jason had sent Owen to his tailor. The suit he wore made him look five years older than he was.

"Hi," Owen said sheepishly.

Rachel nudged him and whispered, *"Your Honor."*

"Your Honor," he said after the fact.

The people in the courtroom laughed.

Rachel glanced behind them to find Jason and his family sitting there in support.

"You gave Miss Price quite the scare. What do you have to say for yourself?"

"Well, Judge . . . I mean, Your Honor. At the time I didn't feel I had any other choice."

She seemed surprised by his answer. "And now?"

"I realized that if I had used a few more of the skills Mr. Collet was teaching me—he's my English teacher—I might have learned that I could have stayed with one of my buddies instead of a foster home until we had a court date."

"Mr. Collet sounds like a wise man."

"His tests are hard."

The courtroom laughed again.

"Hard teachers are always the best," she told him.

"Yes, Your Honor."

Judge Sherman looked at Rachel and then the Colemans. "I'm told you've come to an agreement."

"We have, Your Honor," Mr. Yanez said.

"We have," said Clive.

"I'm listening."

"My clients have decided to drop the petition for custody of Owen Moreau."

Rachel already knew they were going to drop everything, but it was nice to finally hear it aloud in front of a judge.

"I think that's wise," Judge Sherman said. "I take it you're TJ?" She addressed Owen's father.

"That's right, Your Honor."

"What are your intentions?"

TJ looked around the attorneys to stare at Owen. "I want to get to know my son, Your Honor."

Rachel placed her hand on Owen's shoulder.

"With all respect, I don't think a court should force Owen to see me, or his grandparents. The stress this situation has put on Owen and the roadblock I've created by not stopping my parents before they came to the court is something I'm going to have to live with." TJ turned his attention to Owen. "He's turning out to be a fine young man without us, and my guess is that isn't going to change. I hope that one day he will *want* to know me."

Rachel caught Owen moving his gaze to his feet.

"TJ is relinquishing his rights for custody so long as Miss Price remains Owen's legal guardian," Mr. Yanez stated.

Judge Sherman focused on Rachel. "You're in agreement with these terms, Miss Price?"

"Yes, Your Honor. With all my heart."

The judge smiled and lifted her papers. "Let's hope all my cases go this well today. I am ordering Miss Price and Mr. Moreau's passports to be returned and all mobility restrictions lifted."

It is over . . . finally over.

Owen hugged her.

"Not so fast, Mr. Moreau."

Owen froze.

"Being a teenage runaway is a probationary offense."

The air left Rachel's lungs.

"I won't do it again, Your Honor."

The judge had a catlike smile. "I'm sure you won't. And to help you with that wise decision, I'm ordering you to perform twenty hours of community service, to be completed at the local homeless shelter and teenage runaway hotline."

Rachel closed her eyes in relief.

"Really?" Owen asked. "Your Honor?"

"Really!"

Rachel lifted her hand, as if she was in a classroom.

"Yes, Miss Price."

Rachel glanced at Owen, then back to the judge. "I'd like to request *forty* hours of community service."

"What?" Owen cried.

The courtroom exploded in laughter.

"The hard teachers are always the best. And I'm too young to have to start dyeing gray hair."

"Forty hours it is." Judge Sherman hit her gavel to the block. "Case dismissed."

Rachel ruffled the top of Owen's head before pulling him into a hug.

She turned to Clive and shook his hand. "Thank you."

"My pleasure."

TJ approached them once they all walked out of the courtroom. "Owen?"

Owen nodded but didn't say anything.

"I'm going to be in town for a few weeks. I was wondering if maybe we could catch a movie or something."

Owen looked at her, then back to TJ.

"I guess so."

"You sure?"

"Yeah, I mean, as long as I can pick the movie."

"Deal."

TJ turned to Rachel. "Thank you."

"You're welcome."

He turned and walked away, making his parents come with him as they left the courthouse.

Jason squeezed between them and placed an arm around each of them. His brothers and their wives followed close behind. "How are we going to celebrate?"

"I was thinking Machu Picchu," Owen said, deadpan.

"Peru?" Rachel exclaimed.

Glen started to laugh.

"I really am starting to like this kid," Trent said.

"Too much?" Owen asked Rachel.

"Ya think?"

Jason laughed. "It's only a seven-hour flight."

Owen jumped in front of them. "Not a bad idea, right?" He pointed both index fingers at Jason and bounced on the balls of his feet. "Seven wonders of the world. What's not to love?"

"Owen!"

"What?"

"How about dinner and ice cream?" Rachel suggested.

"Peru totally trumps dinner and ice cream," Trent said.

Monica smacked his arm. "You're not helping."

"He has school in the morning." As if Rachel had to talk this crazy clan out of a spontaneous trip to Peru.

"And community service hours," Mary added.

Glen was looking at his phone. "It's eighty degrees there right now."

Rachel turned her unbelieving stare toward Mary and Monica. "These men. How do you cope?"

The door to the courthouse opened, and a rush of cold air had all of them turning toward the icy temperature.

The view was breathtaking . . . or maybe it was the beginning of altitude sickness.

From Rachel's vantage point, she could see Owen running circles around the others. His crazy-ass idea caught a fever within the Fairchild men, and before Rachel could say no, they were tucked in the Fairchild personal jet and soaring at thirty thousand feet.

"I don't remember the last time the three of us went anywhere together like this," Jason told her as they rested on one of the many ancient steps of the Incan temple. She sat half in his lap, her tan legs dangling across his, her head resting on his shoulder.

"Why not?"

"Work. Life. Sometimes we have our eyes set on the golden ring so hard that we lose sight of everything else that's important."

"Didn't your parents already hand you the golden ring?" she asked, watching Jason's profile.

"Up until I met you, it felt more like a baton I had to run to the finish line. Only I never saw the finish line, so I just kept running."

"Sounds tiring."

"Exhausting. I didn't realize how tired I was until I woke up with you by my side."

"Jason." He always had the right words.

He turned to catch her smiling at him. "It's true. I've never felt so alive as I have when I was convincing you to date me."

"When was that? Between putting up my Christmas lights or fighting my legal battles?"

"Somewhere in there."

They both laughed.

"I want this. Exactly *this*, forever," Jason said.

Rachel looked at the panorama before them. The blue sky merged with the deep green of the Peruvian forest that hid Machu Picchu for hundreds of years, the steps where human sacrifices were likely performed, a constant reminder of how precious life was. "You can have this every day if you want."

She laughed.

Jason shook his head and grasped her hand. "Not this." He waved a hand at the land in front of him. "This." He squeezed her hand.

Before she could say a thing, he pointed at Owen taking pictures of his brothers and their wives. "That. I want to be that guy who says . . . okay, Owen, you wanna learn about the Great Wall of China? Let's go!"

"That's crazy."

"Not quite crazy." He kissed the back of her hand. "Maybe a little crazy."

She squeezed her thumb and index finger together. "Tiny bit."

"I'm going about this all wrong," he said.

"Going about what?" she asked.

He hiked her higher on his lap and kept one hand on her hip to keep her from toppling off. Jason's playful smile turned twenty shades more serious.

"I have fallen completely and irrevocably in love with you."

Her jaw fell open.

"I want you, this love, for the rest of my life."

She was going to cry.

"The way I see it is I can spend the next six months convincing you we belong together forever, or we can just get on with our beautiful life."

"Jason—"

He placed a finger over her lips. "Marry me, Rachel. Give me a reason to pass the baton and start living my life again."

She sniffled through her smile. "You're crazy."

"We established that."

"I guess that makes two of us."

His smile fell. "You're serious?"

She nodded through her tears. "Yes."

"Oh, thank God." He kissed her hard, spoke without breaking contact of their lips. "I'm going to make you so happy."

"You already do. I love you," she told him.

He kissed her softer, deeper.

"Hold on." He pulled away and lifted her off his lap and onto the Incan steps and then dropped to one knee. From his back pocket, he produced a small box.

"You totally planned this."

He smiled like a teenager and opened the lid. His eyes glistened with unshed tears of his own. "It was my mom's. I would be honored if you would wear it."

Ugly tears ran down her cheeks as her heart burst with pride and happiness. Then she looked at the ring. "Your dad had great taste."

Jason removed the ring, wiped his cheek, and lifted her left hand.

They both stared at it for several seconds, the enormity of the step they were taking circled around them with a loving band of joy.

"This is really happening?" she questioned.

"Oh, this is on. We are doing this."

He stood and pulled her into his arms.

Their kiss was broken by the round of applause from below.

Owen pointed his camera lens their way and put a thumb up in the air after checking the image.

"Was he in on this?" Rachel asked under her breath.

"They all were." Jason waved.

"You're all nuts."

"Not quite."

Epilogue

Light bounced off the lake and caught Owen's fishing pole as he tossed a line off the side of the boat. Nathan sat on the opposite side, directing him. Summer was quickly fading into fall, signifying the year since she'd moved.

Rachel felt the weight of the ring Jason had placed on her finger that day in Peru, and the band he'd added to it the afternoon six weeks later when he made her Mrs. Jason Fairchild.

The memory of Jason flying her and Owen back to California to place flowers on Emily's grave on the anniversary of her death wasn't something Rachel would ever forget.

Their marriage was saluted by most and doubted by others.

Neither one of them listened to what anyone else had to say. Even when her promotion to the head of the marketing department was talked about under hushed tones around the water cooler, Rachel kept her head high and her ego in check. It helped that Julie reminded employees that it was Rachel who brought Fairchild Charters one of the largest accounts they'd acquired in over five years.

Jason's even footsteps sounded behind her as he walked outside.

He kissed the top of her head and took a seat beside her. "Has he caught anything yet?"

"I don't think so."

Jason kicked his feet up on the double chaise longue and pulled her into his arms. "Do you think he suspects anything?"

"I'm pretty sure he knows there's a party planned."

"And the car?"

She cringed. "I'm not ready for him to be driving."

Jason laughed. "He's a good driver."

Yeah, and his sixteenth birthday was the following week.

"Where did you leave the car?"

"Trent's house."

Buying Owen his first car wasn't something Rachel could talk Jason out of.

"One crash and we buy him a beater."

"He'll be fine."

She sniffled. "He's growing up too fast."

Jason hugged her, and when the waterworks didn't end, he stopped teasing. "Are you okay?"

She sighed, watched Owen tugging on the line. "It's just hormones."

"Ahh." Jason settled against her. "Is it an emergency chocolate kind of night, or a glass of wine?"

It was now or later. "I'm probably better off with pickles and milk," she said, deadpan.

"Oh, God, that sounds horrible—"

Jason snapped up to a sitting position on the chair and leaned over her. His gaze moved to her stomach. "Pickles?"

Rachel placed a hand over their unborn child and let her smile show.

"You're serious?"

"Took the test this morning."

He patted her stomach as if he was afraid to touch her. "You're pregnant?"

"I'm surprised it didn't happen sooner. It isn't like you've left me alone since Costa Rica."

"I'm going to be a dad."

Rachel started to laugh. "You catch on quick, Fairchild."

"Oh my God." He leaned down and kissed her stomach before resting his ear on it. "What was that?" He jumped up.

"That would be my stomach. I'm hungry."

"You're hungry . . ." He scrambled off the chair. "Okay. I'll get you something to eat. What do you want? Pickles? I can cook pickles."

Rachel started laughing.

Jason took two steps toward the house, then turned back around and pulled her off the chair and spun her around. "I love you. Every day I love you more."

"I'm getting dizzy."

He stopped spinning her just as abruptly as he'd begun. "Are you okay? Did I hurt you?"

She started laughing again. "I was just as pregnant last night when you had me bent over the pool table."

"Oh, that's bad."

Rachel shrugged. "I don't know. I had a good time."

He kissed her soundly, then stepped away and lifted both hands in the air and shouted, "I love this woman!"

He caught the attention of Owen and Nathan on the lake.

Owen placed his hands around his mouth to amplify the sound. "What's wrong?"

Jason ran several yards closer. "You're going to be a brother!"

"What?"

"Rachel is pregnant!"

Owen stood in the boat. "Pregnant?"

Jason nodded several times.

Owen pounded a fist in the air, and two seconds later was standing chest deep in the lake, Nathan hitting the back of his head.

Rachel laughed. "That just cost us two cell phones."

"Cell phones? You're carrying my child and muttering about phones."

"We're going to start muttering about food soon if we don't get something to eat."

Jason picked her back up and spun her once. "We. Oh, God I love you. I'm so happy you ran me off the road last winter."

"I did not run you off the road."

Jason lifted her into his arms, carried her into the house, and spoke to her stomach. "She totally ran me off the road."

Rachel held on to his neck and let him carry her through their crazy life.

Acknowledgments

It has been an absolute joy to write this series. If it wasn't for the short time I worked the graveyard shift at Denny's when I was eighteen, I would never have thought of the opening scene between Jack and Jessie in *Not Quite Dating*. Now look where I ended up. It's nothing short of spectacular.

Here are a few shout-outs to the people who helped make this final chapter in the series complete.

Thank you, Kayce Harding, for jumping on a plane with me to visit New York in the dead of winter. I still dream about that duck we had in that little French restaurant. Love you, Cousin.

For Denise Placencio, my kick-ass female attorney who is a joy to watch in the courtroom, thanks.

A special thanks to Jane Dystel and Miriam Goderich, who encouraged me to use the Manhattan subway after my three-hour Uber drive from hell. I feel so very grown-up now.

Back to Kelli Martin. You've been my editor since Jack and Jessie and have taken every step alongside me for five years. Publishing has pulled us into the same world, but our friendship spans the universe. I adore you, even the parts that have to be told what the joke is at times. You are truly the blondest black woman I have ever met, and I wouldn't change one thing about you. We are sisters from a different mister, and I look forward to the many years of spirited friendship we will share. Thank you for making my work pop, and for always keeping it real.

I love you, my friend.

Catherine

About the Author

Photo © 2015 Julianne Gentry

When Catherine Bybee fell in love with the first romance novel she ever read, she promised herself she would one day become a published author. Now she's written twenty-seven books that have collectively sold more than four million copies and have been translated into more than eighteen languages. Along with her popular Not Quite series, she has also penned the Weekday Brides series, the Most Likely To series, and the First Wives series.

Raised in Washington State, Bybee moved to Southern California in hopes of becoming a movie star. After growing bored with waiting tables, she returned to school and became a registered nurse, spending most of her career in urban emergency rooms. Catherine now writes full-time. Fans can learn more at www.CatherineBybee.com.